– Trespassing –
AND OTHER STORIES

Valerie Miner is a highly acclaimed novelist and critic. Her novels reflect concerns and challenges of contemporary women. *Blood Sisters* is about working-class Irish women and the IRA. *Murder In The English Department* concerns the climate of sexual harassment and rape on an American college campus. *Winter's Edge* depicts the challenges facing two old women in San Francisco. *Movement* follows the spiritual, political, emotional and geographical movement of a young woman through the 1970s. *All Good Women* captures the experiences of four friends sharing a house during the Second World War. She is co-author of *Tales I Tell My Mother*, *More Tales I Tell My Mother*, *Her Own Woman* and *Competition: A Feminist Taboo?*

Born in New York City, Valerie Miner grew up in New Jersey, the Pacific Northwest and California. She lived abroad for seven years, writing and travelling in Britain, Africa, Canada, Australia and Latin America. Her work has been translated and published in a number of countries, and she has won a number of literary awards and writing prizes. She teaches Humanities at the University of California, Berkeley.

Also by Valerie Miner
*available in Mandarin Paperbacks

*Movement
*Blood Sisters
*Murder in the English Department
*Winter's Edge
*All Good Women

as co-author

Her Own Woman
Tales I Tell My Mother
More Tales I Tell My Mother

VALERIE MINER

– Trespassing –
AND OTHER STORIES

Methuen · Mandarin

A Mandarin Paperback

TRESPASSING AND OTHER STORIES

First published in Great Britain 1989
by Methuen London
This Mandarin edition published 1989
by Methuen · Mandarin
Michelin House, 81 Fulham Road, London SW3 6RB

Mandarin is an imprint of the Octopus Publishing Group

Copyright © Valerie Miner 1989

Some of these stories originally appeared
in the following publications:

Conditions
More Tales I Tell my Mother, Journeyman, London, 1987
Sinister Wisdom
Ikon
The Berkeley Monthly
A Faith Of One's Own, The Crossing Press, USA, 1986
The Last Word won the PEN Syndicated Fiction Prize, 1986

British Library Cataloguing in Publication Data

Miner, Valerie
Trespassing and other stories.
I. Title
813'.54

ISBN 0–7493–0086–8

Printed in Great Britain
by Cox & Wyman Ltd, Reading

This book is sold subject to the condition that it shall not,
by way of trade or otherwise, be lent, resold, hired out,
or otherwise circulated without the publisher's prior
consent in any form of binding or cover other than that
in which it is published and without a similar condition including
this condition being imposed on the subsequent purchaser.

For *Peggy Webb*

Contents

I Home

Trespassing	13
The Last Word	30
Dropping Anchor	37
Misty, Tiled Chambers	58
Guest of Honour	66
Valentine's Day	82
Objectivity, She Said	93
All Those Dead Horses	98

II Transfer, A Novella — 107

III Away

Worms and Women Have Spun Magic	157
Uncommon Ground	159
Deutschmarks and Venetian Blinds	171
The Giants Haven't Won a Pennant Since '62	181
Interval	197
On The Way From China	198
Smoking	201
You Remember Sophia	229

– Trespassing –
AND OTHER STORIES

I
Home

– *Trespassing* –

Exhausted from four hours of traffic, Kate and Josie almost missed seeing the two doe and their fawn drinking at the pond. The women waited in the car, cautious lest the noise of opening doors disturb the animals. The deer lingered another five minutes and then stepped off gracefully into the wings of sequoias. Last sun settled on the golden hills. Night noises pulsed: frogs, crickets, mallards. Wind whispered across dry grass. Jays barked from the top of the hill. As the sky grew roses, Kate and Josie watched Jupiter blaze over the Eastern mountains.

They unloaded the Chevy quickly and sloppily, eager for the comfort of the compact wooden cabin they had built with their friends over five summers. Josie opened the gas line outside the house. Kate lit a fire, reflecting on the joys of collective ownership when the rest of the collective was absent. She could hardly believe it – two whole days away from Meredith High School; forty-eight hours of privacy and peace.

Suddenly starving, they decided to eat right away. Afterwards they would sit in front of the fire and read to each other. Kate chopped salad while Josie made pasta and whistled. The sky got redder and then, abruptly, the cabin was dark. With heavy reluctance, Kate walked around and lit the lanterns.

'Oh,' Kate said.

Josie turned and caught a flick of brown before her, like an insect crashing on a windshield.

'Damn bats.' Kate shook her head and picked up the broom.

'Bats!' Josie screamed. 'I thought Iris got rid of those gruesome things last month.'

'Must still be some holes in the sun porch.'

A dark object dropped beside Josie, like a small turd falling, from the eaves. It disappeared. She fretted the wooden spoon through the pasta, watching another tiny brown mass cut its fall in mid-air and swoop across the room. It was too much. 'Bats!'

Josie ran outside. She felt safer in the dark.

Kate stayed in the house, sweeping bats out of the windows and back door.

Staring up at the stars, so benign in their distance, Josie considered vast differences between Kate and herself. Rational, taciturn Kate was probably calculating the increasing velocity of wing movement as the bats ignited to wakefulness. Josie, herself, still cringed at Grandma's tales about bats nesting in little girls' hair. And raised as she was in a wilful family where intentionality was more important than action, where danger didn't exist if one closed one's imagination to it, Josie was given to the substitution of 'good thoughts'. Let's see, she forced herself to concentrate on a pleasant memory: how she and Kate met. It was a miracle if you thought about it; *who* would have expected romance at the school xerox machine? But there was Kate copying quark diagrams for her physics students while Josie waited to xerox a new translation of *La Cigale et La Fourmi*. If Kate hadn't run out of toner, they might never have become acquainted.

'All clear,' Kate called. There was no disdain in her voice for she had always envied Josie's ability to show fear. She should tell Josie this.

Josie craned her neck and stared at the sky. 'Glorious night,' she called back. 'Wanna see?'

Ducking out the front door, Kate ran through the pungent pennyroyal to her friend. Josie took her hand. Together they stood quietly until they could hear the frogs and the crickets once more.

They slept late and spent the next morning eating eggs and fried potatoes and rye toast. Josie noticed some wasps dancing around the table, so they cleaned up and went outside to lie on the warm deck.

Later they spent an hour fitting moulding around the edges of the sun porch's glass door, sealing the house seams against nocturnal trespassers.

At noon the women drove five miles to town for forgotten country necessities – ice, water and flashlight batteries. Josie secretly checked the grocery shelves for bat killer, but she didn't find any and she knew Kate wouldn't approve.

As they drove back to the land, Josie tried to renew her enthusiasm for the weekend. She stopped in front of the cabin. Kate, now completely restored by country air, bounded into the house with the grocery bag.

Josie moved the Chevy into the shade of an oak tree which was being gradually occupied by Spanish moss. As she locked up the car, she saw a fat man with a rifle waddling out of the forest. He wore a yellow cap, a striped T-shirt and bluejeans.

A giant bumblebee, she thought. Then she warned herself to get serious. The land was clearly posted, 'No Trespassing. No Hunting'. A shiver ran along her collarbone. They were half-a-mile from the highway here. It could be weeks before anyone investigated.

Josie decided to be friendly and waved.

'Hello there.' He was winded, hustling to meet her.

Josie closed her eyes and hoped Kate would stay in the house until it was all over.

'I got lost,' he said, nodding his whole body. 'How do you get back to the highway?'

'That direction.' Josie tried to calm herself. 'Up the road there.'

He looked her over. 'You got any water? A glass of water? I've been walking for hours.'

Biblical tales filled her head. 'The Woman at the Well', 'The Wedding at Cana', 'The Good Samaritan'. 'Sure,' she said as noncommitally as possible. 'I'll be right back.'

'Who's that?' Kate greeted her.

Josie tried to be calm. 'Water man. I mean, a lost man who needs water.' She watched Kate's jaw stiffen. 'Now let me handle it. He just wants a glass of water and then he'll be on his way.' Josie poured water from a plastic jug into an old jam jar they used for drinking.

'Water, my foot, what is he doing on the land? It's posted "No Trespassing", for God's sake.'

'Listen, Kate, he was hunting and . . .'

Kate took the glass and poured half the water back into the jug. 'Don't *spoil* him. He may return.'

She stalked out to the man, who was leaning on their car, his gun on the ground. Josie stood at the door, watching.

'Thanks, ma'am.' He reached for the water.

'No shooting on this land,' Kate said as she released the glass.

'Sorry, ma'am. I was hunting up there on the North Ridge and I hit a buck. But he got away. I followed, to make sure I got him good. Then I got lost and I guess I wound up here.'

'Guess so,' Kate said. She held her hand against her leg to stop it from shaking.

'I'll be off your land soon's I finish the water,' he promised.

'That's right.' She kept her voice even.

'But I'll need to be coming back to get the buck. See, I finally did get him. But since I was lost, I couldn't drag him all over tarnation.'

'We don't want a dead buck on the land,' Kate conceded. 'When're you coming?'

'Tomorrow morning?' he asked. 'About eight o'clock?'

'Fine, and no guns,' she said.

'No, ma'am, no guns.'

'Right then.' She held her hand out for the jam jar. 'Road's that way.'

'Yes, ma'am.'

Kate watched him climb the hill and walked back to the house, shaking her head. Josie reached to hug her, but Kate pulled away. 'God damned hunter.' She was on the verge of tears.

'How about some coffee or lunch?'

'Naw, are you nuts, after all we ate this morning? No, I think I'll just go for a walk. See if I can find the buck. If there *is* a buck.'

Josie nodded. 'Want company?' She wasn't keen on viewing a dead animal, but she didn't care to admit being afraid to stay in the house alone, not after her melodramatic performance with the bats last night.

'Sure.' Kate was grateful. 'Let's go.'

Josie locked the ice chest and dropped the jam jar in the brown paper garbage bag on the way out.

It was hotter now, about 85 degrees. The pennyroyal smelled mintier than last night. The day was dry and still—bleached grass, golden hills scumbled against teal sky. A turkey vulture glided above the oak grove. As they walked around the pond, they could hear frogs scholop into the water. Kate stopped to inspect the eucalyptus trees they had planted in the spring. Four out of five still alive, not bad. Further along, a salamander skittered across their path. Josie felt cool even before she entered the woods. In a way, she hoped they wouldn't find the buck. But if there was no buck, who knew what the bumblebee man really wanted?

The woods were thick with madrone and manzanita and poison oak. It was always a balance on the land, Kate thought, pleasure and danger.

Josie wished she had worn sneakers instead of sandals. But Kate didn't seem to be bothered about her feet as she marched ahead. Right, Josie reminded herself, this wasn't a ramble. They continued in silence for half-an-hour.

''Round here, I guess,' called Kate, who was now several yards ahead. 'See the way branches have broken. Yes, here. Oh, my god, it's still alive. God damned hunter.'

They stared at the huge animal, its left front leg broken in a fall, panting and sweating, blind fear in its wide eyes.

'I told Myla we should keep a gun at the house,' Kate cried. 'What are we going to do?'

Josie didn't think about it. She probably wouldn't have been able to lift the boulder if she had thought about it. But she heard herself shouting to Kate, 'Stand back,' and watched herself drop the big rock on the buck's head. They heard a gurgling and saw a muscle ripple along the animal's belly. Then nothing. There was nothing alive under the boulder.

Josie stared at the four bullet wounds scattered up the right side of the buck. The animal's blood was a dark, cinnamon colour. She noticed sweat along the hip joints.

Kate walked over to her quietly and took her hand. 'Good, brave,' she stuttered. 'That was good, Josie.'

'Yeah, it seemed the right thing.'

Kate hugged Josie and gently drew her away from the dead buck and the broken bush.

They walked straight out to the trail. Neither one seemed to want to stay in the woods for their customary ramble. Kate watched her friend closely, waiting for the explosion. This silence was so uncharacteristic of Josie. Soon, soon, she would erupt with anger and aggravation and guilt and a long examination of what she had done in the woods. For her own part, Kate could only think of one word. Brave.

'Let's go swimming,' Josie said, trying to focus on the trail. 'It'll cool us off.'

The two women stripped on the makeshift dock and lay in the sun beside one another. Kate was slim, her legs long and shapely. She didn't think much about this body which had always served her well. She never felt too thin or too plump. Josie, in contrast, fretted about her zoftig breasts and hips. Her skin was pinker than Kate's, a faint pink. Kate curled up beside Josie, her legs across Josie's legs, her head on Josie's shoulder.

Josie closed her eyes and told herself it was over. They were all right. She had never killed anything before and she felt terribly sad. Of course, the animal had been dying. It was a humane act. Still, her chest ached with a funny hollowness.

'What's that?' Kate sat up.

They listened, Josie flat and Kate leaning forward from her waist.

The noise came again.

A loud whirr.

Like an engine.

Whirr.

'Quail.' Kate relaxed back on her elbow. 'Come on, let's wash off the feeling of that creepy guy.'

She lowered herself into the water from the wooden ladder, surprised as Josie jumped in.

'Freezing!' Josie laughed, swimming around her friend and noticing how Kate's blonde curls sprang back the minute she lifted her head from the water. 'Freezing!'

'You'll warm up,' Kate said, herself breathless from the cold.

'You're always telling me to stop daydreaming, to stay in the present. The present is freezing.' Josie giggled and splashed her friend.

Kate laughed. She ducked under the water, swimming deep enough to catch Josie's feet, which were treading earnestly.

'Hey, watch it.' But Josie called too late. Now she was below the surface, tangled in Kate's legs and the long roots of silky grass. It was green down here and very cold.

They dried out on the sunny dock and dressed before starting towards the house. Often they walked naked across the land, especially after swimming when they didn't want to wear sweaty clothes. Today that didn't feel safe.

Back at the cabin, the afternoon grew long and restless. Both women felt fidgety. Kate put aside her equations and washed all the windows in the house. Josie couldn't concentrate on her translation, so she worked up lesson plans for the following week.

About five o'clock, she glanced at Kate, stretching recklessly to the skylight from the top of a ladder.

'Careful up there.'

'Sure, hon!'

'What did we bring for dinner?' Josie's mind was blank.

'That beef chilli you made last week. And rye bread.'

'Why don't we go out?' Josie paced in front of the wood stove. God, she wished Kate would be careful on that ladder.

'Out? But the whole point of being here, oops,' she tipped precariously and then straightened. 'Hey, just let me get one more lick in here and we can talk. There.' She started down the steps. 'But the whole point of being in the country is to retreat together in solitary bliss. And what's wrong with your chilli? I thought this batch was perfect?'

Josie shrugged and looked out the big bay window across the grass. She told herself to watch the horses ambling along the ridge or the hawk hovering over the pond.

Instead she was caught by a line of lint Kate had left in the middle of the frame. 'I don't know. Not in the mood. Guess I'd like vegetarian tonight.' Her eyes stung.

Kate stood behind her; still, Josie could sense her nodding.

'Why not,' Kate said. 'Be nice to take a ride this time of evening.'

Edna's Café was practically empty. But then – Kate checked her watch – it *was* only five-thirty. Edna waved menus from behind the counter. Josie and Kate said yes.

'Coffee, girls?' Edna carried the menus under her arm, pot of coffee in one hand and mugs in the other.

'Thanks,' Josie said.

'Not just yet,' Kate smiled. Edna reminded her of Aunt Bella who worked in a coffee shop back East.

While Kate studied the menu, Josie excused herself to the rest-room.

Kate breathed easier when Josie returned to the table looking relaxed. She felt a great surge of affection as her companion intently appraised the menu.

'I think I'll have the chef's salad with Jack cheese,' Josie decided.

'Sound's good.' Kate nodded. She was relieved to see Josie looking happy. 'Two chef salads, with Jack cheese,' she called over to Edna.

They talked about plans for the following summer when they could spend four consecutive weeks on the land.

'You two girls sisters?' Edna served the enormous salads.

'No,' laughed Kate. 'Why?'

'Don't know. You kinda look alike. 'Course when I stare straight at you like this, there's not much resemblance. I don't know. And you always order the same thing.'

'In that case, I'll have tea,' Kate laughed again. 'With lemon.'

They ate silently, self-conscious of being the only ones in the restaurant. Kate could hardly get down the lettuce. She'd feel better after she made the phone call. She wouldn't tell Josie, who would get nervous. But it was responsible to report the intruder to the sheriff. 'Excuse me. Now I've got to use the bathroom,' she said to Josie. 'Don't let Edna take my salad.'

'I'll guard it with my life,' Josie grinned.

The sheriff's number was posted beneath the fire station number. She dialled and heard a funny, moist sound, as if the man were eating or maybe clicking in his dentures. She concentrated on the sturdy black plastic of the phone.

'Hello,' he said finally.

She began to report the incident.

'Listen, you're the second lady to call me about this in twenty minutes. Like I told the other one, there's nothing I can do unless the man is actually trespassing on your land. Since you've invited him back tomorrow, he ain't exactly trespassing.'

'We didn't exactly invite him.'

'OK, if it makes you feel easier, I said I'll swing by about eight a.m. That's when the other lady said he'd be coming.'

'Thank you, sir.'

'Sir,' she shook her head as she walked back to the table. She hadn't said 'sir' in fifteen years.

Josie had finished her salad and was doodling on a paper napkin. Definitely signs of a good mood. Kate sat down and stared at her until she looked up. 'So I hear you have a date with the law tomorrow morning.'

Josie smiled. 'Hope you don't think I'm stepping out on you.'

By the time Kate finished her salad, the café was getting crowded.

'Refills?' Edna approached with a pot of coffee and a pot of hot water. 'No thanks, just the cheque,' Josie said.

'Guess you girls didn't mind my asking if you was sisters?'

'No, no, not at all.' They spoke in unison.

It was a warm, richly scented evening and they drove home with the top down. Jupiter came out early again. Josie thought how much she preferred Jupiter to the cold North Star.

They were both worn out as they collapsed on the couch

together. Their feet on the fruit crate coffee table, they watched pink gain the horizon. It was almost pitch dark when Josie reached up to light the lanterns.

She hesitated a moment, remembering last night, and then proceeded. Light, *voilá,* the room was filled with sharp corners and shiny surfaces. Kate picked up her book, but Josie drew it away, cuddling closer.

'Here?' Kate was surprised by her own resistance. After all, they were alone, five miles from town.

'Where then?' Josie tried to sound like Lauren Bacall.

Kate sighed with a breath that moved her whole body, a body, she noticed, which was becoming increasingly sensitive to the body next to her. 'Mmmmm,' she kissed Josie on her neck, sweet with late summer sweat.

When Josie opened her eyes, she thought she saw something. No, they had sealed off the sun porch this morning. She kissed Kate on the lips and was startled by a whisssh over her friend's head. 'Bats,' she said evenly, pulling Kate lower on the couch.

'Don't worry,' Kate said. 'I'll get rid of him.'

Worry, Josie cringed. She wasn't worried; she was hysterical. Calm down, she told herself. Think about the invasion of Poland. This was her mother's approach to anxiety – distract yourself by thinking about people with *real* problems. Worry is a perversion of imagination.

Kate opened the windows and set forth again with the broom, but the bat wouldn't leave. Eventually it spiralled upstairs into the large sleeping loft. Kate shook her head and closed up the house against further intrusion. She shrugged and returned to the couch, where Josie was sitting up, considerably more collected than the previous night.

'It'll be OK,' Kate said. 'It'll just go to sleep. You know, they're not really Transylvanian leeches. They're harmless little herbivores. And rather inept.'

Herbivores. Josie thought about eating salad for absolution after she murdered the buck.

Kate reached over and brushed her lover's breast, but Josie pulled away. 'Not now, sweetie. I can't just now.'

Kate nodded. She picked up her book. Josie fiddled with

a crossword puzzle. At about ten o'clock, Kate yawned, 'Bed?'

'OK,' Josie was determined to be brave. 'I'll go up first.'

'Sure,' Kate regarded her closely. 'You light the candle up there. I'll get the lantern down here.'

They settled comfortably in the double nylon sleeping bag. Kate blew out the light. She reached over to rub Josie's back in the hope something more might develop. Suddenly she heard a whissh, whissh, whissh.

'Looks like our friend is back.' Kate tried to keep her voice light.

'Just a harmless little herbivore.' Josie rolled to her side of the bed, putting a pillow over her head.

That night Josie dreamt that she had become Mayor of Lincoln, Nebraska.

Kate slept fitfully, hardly dreaming, and waking with the first sun.

She lay and watched Josie breathing evenly, blowing the edges of her black hair, her body ripe and luscious in the soft light. If she woke up early enough, they could make love before Mr Creepo arrived. And the sheriff. Had they made a mistake in phoning the sheriff?

The loft grew lighter. Kate lay on her back with her head on her palms, wondering where the bat had nested, about the reliability of her research assistant, whether she would go home for Christmas this year. Then she heard the noise.

Her entire body stiffened. No mistaking the sound of a car crawling down the gravel road toward their cabin. She checked her watch. Seven a.m. Shit. The sheriff wouldn't arrive until their bodies were cold. Maybe Josie would be safer if she just stayed in the house; maybe she wouldn't wake her. Yes, Kate pulled out of the sleeping bag. She was grabbed by the night-gown.

'Not so quick, brown fox,' Josie said sleepily. 'How about a cuddle?'

She was adorable in the morning, thought Kate, completely *dérangé* as Josie herself would admit, before the second cup of coffee.

The noise outside grew closer and Kate tightened.

'Don't you even want to hear how I got elected Mayor of Lincoln . . . ?'

'Not now.' Kate couldn't stem the panic in her own voice.

Josie sat up. 'What is it?' Then she heard the truck's motor dying.

'I'll just go check in with him,' Kate said nonchalantly. 'You wait here and I'll come back to snuggle.' She pulled on her clothes.

'No you don't, Joan of Arc.' Josie stood up and tucked her night-shirt into a pair of jeans.

The two walked downstairs together.

The fat man was approaching the house, empty-handed. His friend, also bulky and middle-aged, stayed behind, leaning against the red pick-up truck.

Kate called out to him when he was three yards from the house. 'Back again.'

'Sorry to bother you, ma'am. As you can see we didn't bring no guns. We'll just get that deer and then git offa yer property as soon's we can.'

His friend shuffled and looked at his feet.

'OK,' Kate said gruffly. 'We don't want dead animals on the land. By the way, we finished him off for you yesterday.'

The man opened his mouth in surprise. His friend moved forward, tugging him back. They closed up the truck and headed into the woods.

Josie watched until they were out of sight. Kate went inside to make coffee.

Half-an-hour later, as they sat down to breakfast, another vehicle crunched down the hill. Josie looked out at the black and white sedan. 'Our hero, the sheriff.'

They walked over to greet the sheriff, a solid man, who looked them over carefully.

'You the girls who called me yesterday?'

'Yes, we did.' Josie smiled.

'Yes.' Kate nodded, the 'sir' gone as quickly as it had come. She didn't like his expression.

'Only ladies listed on the deed to this land, I see. Looked

it up last night. All schoolteachers. Some kind of commune? Something religious?'

'Just friends.' Kate stepped back.

'Edna says she thought you were sisters.' He squinted against the bright sun. 'One sort or another.'

'Just friends.' Kate's voice was more distant.

'Soooo.' The sheriff held his ground. 'You want to run through the nature of that problem again?'

As Kate talked with the sheriff, Josie inspected the hunters' pick-up truck. The bumper sticker read, 'I live in a cave and one good fuck is all I crave.' Inside, dice hung from the rearview mirror. On the seat were a parka and two empty cans of Dr Pepper. The dashboard was plastered with several iridescent signs. The sun glared so that she could read only one. 'Gas, Ass or Grass – No one rides for free.'

The sheriff noticed her and observed, 'Leon's truck. Just as I figured. Leon Bates, a local man. He's, well, he's strayed off the hunting trail before.'

'Isn't there something you can do about him?' Josie felt the heat rising to her face. 'He might have killed one of us. On our property. With a gun.'

'Today,' the sheriff's voice was cool, 'today your friend tells me that he has no gun. That in fact, you said he could come back here to get his buck. That right?'

Josie closed her eyes, feeling naïve for imagining this man might protect them. Now bureaucracy seemed the only recourse. 'Right. Can't we make some kind of complaint about what he did yesterday?'

'Sure can,' the sheriff nodded. 'If that's what you want.'

'What do you mean?' Kate's back tightened.

'You're weekend folks, right?' He lit a cigarette.

'We work in the city, if that's what you mean,' Kate spoke carefully, 'and don't live here year round.'

'None of my business what you all have going on here. None of Leon's business either. But if you file a complaint and we take it to court, well, he's bound to do some investigating and . . .'

'There's nothing illegal about our land group,' Josie snapped.

'Miss, Miss, I never said anything about legal, illegal, but you know there are natural pests the law can't control. And it's better maybe not to get them roused.'

Kate and Josie exchanged glances. 'Well, perhaps we'll check with Loretta; her sister's a lawyer. We'll get back to you.'

'Yes, ma'am.' He grew more serious. 'That about all for today, ma'am? I mean you said they didn't bring no guns with them. You feel safe enough on your own?'

'Yes,' Josie said. 'We're safe enough on our own.'

'Then if you'll excuse me, it's almost eight o'clock and services start early around here.' He stamped out his cigarette and softened. 'Church is always open to outsiders and weekend people, by the way. Just three miles down, on the road by the gas station.'

'I know where it is,' Josie said. 'Goodbye, sheriff.'

They watched him roll up the hill, then returned to the house for breakfast. They were both too furious to talk. Kate hardly touched her food, watching out the window for the trespassers.

About ten o'clock, she saw two pregnant-looking men pulling a buck through the dust by its antlers. Her first thought was how powerful those antlers must be. She tightened and Josie looked up from her book. 'At last.'

It took the men ten minutes to reach the truck. They were huffing and sweating and Josie had to resist the urge to bring them a pitcher of water. She followed Kate out on the front porch.

Leon Bates glowered at them, as if weighing the value of wasting breath for talk. He and his friend heaved the buck into the truck. On the second try, they made it.

Leon's friend wiped his hands on his jeans, waiting with an expression of excruciating embarrassment.

Leon straightened up, drew a breath and shouted, 'That'll do it.'

'Good,' called Kate.

'Gotta ask one question.' Leon leaned forward on his right leg. 'What'd you have to go and bust his head for? Ruined a perfect trophy. Just look at the antlers. Would have been perfect.'

'Come on, Leon,' his friend called.

Kate stood firmly, hands on her hips. Josie tried to hold back the tears, but she couldn't and pivoted toward the cabin.

'The road's that way,' Kate pointed. 'Only goes in one direction.'

Kate stamped into the house. 'Damn them. Damn them!' she screamed.

'Hey, now.' Josie reached up to her shoulders and pulled Kate toward her. 'Hey now, relax, love.'

'Don't tell me to relax. This man comes on our land, shoots living things, threatens us. And you tell me to relax.' She banged her hand on the table.

Josie inhaled heavily and pulled Kate a little closer. 'They've gone now.' She looked over Kate's shoulder and out the back window, which gleamed in the mid-morning sun. 'See, they're over the hill.'

'Out of sight, that's what you think, you fool.' Kate tried to draw apart.

Josie held tight, hoping to melt the contortions from her friend's face.

Kate pushed her away. Josie lost balance, hitting her head against a pane of glass in the sun porch door.

The glass cracked, sending a high-pitched rip through the room.

Josie ducked forward, her eyes tightly shut, just in time to avoid most of the showering glass fragments.

Drenched in sweat, Kate shook her and shouted, 'Josie, Josie, are you all right? Oh, my God, Josie, are you all right?'

'We'll never keep out the bats this way,' Josie laughed nervously, on the verge.

'Josie, I didn't mean it.' Tears welled in Kate's eyes. 'I love you, Josie, are you all right?'

Josie nodded. They held each other, shivering.

Josie stepped forward, 'OK, yes, but I feel a little like Tinkerbell. Scattering all this glitter.'

'Tinkerbell!' Kate laughed and cried and choked. The room seemed to be closing in on them. Hot, tight, airless. She could feel herself listing.

'But you, hey.' Josie frowned. 'Let's go upstairs and have *you* lie down.'

They sat on the bed, holding hands and staring out at the land. The day was hot, even dryer than yesterday and the golden grass shimmered against the shadowy backdrop of the woods.

'We really should go down and clean up the glass, put a board over the shattered pane.' Kate whispered.

'Yeah, if we don't head home soon, traffic's gonna be impossible.'

Kate rested her head on Josie's breast. She smelled the musk from the black feathers beneath her arms. Her hand went to the soft nest at the bottom of Josie's generous belly. Josie slipped off her clothes. Kate followed. They sank down on the bed, swimming together again, sucked into the cool sleeping bag.

'Home,' Josie murmured.

'Hmmmm?' Kate inhaled the scents of Josie's sweat and sex. Forcing herself to be alert, she pulled back. Was her friend delirious? Maybe she had a concussion.

'Home.' Josie kissed her with a passion so conscious as to take away both Kate's concern and her breath.

'Yes.' Kate moved her fingers lower, separating the labia, swirling the honey thicker. 'Yes.'

Josie crawled on top of Kate, licking her shoulders, her breasts; burying her nose in her navel; kissing her thighs. Then she was distracted by a slow fizzzz, as if their air-mattress were deflating.

Josie looked up. Two wasps hovered over them, bobbing and weaving and then lifting themselves abruptly out of vision. Maybe if she just continued Kate wouldn't notice. But it was too late.

'They always come out in the middle of the day,' Kate said drearily. 'For food. For their nests.'

Josie shock her head, staring at the unsteady, fragile creatures.

'What the hell,' Kate shrugged, inching away from Josie.

'What the hell,' Josie whispered seductively. They returned to the pleasures between them. When they finished making love, Josie curled around Kate. She explained how she had been elected Mayor of Lincoln, Nebraska.

The wasps wove over and around the two women. Even as they fell asleep.

– The Last Word –

Rain is threatening. It's a chilly autumn evening. The sun is setting in pale pink and I had hoped for coral to blaze my spirit after a long day of teaching. The grocery store is drafty. One of the back lights is broken, giving the impression that the grocer is going to close before I finish shopping. The grapefruit look as rotten as they have tasted for the last two weeks. I recall Allen Ginsberg's euphoric poem, 'A Supermarket In California', and begin to question seriously the things we learn and teach in school.

Next door the doughnuts in Redimade's window – even the chocolate French twists – seem to be drooping. I remember the Redimade shop on the road home from Dickson High School and how I had to use every ounce of will-power to pass by the chocolate French twists. ('One ounce of will-power equals one pound of fat,' warned my gym teacher, Miss Mendoza, who seemed to subsist on carrots.)

As I turn the corner, I see my favourite dress shop has a sale. 'Some items half-off.' The sign is depressing rather than enticing for I think of Alexa out of work and all those newspaper stories on the declining economy. So I don't stop to check the snazzy purple suit I've been coveting. Instead, I walk home, fiddle around making a cup of coffee and try to figure out what is depressing me. It is more than a lost sunset.

Perhaps it is the fall; the first days of school. This time of year is always unpredictable. Sitting back on my living-room couch, I regard the last shards of pink sky through the drizzle. First days of school. I can still taste the finger paints from kindergarten and smell the egg salad from the damp basement which served as our cafeteria and fallout shelter. Again, I feel the nervousness of my first week in high school, where I seemed like a fraud, the only person in my family to move past the eighth grade. I was silent throughout freshman year and astonished to hear myself speaking French and geometry as a sophomore.

'Miss Harvey, Mrs Wilson, Mr Greenspan, Mrs Richter, Miss O'Leary.'

Sipping my coffee, I realize that I have recited this litany every autumn as the sunsets dissolve in drizzle. I am long past believing in prayer, but I still practise meditation on teachers past. What happened to them, I wonder. Mrs Wilson told me my handwriting was illegible and I still have problems with some capital letters. 'Q' for instance. Miss Harvey looked as frightened as I was. And she was so tactful. Upon hearing my squeaky alto, she promoted me to 'page turner' as the other seventh grade girls sang 'The Happy Wanderer'. Then Miss O'Leary. Why couldn't I forget Miss O'Leary, for God's sake? I wasn't that impressionable – a senior in high school – when she did her deed. It wasn't exactly a deed, rather more like a protracted torture.

*

The torture began one late September day during the third week of my senior year. By then, not only was I speaking French and geometry, but I was making 'A's in English literature. While other teachers had reached out to me, Miss O'Leary seemed to dare me. Every day of class was exhilarating. She even drew out my secret ambition to become a writer. In those days I thought she was old and wise. Now I realize she was only about forty.

I was excited as Miss O'Leary handed back the Matthew Arnold assignments – until I saw Donna wince. I knew I was done for because Donna was ten times smarter than I. Besides, we had talked after submitting our essays and I had learned – much to my delight – that we had made the same arguments. Now I sat peeling the aluminiun off a chewing-gum wrapper, knowing I must have failed terribly. Miss O'Leary stopped at my desk and waited for me to look her in the eyes before handing back the essay.

'A' it said. At first I thought she had made a mistake. Should I report it? We were beginning our discussion of *Tales From a Troubled Land* and I was conjuring Sister Marian to enquire what sin I was committing by not reporting the error. Suddenly a note was slipped under my book.

From Donna, 'What did you get? She gave me "C", the old battleaxe.' My first reaction was relief. No matter which commandment I was breaking, at least the sin only marked the difference between an 'A' and a 'C', not an 'A' and an

'F'. It would be a venial sin. I managed to concentrate on *Tales From a Troubled Land*.

After class, Miss O'Leary rushed over to the faculty lounge where she drank the coffee and inhaled the cigarettes which stoked her mighty breath. She didn't notice Donna and me lagging behind, indifferent to our seventh hour gym class. (PE wasn't interesting until October, when Miss Mendoza, having offered the required month of hygiene lessons, allowed us on the archery range.) Scrupulously Donna and I examined each other's papers without finding any real distinction. Donna had made the same points. I had one more spelling error. Still, I had received an 'A' and Donna a 'C'. At the bottom of her paper was Miss O'Leary's meticulous Palmer penmanship, 'Simplistic and general'. At the bottom of mine was the comment, 'Creative potential'. Whatever the definitions of these phrases, they couldn't mark the distinction between an 'A' and a 'C'. I didn't know what to do.

'Why do you have to *do* anything?' asked Donna as we hurried into our gym clothes. Technically I didn't have to dress down because I had my period, but the least I could do was keep Donna company.

'Because it's . . . unfair,' I managed. Donna didn't disagree.

The next morning before school, I dropped by Miss O'Leary's classroom. She sat camped over her papers with a distressed, resolute posture that reminded me of Dad studying the bills in our dining-room. Embarrassed at catching her in such a private moment, I walked out of the room and then knocked with loud formality on the door frame.

She looked up, her face a blur of motion as if she couldn't decide which expression to adopt. Finally, she said, 'Yes, dear,' with a sympathy that reminded us both that she was the authority and I the supplicant.

'I came about my paper,' I managed.

She smiled more kindly.

'I, I got an "A".' I stammered, struggling to recall the speech which had kept me awake the previous night. 'And,' I spoke more rapidly, 'Donna Gomez got a "C".'

Her face blurred again, the kindness fading to confusion and then disappearing into affront. Her eyes darted briefly to the faculty coffee shop and then back to me. 'And what would you have me do about this?'

'Well, we made the same points on our papers.' I went blank, forgetting just what I *would* have her do about this. 'So, I, uh, guess it would be fair if we got the same grade.'

'Fair. I suppose you "uh guess" you're qualified to make such decisions,'' she said with reflective softness.

I glanced over at the faculty lounge, remembering how awfully Dad behaved before his morning coffee ('Timing,' Mom often admonished me, 'It's all in your timing.').

'What is this,' her voice swelled, filling the empty classroom, 'teenage tyranny?'

'No . . . sorry . . . fair . . . only . . .' my words scattered between us like spilled Scrabble letters. I sucked them in with a quick breath, struggling to reassemble my thoughts. Miss O'Leary coolly flipped through the green marbled grade book, biting her Bic pen and repeating, 'Fair. Fair. Well, I can adjust the situation right now.'

As I watched her long finger travel past Gomez, to the bottom of the alphabet, I knew just how she would adjust it.

My grades remained 'C's' for the rest of the year. No matter how many times I rewrote an essay, no matter how much creative potential I tried to tap, I always got a 'C'. This class would have lost me a scholarship, but luckily I was sailing through social studies where we were doing a long section on ethics. And the funny thing – I think it's odd even now – is that she didn't stop me from loving English or from wanting to be a writer. I worked twice as hard trying to get out of 'C'. Writing and rewriting and rewriting. Doing extra work. Miss O'Leary went through my papers with a microscope. My spelling cleared up as if I had swallowed a dictionary. Donna somehow made her peace with Miss O'Leary and emerged with an 'A–'. I was 'C' all the way, right up to the final report day, which was also the afternoon that Miss O'Leary signed our yearbooks. 'Keep in touch,' she jotted in mine, 'and send me a copy of your first book.' The report card said 'C'.

Actually, I did intend to invite her to the first book party. But something stopped me. The style was stiff in places. She might find a punctuation error. 'Funny,' Donna smiled over the champagne, 'this would have been a good way to show Miss O' her place.' I was relieved to know I wasn't the only person haunted by her. I also realized I hadn't yet made the mark I wanted.

Several years later, with my second book published and a new job at the state college, I found myself driving out to Dickson High School. I got to campus at three-fifteen, after class but early enough to find her there. As I walked down the Lilliputian corridor, past the teachers' lounge, I sensed that something was wrong.

No, I sighed, her door was ajar as usual. Already smelling her nicotine and caffeine greeting, I knocked rapidly. Inside, a strange voice called, 'Door's open.' It was the same room. Matthew Arnold still presided from his battered frame. The 'most misspelled words' were listed in her perfect handwriting next to the window. Apparently kids continued to have problems with 'Manila'. The tattered posters of the Lake District hung over the chalkboard.

'Help you?' A young woman rose from behind a huge packing crate. She looked remarkably like Angie Truman, our head cheerleader, but just as she was too young to be Angie, she was too old to be Angie's daughter.

'I . . . look . . . long . . . time,' the whole Scrabble game spilled before us. I was astonished by my nervousness at returning to the sanctuary.

'Looking for Miss O'Leary?'

By the cheerful way she asked, I could tell Miss O' wasn't dead. I hadn't seriously considered the possibility. She seemed indomitable.

'She's OK, now . . .' I heard fragments of the young woman's voice between my memories, 'hospitalized last month for emphysema.' ('An ounce of will-power . . .' Miss Mendoza had, no doubt, also advised her.) 'She took an early retirement and I'm helping to pack up.' *Cry the Beloved Country. Culture and Anarchy.*

'A former student?' she persisted with implacable friendliness.

'Yes.' I nodded reluctantly. What did she know about it? Perhaps she, too, was one of Miss O's former students. Suddenly my discomfort crystallized in rivalry.

'Her students are her life,' she spoke with a detachment revealing she had never had the privilege. 'See over there, the scrapbooks.'

I was lost at that shelf for an hour. Yearbooks. School newspapers. Albums. John Costello passing the bar. Martha Killam singing in New York. Donna Gomez getting married. I was nowhere.

Until I found the rose notebook. All about me. Clippings describing my scholarship and graduate fellowship. An article about me in *The Standard*. Then reviews of my books, all meticulously situated under glossy plastic. My own mother couldn't have done better.

'Got to close up now,' said Angie Truman in her school spirit voice. 'I'm sure Miss O' would love to hear from you.'

'I'll be in touch,' I answered brusquely.

'Who shall I say called?' she continued.

'I'll be in touch.' I left, eager to conceal the red around my eyes and the confusion in my voice.

I drove back from Dickson High School puzzled. Puzzled at my own sadness, my reluctance to give a name. I was irritated that after all these years I was still baffled by Miss O' while she knew my whole story, had organized it in plastic, for God's sake. What effect did she really have on me? Had she intended to provoke, to draw me further? Did she know that for years, still to this day, I rewrote for the precise phrase, the deeper description? Did she know that nothing had ever compelled me more than that little phrase on my essay, 'Creative potential'? Or was she simply a sadistic, cold woman who found rough consolation breathing smoke and stale coffee?

Of course I recognized that I was taking this too seriously. I resolved to visit her. Perhaps I would phone. Finally, it occurred to me to dedicate my third book to Miss O'Leary. Yes, I would wait for this, wait to hand her *our* book.

The publication was delayed a year because I had several

complicated terms at school and a very tough time with the final draft.

When Donna phoned, I was more surprised by the sorrow in her voice than by the news itself.

'Did you know that Miss O' died last week? Lungs.'

We made plans to see each other. However, like so many plans that year, they fell through until the book appeared. At the publication party, Donna was taken aback by the dedication.

'To Miss O'Leary, who had the last word.'

*

My coffee is turning cold now. The whole apartment is cold. I must fix the heater; my friends have been complaining. I stare out the window wondering how Miss O'Leary lived – with her family, a friend, alone? Did she have a wild life outside Dickson High School? A visit from me after graduation might have meant a lot to her. Or perhaps she preferred the distance. It is almost dark. The rain continues to sputter. Still, there is always creative potential. I am drawn back to the typewriter, ignoring the gurgling in my stomach and the familiar craving for a chocolate French twist.

– Dropping Anchor –

> The sailor leaves his ship, picks up an oar and walks inland. He cannot stop until someone asks, 'What's that you're carrying?' Then he can rest.
>
> *The Odyssey*

Grey. Brown. Beige. The colour of this high desert eludes her. The mountains are rocky ladders to a flat, pale sky. Macro arrowheads. Otherwise, scrub stretches for miles to the horizon. This reminds Patricia of travelling in the South. Perhaps because of the bus. She hasn't taken a long bus journey for fifteen years.

A Black woman across the aisle places a yellow-flowered pillow next to herself so she doesn't have to share the seat when they make the next stop at Murdoch. Patricia had heard the woman tell the young Chicano soldier behind them that she is travelling from New Orleans to visit her sister in Los Angeles. She needs the space to stretch. Who could argue?

A day-and-a-half in this bus, muses Patricia, who has less than four hours to ride from the El Paso airport to Murdoch, New Mexico. She glances at the blond sailor sleeping next to her, head jiggling against the window frame, snoring beer breath in and out. Now she watches his fog on the cold window, almost clearing when he inhales, then returning the net of moisture over the glass. Outside the window it is white: snow on the cactus, on the telephone poles, on the road ahead.

Patricia closes her eyes and tries to imagine what her father will look like. Instead, Mother's face appears, objecting to this visit. Patricia argues back, that he is more her father than Mother's ex-husband. Her father. Patricia reflects that she was sixteen when he left the family and she has hardly seen him in twenty years. Oh, they have had the obligatory dinners and brunches when they happened to be in the same port. Three years ago in New York. Five years ago in London. Once in San Francisco. But these infrequent, indigestible meals were ritualized encounters. *She has always been better at observing rituals than at participating in them. Even as a devout child, she found the Eucharist stuck to the roof of her mouth.* Sometimes she wonders if Dad sent a stand-in to the dinners and brunches. Any number of people could have imitated that Boston Irish accent and affected the racial epithets. She wonders again why her father, a merchant seaman all his life, has retired to the desert to raise chickens.

The sailor shifts, disturbing her reverie and she opens her eyes. Snow falls steadily as they approach a town. She consults her watch – almost two o'clock. Yes, 'The Rotary Club Welcomes You To Murdoch, New Mexico. Population: 1,376. Elevation: 4,095 feet.' Patricia never thought her father would get this far above sea level before he died. She had spent years praying for his death. Now he is seventy years old. He is a hoary, fat old man waving to her from the door of the small Greyhound station.

Patricia is the only passenger to disembark at Murdoch. Do the others know something she doesn't? She resists the impulse to turn and wave to the woman with the pillow; the friendliest gesture she can make is to hustle off this bus so that they can get on to Los Angeles.

Dad waves again as she emerges. He stays inside the station until the driver disengages her bag from the storage compartment. Then her father waddles towards her, pulling a poodle. A standard grey poodle, she notices, like the one they had when she was little.

'Hi there,' he says.

'Hi.' She smiles and pecks his cheek. 4711. Even in the frozen desert, he wears 4711 cologne.

'You like him?' His accent is stronger. Until now, he might have been any retired rancher. Now, she knows he is her father, displaced from Newton, Massachusetts, and from Dun Laohaire before.

'Cute,' she manages.

'Guards against the spics,' he says.

Testing her already, or does he always talk like this? She realizes she can swallow the bait. He would love a fight. But it's only sport to him.

'I call him Fritzie. Got two more at home. They couldn't all come to welcome you. So I brought Fritzie. He's the quietest.'

'Nice to meet you, Fritzie.' She scratches the dog's neck and he rubs himself against her long, quilted coat.

'Better get you in the car,' he says, 'before you freeze. Crazy weather for New Year's. I said come for New Year's because it's usually hot.'

'Weather doesn't matter,' she shrugs. 'I'm here to see you.' It comes out naturally enough because it is the truth. She *has* come to see him. Now and then. She has come to be kind to him. She has come because he may die soon – how can he survive with all that weight? – and she would feel guilty if she hadn't come. Still, she is taken aback by her statement, so intimate and direct.

He walks up to a small, green Datsun truck. She is mildly surprised that it isn't a big, old Pontiac they could sail down the highway. However he is a chicken rancher now.

'Mind if Fritzie rides with us? It's a little cold for him in the back.'

'Not at all.' She holds one bag on her lap, pushes her suitcase on the floor in front of her and draws the dog closer. The truck smells of country. She checks herself in the rearview mirror: a tall, redheaded woman looking a little younger than usual.

'Sorry I couldn't pick you up at the El Paso airport,' he grunts, getting behind the wheel. She feels the truck lower a foot towards the ground. 'But those roads were slick and I don't have chains. I knew you'd make it fine, though. Once, I took a bus down the Jersey turnpike in weather like this and we made it fine. Who would have thought – chains in the desert?'

'It *was* fine. Really. I thought about the years I spent on buses, doing organizing at those mills in the South.'

'Unions.' He clears his throat of phlegm and pulls onto

the highway. Fritzie barks frantically. 'I still can't believe you threw away your college education to become a union organizer.'

She stares ahead into the thick fog and prays they will make it safely to the ranchero. Suddenly, she is overwhelmed with memories of Dad, lit up like a tree and swerving all over the road to Somerville on the way to spend Christmas at Grandma's. But the strongest thing she has smelled today is 4711.

'Didn't hear from Art at Christmas.'

'Oh.' She reminds herself that she has promised not to get involved in the feud between Dad and her older brother. 'How about Henry? Did Henry call?'

'Your little brother always calls.' His voice loses its edge. 'Henry's doing great. Made assistant manager of the dealership last month.'

'Yes.' She smiles at the thought of her gregarious baby brother.

'Say, seriously now, how's your work? Your job going OK?'

He's trying, she thinks. The last time they met he didn't ask a thing about her.

'Fine.' She nods. 'We're working on a new contract. Management seems flexible. We'll see.' She wished she could be forthcoming; wishes she could trust him more.

'The dentist liked your book.' He clears his throat again. 'He's a reader, that guy. He was impressed that I had a daughter who wrote a book. So was I.' He looks at her.

Patricia is glad the weather is so cold; perhaps her blush will disappear quickly. It's a modest publication; more a handbook, really. She remembers a wonderful trip they once took together, just the two of them up the coast. 'Tell me about the chickens,' she says.

'Well, I got bantams and Rhode Island Reds . . . you'll see. Best this year are the pheasants. And I've got one terrific peacock.'

'Peacock?'

'Yeah, a gorgeous male, wait till I show you.'

She knows his place before he turns up the driveway. The flagpole is an exclamation point in front of the house of

Walt Lester, American citizen, who hated all the ports he visited and couldn't wait to retire at home. The front yard is filled with pastel gravel. She sees her father's wife, Dagmar, standing in the living-room window.

'Home, Fritzie, whadya say, boy? Glad to be home?'

The dog presses his nose on the windshield, yapping wildly.

A chorus of higher and lower-pitched barks greet him. As soon as her father cuts the motor, Dagmar releases the other poodles from the front door.

'OK, OK, now,' he shouts. 'Down, boy. Down, girl. That's it, that's a good dog.'

Patricia sits in the car, amused and touched by the chaos. Why is she taking it so good naturedly? He used to drive her nuts.

'It's all right.' Her father looks over, 'They won't bite.'

'Oh, I'm not worried about that,' she begins defensively and hops out of the car.

'Welcome, Patricia,' the tall, blonde woman says. She begins to hug her and then remembers the cup of cocoa in her hand. 'To warm you up, after the trip.'

'Yes, thanks.' Patricia nods, accepting the cocoa. Should she stand here and drink it? Won't Dagmar freeze if she stays outside in her slippers?

'That's it; that's it.' Her father is still talking to the dogs.

Patricia sips the cocoa. 'Delicious. Perhaps we should get in the house?' She shifts her shoulder bag and reaches for the suitcase.

Dagmar claims it. 'This way, yes, what was I thinking about, serving you on the ice-cold driveway?'

They leave him outside with the dogs. She shivers at the familiar sensation of being abandoned. She remembers, as a little girl, waving goodbye at the side of a big, white roaring ship. Why the panic? He's just gone to quell the dogs.

'Sit,' Dagmar instructs, 'I'll show you the guest room in a minute. But relax here on the couch. You can see two mountain ranges when it's clear. He's been talking about your visit for months. And he gave your book to the dentist two weeks ago so as to talk with you about it. We're not much on reading.'

Patricia looks out the big picture window at the heavy mist sweeping down the street. The barking has grown fainter and she guesses her father has gone to check on the chickens.

'I've taken to watercolours myself.' She bobs the marshmallow up and down in her cocoa. 'I did oils for a while, but the texture wasn't right for the desert. Too rough. You have to look close to see things here. Sometimes in the middle of nothingness, miles of nothingness, there will be a small gem – literally a gem, or a flower – you know and oils are just not delicate enough for that. I don't suppose you paint. You must be too busy.'

Patricia wishes she could excuse herself to lie down for a few moments. 'I don't have the talent for painting, for creative things like that.'

'Don't be modest, an educated girl like yourself,' Dagmar turns. 'Oh, now, dear, brace yourself for an invasion.'

He walks in, followed by three huge poodles. 'Behave,' he warns them. 'Come meet Patricia and behave, you hear me?'

He introduces Schooner, Taffy and Fritzie again.

'Sometimes he gets mixed up,' Dagmar laughs, 'calls them your names, "Art, Patricia and Henry". Can you believe it?'

Patricia smiles thinly and gulps the cocoa.

'Oh, here, let me get a refill. And some cookies. Your father has been baking all week.'

He always did this before he went to sea, Patricia remembers. The house would rise with delicious aromas as he canned peaches and tomatoes and made sauces for Mother to serve when he was away. Then he would disappear. For three months. Six months. 'It's his job,' Mother would explain. 'He doesn't like it any better than we do.' Patricia knew she should trust her parents; she knew she was exaggerating her fears. But even when he got a shore job, he would be gone for weeks loading cargo. Then one day, what she had always suspected happened: he left for good.

The dogs continue to bark. Dagmar continues to talk.

Patricia and her father exchange stale items of family news. The sky outside grows dark and, finally, Dagmar beckons Patricia to her room at the back of the house.

'It's my room, actually, I can't sleep with your father's snoring. Sounds like a bull elephant, you know.'

Patricia thinks how Mother would be happy to hear the old buzz saw at night. Surprised by the reflex to defend Mother after all these years, she declares, 'Very cosy. I like the colours.' She glances surreptitiously at the silver crucifix knotted with palm leaves and hanging over the bed. She has forgotten that Dad persuaded Dagmar to convert to Catholicism. He had talked his way into an annulment and remarriage, protecting his immortal soul. Our father. It's all coming back.

'I'm glad you like it. I sent to Santa Fe for the curtain fabric . . .'

That night, as Patricia brushes her teeth, she reads a prayer tacked to the mirror. 'Please God, help me remember that silence is golden. When I open my mouth to speak, let me breathe in the glory of your universe . . .' She has been judging Dagmar too harshly. So she stole Dad from Mother twenty years ago; surely she's had second thoughts. Besides, Mother is probably better off alone. She's more independent, more outgoing than she ever was when Dad was around.

Patricia climbs into the warm bed and considers the first day. She is confused by the great affection she feels for him. Of course he is still bombastic and single-minded. But she keeps having glimpses of him in the past – driving her to a basketball game; winning double pinochle with her against Mother and Henry. They had some good times when he was in port and sober. She reads for a while, then slips down beneath the rustling comforter and fresh yellow-flowered sheets. Yellow flowers. She thinks of the woman on the bus and wonders how many hours she has to go before Los Angeles.

The noises start before light. Roosters. High, shrieking whistles. Dogs barking. Patricia puts the pillow over her head and falls back to sleep. Sun creeps into the room and the back door bangs. Dad going out to feed the chickens. Six o'clock. He always hit the deck early. She draws down the shade and crawls under the pillow again. She dreams she is at Olduvai Gorge.

The barking wakens her. Eight o'clock, well, she doesn't want to be a slouch. Tentatively she sticks one foot out of the warm covers and pulls it back. She reaches over and raises the shade to find the street still socked in with fog. Yawning, she gets up; rushes into her clothes.

'You didn't have to get all dressed,' Dagmar greets her in the kitchen. 'I'm not usually decent until nine or ten. Your father, sometimes, he wakes the rooster.'

He walks in, brushing his hands. Patricia is filled with fondness. His gesture reminds her of a past moment she cannot quite place.

'Ready for a real breakfast?' he asks.

'Starving.' Then she remembers how much he piled on her plate the previous night. 'Medium starving.'

'Your father is such a cook,' Dagmar sighs. 'Especially this season. When we had Father Bailey over for spaghetti and meatballs, he spent the whole day preparing. I tell him, "Walt, relax, you don't have to sustain people for the next ten years; it's only one meal." But he loves it. Loves it. I just wish he would love to wash the dishes.'

'Thought we could go visit Admiral Dirk, the breeder, while Dagmar's at the picture framer's today. I mean, we could all drive to town and you and me could check out the new birds.'

'Now, Walt, remember, you yourself said we didn't have room . . .'

'All right. All right. Doesn't do an old man harm to browse.'

Patricia remembers her mother's warning that his backyard tomato patch would take over Massachusetts.

'Well, Patricia will be with you. I'm sure that will keep you sensible.'

Mother had said this when he went up to Portland to load cargo. Patricia read while he was at work. Then he took her out to dinner and introduced her to that nice woman, Dagmar, who was staying at the same hotel.

In the truck, Dagmar makes Patricia promise that she will drag him away from the birds by ten o'clock, complaining about how he had to extend the pens twice that autumn after shopping sprees. Patricia tenses, resentful of Dagmar's intimacy with him. What does she expect; they have been married for eighteen years. Still, Patricia can't relax until Dagmar disembarks at the picture framer's.

Silently they proceed to Admiral Dirk's. Patricia watches the flat landscape, considering how like the ocean it feels — empty and endless and bare. Dad is captain of his ship as he has never been at sea; Dagmar is his trusty first mate. He hasn't retired so much as gone to heaven.

Admiral Dirk is a few years older than her father, a tall New Englander, cut from a richer crust than the Lesters, but rank disappears as the men inspect the new birds. The cages are smelly, crowded and dusty. The two friends consult about incubating times and pen temperatures. Patricia is drawn away to the high-pitched squawk of a peacock in the far pen. As she approaches, he turns his back, raising his feathers; a fire of iridescent greens and blues. Patricia aches to see him in the sunlight.

'I call that one "King Walter", in honour of your Dad.' Admiral Dirk comes up behind her. 'Likes to show off before the ladies. Best feathers in town.'

'Don't listen to this old coot.' Her father slaps his friend on the back. 'We really call that one Emperor Dirk.'

She watches the two men laughing and wonders how anyone can be so easy with her father.

'Promised Dagmar I wouldn't bring anything home,' he chuckles. 'She sent this one as watchdog.'

'OK, Walt, see you soon. Happy new year. To you, too, miss.'

Dagmar is waiting outside the frame shop, slapping her hands together against the cold.

She hops in and blows fog on the windshield.

'Whadya waiting in the cold like a dummy for? You'll get pneumonia.'

'I was just trying to make it easier on you.' Dagmar shakes her head and turns to Patricia. 'He's something, isn't he? You do him a favour and he complains. Hey, Walt, where are you going?'

'Home.'

'You forgot that I have to pick up the pattern for Mrs MacLeod. And the basket of fruit for Hunter.'

'God damned church people. You're always running around doing things for them. And here we have our own family visiting.'

'He's such a gentle soul.' Dagmar winks at Patricia. 'I've got an idea. You two take a ride around town while I run errands. It will only be twenty-five minutes. You'll hardly notice. Here, pull over just here, will you, Walt?'

He checks his watch. 'Ten-thirty, sharp. But wait inside Nedley's Grocery, don't stand out in the cold. You'll catch your death.'

He rips away from the curb and Patricia thinks how her brother Art was grounded a whole month for making the family car screech like that.

'Well, I guess I can show you the new residential park. Can't for the life of me figure why people come to the edge of nowhere and live in a housing tract.'

As they drive, she tries not to be frightened. He's with her now. They're together for a while. And this time she'll be the one to leave – to return to her own apartment in Boston.

'Dagmar has these friends who like to eat out. Now I enjoy a good meal, but there's only one decent restaurant here – a Wop place over on the south highway. Anyway, her friends like to eat at 'Sitting Pretty', ridiculous name for a restaurant. And the food is like frozen dinners, not always thawed. Or they like the Chink place down the street. Not bad for a Chink place, but they put in so much MSG you can't see straight for three days.'

'You all compromised on the Italian restaurant?' Patricia asks.

'Naw, we don't go out with that couple at all no more. Dagmar said I let off my big mouth once too often. We used to go out with the Wops, themselves. They're bigshots in the church. Dagmar met the wife at some knitting thing. But him and me got into a fight about the mob and we don't see them no more. Here, I'll show you where they live in the housing estate – see that pink palace up there, lording it over all the other ticky tackys. That's them, the Antonelli's. If that don't sound like a mob name, I don't know what does.'

'Remember Father Antonelli at St John's?'

'Yeah, well, a big family.'

The following day he drives them to the taxidermy studio in Silverton. Patricia sits in the back seat, next to a carefully wrapped pheasant. The bird has keeled over suddenly, a perfect specimen. Well, she has wanted to know her father's life. Still, she hasn't bargained for Dagmar's constant chatter. Poor woman, Patricia tells herself, she's lonely. She is doing her best to adapt with the painting and the church activities and the social life Dad keeps ruining. Still, Patricia is beginning to feel like a kidnapped ear.

'. . . So what do you think about that, Patricia?' Dagmar asks.

'About what, sorry, I was looking at the scenery.' She regrets speaking brusquely, then feels mad at Dagmar for making her mad with herself. As always, Dad seems out of anger's range.

'Leave her alone, Motor Mouth. Let her enjoy the country. She has to get back to that damn city soon enough.'

'I didn't mean . . .' Patricia rubs her right shoulder, for she can feel the migraine ticking. 'Sorry, what did you ask?'

'It's OK.' Dagmar sits straighter and peers across the flat scrub as if scouting for the Strategic Air Command. 'Let's just enjoy the world around us for a while.'

Patricia tries to stretch away the tension, her hand falling on the dead bird's head. She shivers and stares out the window, counting cactus.

Murphy's Taxidermy Ltd is an inconspicuous enterprise in a green Quonset hut on the edge of town. One could easily miss it. Her father is clearly a frequent patron.

Dad grows enthusiastic as they make their way through the dimly lit, vacant waiting-room. 'Come on back. They all work here.'

Dave Murphy, a big man wearing casual clothes and a baseball cap, raises one hand in salute. He continues to stitch with the other hand. Nell Murphy turns and rushes to Dagmar. A skinny young man, probably their son, is eating a MacDonald's hamburger at a sawhorse in the middle of the room.

'Like you to meet my daughter,' her father calls to Dave.

Dave nods, 'Welcome.'

Patricia reads 'Dodgers' on his cap and wonders if the bus has made it to Los Angeles.

'Brought up that pheasant,' her father says nervously.

'Get right to it, after this squirrel. One of Leonard's pets – you know the two he fed in the front yard? Just expired.'

'Could have been the cold,' her father says.

'Yep.' Dave concentrates on the small, neat stitches. 'Speaking of which, help yourselves to coffee over there. And Skip, hey Skip, offer the visitors some of them fries. Wouldn't mind a couple myself.'

'Sure, Pop.' The boy unfolds himself and stands about seven feet tall. Even if Patricia had been hungry in the midst of all the carnage, she wouldn't consider taking potatoes from this rake of a lad. Her father grabs a handful and pours her and himself coffee.

She accepts the cup and walks around the cold room. She has never visited a taxidermist or a mortician before. The chill reminds her of church. She stops at one trophy, then the next and the next, hanging at evenly spaced intervals from the wall, like stations of the cross. An elk shot in its prime. A raccoon growing threadbare. Two pheasants. A quail. A blue jay. Suddenly she is exhausted, almost faint. How long are they going to stay here anyway? She notices Dagmar and Nell Murphy sitting at a table of feathers, laughing. Dave and her father are arguing football as Dave sews. Skip is munching his Big Mac. They can't have been here long, she tells herself, if he is still eating the hamburger. Yet she has had enough of the gallery and wanders into the waiting-room.

How had she thought the room was vacant? A grizzly bear feigns menace from the corner. You have to look close in the desert, Dagmar said. A defeated moose hangs his head from the wall over the clock. A coyote prances on top of the wide screen television. *Dad brought her dolls from Japan and fabric from Brazil. She always wanted to say, forget the presents and stay a while. But she had to avoid his answer, which would have been a lie.* Patricia sinks down into the naugahide couch and picks up a copy of *Taxidermy Today*.

An hour later – she has consulted the clock every five minutes – Dagmar and her father come looking for her.

'Always reading,' he turns to his wife. 'Always that way as a kid. She didn't get it from me.'

'How about lunch?' Dagmar enquires.

'Sure,' he says. 'There's a great steak house on Main Street. You feel like steak, Patricia?'

'To tell you the truth,' she says, 'I feel like a little air. Why don't I just walk around town while you and Dagmar have lunch.'

'What's wrong with you anyway? You used to like to eat. You trying to turn yourself into one of them Twiggies?'

'No, I'm just not hungry. And I wouldn't mind some exercise.'

'Let her do as she likes, Walt.'

He begins to protest, then his attention is caught by the grizzly. 'Ralph Foster got that one, on his last trip to Alaska.'

'Why didn't he take it home?'

'Well, it was a tie. I mean Ralph didn't last much longer than it took to fly back to El Paso. Heart attack. His wife knew he'd want the bear stuffed, but then she couldn't bring herself to put it in the house.'

'So what's it doing here?' Patricia is appalled by her morbid curiosity.

'For the grandchildren,' explains Dagmar. 'The Murphys are saving it for Ralph's grandchildren.'

They drive through Silverton in silence, stopping at the Carousel Steak House.

'Sure you're not hungry?' he asks. 'They have a salad bar with garbanzo and kidney beans.'

She smiles, touched that he remembers her favourite beans. 'No, no thanks. I'll just wander around the shops. Maybe I'll join you for coffee.'

An hour later Patricia enters the loud, smoky restaurant, feeling revived by her solitude. 'Hi!' She waves, glad to see them. 'Hey, I got a surprise for dessert. A lottery ticket for each of us.'

'Oh, let me see,' Dagmar says. 'We need coins to rub off the markings. No, no, I didn't win a thing. How about you, Walt?'

'No, two of a kind, but not three.'

'No,' Patricia shakes her head, 'I didn't win either.'

She rises early the next morning in the hope that she will get some time alone with him. Maybe they can feed the birds together. She pours coffee from the thermos and pulls on her coat. Walking along the pens, she is amazed how quickly the chickens skitter, seemingly oblivious to the cold. Her father has explained the elaborate heating system and now she understands how complicated it must be. Sweet that he would go to such lengths for the birds. It is begging the question to ask why he couldn't nurture his own children.

Turning a corner by the pheasants' pens, she sees him, bent over, digging seeds from his bag; his white hair swirling around red earmuffs; his cheeks ruddy; his eyes almost bulging from the strain of stooping so low. Suddenly she notices his hands – small and thick–the fingers more like the dried, cracked legs of a turtle than digits of a man. She has always wondered where she got her tiny hands, for Mother's are large and competent. She is at once repelled and relieved. She had thought there was a mutant gene.

'Shhhh.' He turns, as if he had seen her all along. 'Come this way, the Prince of Hearts is displaying this morning.'

She tiptoes over the sawdust and straw, inhaling the pungent birdshit and taking a step back upon seeing the peacock, even more glorious than the one two days before. The sun is bright now, a crisp, unfiltered morning sun that ignites the peacock's colours, his feathers like rainbows rippling across a lake. He moves the radiant tail slowly, bestowing his gift.

'Beautiful,' she says, regretting she doesn't sound more intelligent, 'beautiful.'

Her father winks.

Her breath catches at his boyishness, at the clarity of the morning, at the power of forgiveness.

'Here,' he hands her the bag with a plastic scoop. 'You feed him. I'll take care of the bantams.'

The Prince scrutinizes her. He waits until she finishes pouring his food. Carefully he tucks away his glory and walks, as if in stiletto heels, to the dish. He stares at her. She steps back. He begins to eat.

'Good,' her father calls. 'He never lets anyone watch him eat. You made a friend.'

She looks up and smiles.

'How about a ride to Mexico? Just the two of us. Dagmar said we should spend some time alone. I've got a couple of errands. Things are ten times cheaper there, you know.'

'Sure,' she says, but she is reluctant to leave the bird.

Over breakfast he checks his shopping list. The dogs are barking to join them. 'No,' he shouts back, 'can't take you to Mexico.'

Dagmar counts the cash from a canister. 'Be careful,' she says.

Patricia excuses herself to the living-room while they complete their transactions. Fog still shrouds the mountains. It does seem strange weather for the desert. Maybe it will clear tomorrow before she leaves.

'Be careful,' Dagmar hugs her. 'They pretend they don't speak English and cheat you every opportunity.'

'She speaks Spanish,' her father explains, with pride or irritation, Patricia can't tell.

'Then take care of him.' Dagmar remains anxious.

'We'll be fine,' he calls gruffly. 'Back about three o'clock.'

The ride is flat and white and peaceful. They are silent. He never said much when she was a child. She wonders how he can stand Dagmar's chatter, but she doesn't know him well enough to ask. Maybe next time. Yes, perhaps she will come back. It hasn't been a bad trip. They have been close, on and off. He has made a great effort baking cakes and cookies, loaning her handbook to the dentist, driving up to Silverton and now down to Mexico. So he is still loud and cranky and destroying himself with too much food. She is no longer a child; how can this affect her so? His grammar and lack of sophistication – which used to embarrass her – now seem almost the hallmark of his success in the world. After all, he immigrated with nothing at the age of seventeen. And here he is, owner of a ranch house, friend of Admiral Dirk, caretaker of the Prince of Hearts and father of someone who has been published. Yes, she is gratified that he would count her book among his trophies.

The car is slowing down. Ahead the sign reads, 'Mexico. *Bienvenido!*'

'Just wait in the car. With the doors locked. I'm going to change some money.' He points to a row of wooden huts. 'Be right back.'

'Be . . .' she begins, almost repeating Dagmar's warning.

'I'll be fine; don't worry.'

He returns promptly. The tyres squeal as he speeds towards the border gate. The air in the car is moist and she tries to ignore his heavy dose of cologne which is making her stomach turn.

'*Buenos Dias,*' the guard greets them.

'No speak Spanish,' her father says as if he were refusing an exchange of pornographic jokes.

The guard straightens slightly. 'Good day. Do you have anything to declare . . . ?'

She wants to speak up, to temper her father's rudeness, but she knows that neither man would appreciate the intrusion.

Mother cried for a month after he filed for divorce. Patricia had tried to hold them together, had tried to explain one to the other. She couldn't comfort Mother because for years Mother had comforted her, promising that he would return, that one day he would return for good. And she was wrong.

They are admitted to Mexico.

Los Altos is a small, poor town of tarpaper shacks and muddy roads, made almost impassable by the weather.

'Snow in Mexico; this is ridiculous,' her father sniffs as he tries to pull the truck out of a rut.

'We've only driven twenty miles,' she snaps in spite of herself. 'Did you expect the equator?'

'If they maintained the damn roads, it would be all right. How do they plan to do trade when you can't get in and out of their damn . . .' The engine goes whizz-whizz and suddenly they are out of the rut, almost running over a little boy playing nearby.

'*Madre Mia!*' the boy's father shouts, shaking his fist.

Her father shakes his fist back, then proceeds gingerly over the corrugated road.

'Damn Mexicans, letting their kids play in the street.'

She closes her eyes, knowing not to provoke him for they will wind up in jail if he gets any angrier. *She remembers him sitting in his undershirt and boxer shorts drinking beer in front of the TV and yelling at the umpire, at Edward R. Murrow, at Sergeant Bilko. After a while her girlfriends stopped visiting when he was on leave. She didn't know if it was the yelling or the boxer shorts which kept them away.*

'Here we are,' he said abruptly. 'Señora Garcia. The only honest woman in town.'

They walk into a shop lined with bottles of liquor; boxes of detergent; cans of car oil: an extraordinary assortment of American goods. As Patricia's eyes adjust to the light she finds a white-haired woman knitting behind the counter. An orange cat sits on the empty shelf behind.

'*Buenos Dias,*' he has suddenly become a linguist.

The old woman nods, without recognition.

'Nearsighted,' he whispers to Patricia.

'*Señora* Garcia,' he says more loudly, moving closer.

'*Si,*' she says, still apparently without recognition.

'She'll remember me. Dagmar sent a box of clothes for her daughter last month. And once I gave them a fan.'

The old woman stands up and asks if she can help.

'*No Espanol,*' he says gently, with a touch of pique. He turns to his daughter. 'She speaks perfect English.'

'Mr Lester,' he explains. 'From America.'

The woman nods. 'Welcome,' she says finally.

He smiles triumphantly at Patricia. 'See. Now what do

you drink? We'll send you back to Boston with something to see you through winter.'

'Oh, I don't know.' She is suddenly embarrassed. 'I don't drink much.'

'Don't give me that bull.' He is offended. 'You've had a drink with me and Dagmar every night since you been here. Whiskey, I know.' He turns to the counter. 'What's your best Irish?'

She frowns.

'Ah, never mind. I see some Bushmills. No, Jameson. We'll send you back with a big Jameson.'

'Dad, really.'

Señora Garcia is climbing a step-ladder, reaching for the bottle.

'See, I told you they speak English when they want to.'

Patricia can feel the headache rising up the side of her neck.

'And we'll take two Beefeaters. Two Bacardis. One big Johnny Walker Red.'

Silently the woman places bottles in a box. She writes down the price on a scrap of brown paper bag.

'No way,' he explodes. 'No way; that's eight hundred pesos too much!'

The woman shrugs, remaining steadfast about the amount.

'You're not gonna rip me off just 'cause you gone mute,' he shouts.

Señora Garcia returns to her stool and watches him.

'Eight hundred pesos too much!' he declares.

Patricia hears a giggle and turns to find five children grinning in the doorway.

'Dad,' she whispers. 'Eight hundred pesos is less than a dollar.'

He glowers at her. She remembers years of vengeful silence at home and can't stand this any more. 'Perhaps if I translated.'

'Translation isn't the problem.'

'Well, somebody doesn't understand something,' she tries.

'It's a question of principle. It's not the dollar. These

people will rob you blind in a flash. She knows the price. I buy here all the time.'

Her father puts both hands on the counter and stares at the old woman, like a belligerent teenager. The woman has retreated behind heavy eyelids. The cat purrs.

Patricia looks from one person to the other in dismay. They could stand here all day. For the rest of their lives. Maybe they should call in Skip Murphy to stuff them and create a diarama for twenty-first century tourists.

Patricia has an inspiration. Turning to the children, she asks, *'Tu Abuela?'*

A little girl steps forward, saying yes, she is the old woman's granddaughter. Patricia walks to the doorsil and hands the child two dollars. *'Por Tu. Por Tu Abuela. Por Navidad.'* The child's face lights up.

'Hey, hey,' her father calls. 'Don't play with those kids, they'll ring every last penny from you. They always want pennies. Pennies add up.'

Patricia knows what she has done.

Señora Garcia, who has followed the exchange from behind closed eyelids, glances at Patricia neutrally.

Patricia stares at her feet.

The woman stands up to the counter.

'So you've decided to be honest,' her father barks, his voice betraying his relief.

She ignores him and crosses out the first sum, noting down the amount he has demanded.

He pays her, picks up the box and leaves, tugging on Patricia's sweater.

Patricia looks back with a mixture of shame and resignation. As a child she knew everything would work out perfectly. It had taken years to develop her dubious talent for compromise.

They cross the American border at the far gate, manned by a friend of her father's. They ride back to Murdoch in strained, not companionable, silence.

Dinner is his famous meatballs and spaghetti. With lots of red wine. And Jameson afterwards. He is sweating as they take their drinks to the living-room. She knows he is worn out, creating the perfect farewell.

The snow is heavy as they drive to the Greyhound depot. Dagmar has stayed home so Patricia can have a last private moment with her father. And Fritzie.

'I would of drove you to El Paso,' he begins.

'No chains,' she says.

'Yeah.' He is nervous. 'But you'll be fine. Those buses are equipped.'

'Yes.' She stares at the fog.

'I seen worse snow. Once in Jersey, when I was taking a ship out. Why the bus just crawled along the turnpike. I thought I'd never make it. Hell, forget the ship. I thought I'd never make it to the dock. But it was fine. The bus was fine.'

'Yes,' she says, patting the dog. 'Don't worry.'

As they pull up, the Greyhound driver is loading bags.

'Well, this is it, honey. Thanks for coming.' He stands stiffly, holding the dog by a leash.

'Thanks for having me.' She reaches up and hugs him, resisting the mad impulse to pull him on the bus with her. She used to imagine him carrying her onto his ship just before the gangplank was lifted.

'For the trip.' He pulls a brown sack from his pocket. 'Meatball sandwich and some cookies.'

'Thanks,' she says, unable to speak more for fear of crying. She can't hold herself this tightly for long and she is grateful when the driver opens the door.

'Hey, don't forget the booze.' Her father hands her a shopping bag. The passengers surge forward. She wishes he would let go of it, so she can get on the bus. She is having a hard time breathing.

'OK.' She pulls on the bag and just at that moment someone knocks into her from behind. She teeters to keep her balance. Turning, she sees a large Black woman and for a second wonders if this is the lady returning from Los Angeles.

'Shit,' her father shouts.

She hears a crash.

'Damn hippopotamus, can't watch her step.' He is shouting at the woman, who has the good sense to ignore him and claim her seat on the bus.

'No, Dad, it's good luck, really.'

Patricia rushes to save the situation. 'Sort of like christening a ship as it's launched.'

He stares at her for a second, his jaw clenched, his brows knit and then he shakes his head. 'Yeah.' He is almost smiling. 'Good luck.'

They walk to the bus door and he waves her a kiss as she hands the driver her ticket.

'You'll be fine.' He is talking to the bus driver. 'Once I took a bus down the Jersey turnpike, snow so thick you couldn't see a foot in front. You'll make it fine.'

– Misty, Tiled Chambers –

'Nine is old enough to learn to swim,' Mom said, letting me have the window seat on the bus.

'But *you* don't know how to swim,' I protested.

'Exactly!' she pronounced with the infallible logic she always used when refuting arguments with my own words.

Mom made me wear my heavy jacket and her own long, wool scarf. She wore the old red coat and her neck looked too long that morning. When I was mad at my mother I found fault with her appearance – especially with her skinny face and bow legs. I was furious with her today because it was 20 degrees outside and she was dragging me all the way to Hackensack for swimming lessons.

'But, Mom, it's too *cold* for a bathing suit. Why don't we wait for summer?'

'It's crowded in the summer. This way you'll be able to swim at the pond when the hot weather starts; won't that be nice?'

'I'd rather learn piano.'

She looked past me at snowmen guarding white lawns along Madison Avenue.

'Why can't I take piano? Jackie has lessons.'

'Music lessons are expensive, dear. Besides, you'd have to practise. We could hardly afford a *piano*.'

I stared at an icicle forming on a telephone wire. 'I could practise on Jackie's.' I looked back with expectation.

She was picking absentmindedly at a callous on her palm. It was about to bleed and I tapped her. 'No, don't do that; it's bad for you.'

She smiled, then peered out the window again. We were silent for the rest of the trip.

As we pulled into Hackensack, she took my hand, 'You'll like swimming. Give it a chance.'

The YMCA was an imposing building, but lacking the

ornate drama of St Mary's Catholic School. Here I noticed one crucifix, no statues, a lot of plain windows and a big desk. A woman with kinky, blonde hair gave Mom a form and took some money. She nodded at me insincerely. Soon Mom was marching me down a dark corridor and I remembered a movie where ancient people sacrificed their children to the gods.

The locker-room had a green smell. It was hot and humid, like July. I caught a glimpse of a fat woman without any clothes, before Mom hauled me over to a stall and handed me the regulation suit. The dark blue knit material was scratchy and stank of disinfectant. I thought about Mom taking me to the doctor, telling me to get undressed and lie on the table while she stood by, tall and invulnerable in that horrid red coat. How could she wear a heavy coat in this muggy room? This wasn't the first time I had doubted her sanity. Maybe I could run away to Jackie's and sleep under the piano.

'Hurry along, dear, we only have five minutes before we meet your teacher.'

Mitch was waiting for us outside the ladies' dressing-room. He was a tall man with red hairs on his chest and head. At first glance, he reminded me of Buster Crabbe. Shyly, I stared at the locker-room door. The italicized 'Ladies' was so much more adult than the block lettered 'Girls' marking the bathroom at school. 'Ladies.' I tilted my head at the same angle as the white letters. I would tell Jackie about this.

'How do you do?' Mitch had a broad smile, but I didn't register the rest of his face because he reached down to shake my hand. And I noticed that he had several fingers missing. I watched the goosebumps rise along my arm.

Mom nudged me. Maybe she saw, too, and we could go home now. Instead, she said, 'Say "How-do-you-do?", Gerry.'

I knew it was rude to stare at people's handicaps. I knew I should be too adult to mention it. And yet I imagined his hand sticking in my throat, right above the 'How-do-you-do?'

'Well, a lot of people are shy at first.'

I noticed he was talking to me rather than to my mother.

'You'll be fine once we get in the water. Shall we test the temperature?'

He took my hand and I tried not to *feel*, just as I would try not to smell when I went to the bathroom at the movies. Instead, I concentrated on the high, winding echoes of the Hackensack pool. For the first time I noticed that there was a whole class of swimmers in the far end – the deep end – of the water. Mitch nodded toward the wading section.

He turned gently to Mom. 'You'll want to sit up there,' he said, pointing to the bleachers. 'That way you won't get wet.'

Coward, I thought, as she found a seat and let the strange man lead me down the cold metal ladder. I soon forgot her when he showed me how to dunk my head in and out of the water. Then I experienced the miracle of floating. I hardly thought about his hand until he lead me back to my mother beneath the italicized 'Ladies' sign.

'A natural.' He patted my shoulder. 'Regular mermaid. See you next week, Gerry?'

'Oh, yes, next week,' I answered, surprised by my enthusiasm.

It was a very cold winter, but each week we took the bus to Hackensack. Once I had learned to dog-paddle, Mitch graduated me from the wading section. Every so often I would look up and see Mom watching closely and pretending to be brave. After the lesson she always took me to Woolworth's for an egg salad sandwich and a ginger ale. I had completely forgotten about the piano. I hardly saw Jackie any more because she spent so much time indoors, practising.

One night I dreamt I was sitting on the edge of the pool, dangling my feet. The water had turned black and I was singing, trying to entice the missing fingers to surface from the bottom of the water.

During the day, I tried not to think about Mitch's hand. I never mentioned it to Mom. At first I thought it would be impolite to talk about his handicap – for surely she must have noticed it too. Then I worried that she hadn't noticed and that if I told her about the missing fingers, she would cancel the lessons. None of the reasons made sense, but it seemed important to remain silent. I succeeded in forgetting about Mitch's hand until the week we began diving lessons.

He took me to the deep end, dove in himself, cutting the water sharply, swimming underneath, graceful as a dolphin. He surfaced with a big smile. 'See how easy it is?'

'Sure.' I stood shivering, suddenly remembering this was late January and it was sleeting outside.

'Just try jumping first,' he called. 'I'll catch you.'

I stood there, bolstered by his smile. Then I glanced over at Mom's encouraging face. The air was an endless expanse; the water, I knew, would be worse, for it went down fourteen feet. Suddenly I jumped. Down. Down. I couldn't decide between terror and exhilaration, and then I was safe. Mitch was holding my hands; we were looking at each other, sputtering and laughing.

'Brave girl,' he said.

I laughed, pumped my feet up and down and held onto his hands. Suddenly I was conscious of the missing fingers and panicked about drowning.

'Don't worry.' He caught my frown. 'Just hold on and I'll swim us to shore.'

Those four feet were interminable as I struggled to keep afloat, to hide my revulsion, to keep from throwing up.

'There,' he said as we reached the safe metal ladder. 'It's a little early to knock off, but you've done a lot for one day.'

I nodded, not daring to meet his eyes, for he must have known the cause of my distress. 'Thank you, Mitch. See you . . . next Saturday.'

I couldn't eat the egg salad sandwich. When Mom asked what was wrong, I broke down and sobbed, finally managing to confess.

She regarded me carefully. She listened as all my fears spilled out. Did he have a kind of leprosy? Was it catching? Or polio? Sometimes the Salk vaccine didn't work and I knew kids got polio from swimming. Were the missing fingers dangerous? Would he lose his grip and let me slip to the bottom of the pool? Mom patted my perfectly formed hand and reassured me that I was safe. She speculated on how he might have lost his fingers – in an industrial accident, in the war.

The war, I decided. That night, watching a World War II movie on TV, I imagined Mitch on the frontline, perhaps the scout who went ahead of other soldiers to clear the way for his buddies and in the process . . .

Sergeant Mitch taught me the crawl, the side-stroke, the breast-stroke, the elementary back-stroke. I still had trouble diving. But he was impressed with my progress and told Mom I was his best student.

I liked the side-stroke because I could see all around me. I would look up at the ceiling and consider the funny, yellow light pouring through the high windows. I liked to peer down the length of the pool and watch the fat lady doing her laps and the toddlers splashing each other. Searching the bleachers, I would wave to Mom, who smiled as I swam past her fears. When I looked up at her nowadays she seemed more relaxed. Sometimes she even sat back in her seat with her feet out on the bench in front of her.

The side-stroke made me feel like a graceful machine or one of those scissor bugs at the pond. It always put me in a quiet mood. I found the back-stroke too slow just as I considered the crawl too fast. With the breast-stroke, I could fly, clearing a path through the cool water with my strong arms. Sometimes Mitch and I played tag and he would dare me to chase after his sleek shadow on the chlorine floor.

The locker-room felt more comfortable now. I watched steam weaving around the dented grey lockers and I imagined this mist as angelhair breathing from the naked female forms. Mom made me get dressed in the cubicle, but many swimmers, particularly the older women, weren't at all shy. The different shapes were fascinating: tall, lean women with tiny breasts; others with chubby legs and big tummies. Everyone with that triangle of fur above the legs. I had a big curiosity because my mother was always very modest about her own body. Despite Mom's efficient method of whisking me in and out of the dressing-room, I learned a lot. One woman always creamed her legs, slowly, as if she were putting on delicate silk stockings, her hands rising higher and higher until she almost touched the triangle. Everyone had a different system for attaching the bra – some would snap it in front and then ponderously turn the bra around before putting their arms through the straps. Others were astonishingly quick at hooking from behind. The bras came in all sorts – flimsy cheesecloth models like the one my friend Karen wore; lacy, black styles and large, white contraptions with metal supports which made me think of the hairshirts Sister Martin talked about. Maybe women saints wore metal under their breasts. I loved the mingling scents of talcum powder and deodorant and perfume. I eavesdropped on the ladies' quick conversations about gaining and losing weight, raising kids and shopping. By late February I was a regular; several women began to greet me by name.

Sister told us we could write about anything we liked, so I was surprised when she asked me to stay after school to discuss my essay on Mitch's swimming lessons.

'Sit here,' she said in that voice she reserved for serious talks. 'Is it true, what you've written in your paper?' she asked slowly.

I looked into her long face, relieved that I could reassure her it wasn't a lie, that I had, indeed, mastered four strokes although my diving was still giving me trouble.

'Very nice, dear. But is it true that you're taking lessons at the YMCA?'

'Yes, Sister,' I answered proudly. 'All the way in Hackensack. Every Saturday.'

She breathed deeply and looked at me with kindness. 'But what can your mother be thinking about? The YMCA is a *Protestant* organization.'

'Oh, I know that, Sister. There are no statues, anywhere. It's a very plain building. But the pool is pretty, with lots of blues and greens . . .' I stopped at her impassive face.

'Dear, remember what we learned in catechism class about the First Commandment. You shouldn't be participating in a Protestant organization.'

'Oh, I see,' I said, in that voice Mom used when she didn't want to make a decision right away and planned to talk with my father first.

She changed her tack. 'And swimming in the middle of winter? Hackensack is a long way to travel. Have you considered piano? Mrs Sullivan teaches piano in her home.'

'No.' I shrugged. 'Swimming is more useful.' The anger rose suddenly in my throat. 'Music requires too many fingers.'

Sister decided not to pursue this last point. She tapped my knee and said conclusively, 'Gerry, I'm afraid that you'll just have to stop going there.'

'I see.' I wasn't sure how convincing my neutrality was because I was concentrating on holding back the tears.

The next week Mom and I were back on the bus to Hackensack. Mom explained that Sister was mistaken. She couldn't have understood that I was just learning how to swim, that it involved no religious instruction.

I stared out at the grey slush and the lawns peeking through the snow. This was a moral crisis for me because I didn't want to displease God. I didn't want my attendance at the YMCA to damn me to hell – what good would swimming do me there? On the other hand, I loved that old building and my new friends in the locker-room. And Mitch.

'Don't worry,' Mom repeated. 'Trust me. Sister Martin means well, but sometimes the nuns are a little . . . innocent about the world. They could get lost in their rules and regulations.'

I shrugged, but I felt very grown up. Although Mom complained about the nuns to Dad, this was the first time she had ever said anything to me. I tried to conceal my satisfaction.

'Trust me. Wasn't I right about swimming being fun?'

That was the day I did it. I wasn't sure what had got into me. I walked out to the fourteen foot sign, put my head down and dove straight into the green water.

'Perfect,' Mitch called, treading gracefully, holding out his hands to congratulate me.

'Perfect,' Mom called from the bleachers.

'Perfect,' I surfaced, reaching eagerly for his hands.

All winter during my ninth year I took the long bus ride from Dumont to Hackensack. Through the snow I travelled to those misty, tiled chambers where I learned how not to drown.

– *Guest of Honour* –

The parking lot at Leo's Prime Ribs was packed. They couldn't have all come to hear her, Anna reminded herself. This was a popular spot on weekends, with several banquet halls. 'The Pavilion Room,' Mr Swenson had instructed. Anna had promised the man with the slight Swedish accent that she would read her poetry at The Seattle Writers' Gathering tonight. She was feeling shy and tired, but she had agreed six or seven months ago to be their guest of honour. And her editor, Marilyn, said these speaking engagements were good for one's reputation. She took out her box of books and locked the car.

Making her way through Leo's noisy corridors, Anna sniffed succulent odours of dinner to come, realizing that she had skipped lunch. Maybe they would have hors-d'oeuvres at the cocktail hour. The Pavilion Room was four doors up on the right, a busy waiter, whose badge identified him as, 'Hi, I'm Goodwin', pointed and gave her a quizzical look.

Inside the Pavilion Room, she found dozens of men in parkas and heavy flannel jackets. The room was smoky and reeked of beer.

'I'm Anna Lanthier.' Anna tried not to imagine the source of this group's curiosity about women's poetry.

A ruddy faced young man looked her over sympathetically, 'You want the Western Decoy Association?'

'No, I mean, I was told the Pavilion Room, this is it, isn't it?'

'Yeah, lady, the Awards for the Western Decoy Association.'

Anna inhaled sharply. It *was* the fifteenth of November. It *was* Leo's Prime Ribs. 'Do you know where the writers are?'

'In the newspaper, I expect.' He laughed, then took pity

on her again. 'Hey, Walt, you know where a writers' group is meeting tonight?'

'Tell her to go back to the lounge and ask for Marv.'

'Thank you,' she managed, hiking her box of books higher on her hip.

The bar was dark and empty. She knew it would be busy soon enough because Leo's Lounge had a reputation around town.

'Where would I find Marv?' she asked the bartender, whose nametag said, 'Hi, I'm Beatrice'.

'He's sick tonight.' Beatrice inspected Anna. 'Besides, I think he has enough girls. Honey, do yourself a favour. You look a little delicate for that line of work. Try typing or something. I typed for years myself and it's not so bad.'

Abashed, Anna decided to move on. She considered her red silk dress and high heels. Perhaps she had overdressed a little in her nervousness. But surely Beatrice hadn't pegged her because of the cliché clothes. Well, maybe all the other young women who 'asked for Marv' as she did, had a particular objective. Calmly, she walked to the front dining-room. Damn heels; her feet ached already.

She found the *maître d'* and inquired confidently. 'I'm looking for the Writers' Gathering. What room have they been moved to?'

'Oh, that group, let's see, they called to say it would be a small crowd tonight, so they've moved to the Cosy Corner. Five doors down on your right.'

Ten past six, still, it was hardly her fault they had relocated without informing her. Small crowd, she tried not to take it personally. Maybe people couldn't handle this cold weather. The Cosy Corner was a brightly lit, pleasant little *vacant* room.

A harried waiter – Goodwin again – hustled across the floor and did a double take. 'Somehow I didn't think you was with the decoy folks.'

'Do you know where the writers are?' Anna tried to curb her desperation.

'Let's see.' Goodwin observed her more closely. 'Yeah, you look more like a writer.' Then he pulled a schedule from his back pocket. 'Writers' Gathering: Cosy Corner: minimum table settings.'

He watched her face rise and fall. 'Are you Anna Lanter?'

'Lanthier.' She felt pathetically grateful.

'Guest of Honour.' His tone was more formal. 'Says right here, next to your name.'

'Yes.' She blushed. 'Thank you. I think I'll just wait here.'

'Right then. They're scheduled to arrive at six-thirty. Should be any time now.'

'Thanks,' she said.

'Can I get you something?' he frowned. 'Coffee? Cocktail?'

'No, thanks.' She smiled.

Bored after five minutes of sitting on a distinctly uncosy folding chair, Anna stood and arranged her books on the front table. Stepping back, she admired the display. Two volumes by Anna Lanthier. Two books published. Six years ago she wouldn't have believed it. She was lucky. She should be honoured that they invited her. Half-an-hour off – she was sure he had said six sharp, that he would meet her here and help her set up the books – what did it matter?

Two women walked down the hall. 'I know it's here somewhere,' said the younger woman. She tugged on a curl. 'The Pavilion Room is where we met last time, isn't it?'

Anna wanted to call out to them, 'It's the Cosy Corner this month.' But she felt too foolish – being the guest of honour standing in the smaller room all alone admiring her own books. Maybe she could go to the toilet and return after they had discovered the corner, but she would have to pack up the books again. While she was waffling, the two women walked back.

'Here it is, Loretta, the Cosy Corner.'

'Yes,' the older, heavier woman sighed. 'And none too soon.' She set down a cash box and a red folder.

The younger woman noticed Anna first. She hesitated for a second and then offered her hand. 'Are you here for the Writers' Gathering, dear?'

'Yes.' Anna stood. 'I'm Anna Lanthier.'

'Ohhh, the guest of honour,' Loretta said. 'Welcome.

Welcome. A poet, I understand. A feminist poet, Darlene.'

Anna smiled and nodded.

Darlene smiled too. 'If you're anything like me, you always get to a place an hour ahead of time.'

'Half-an-hour,' Anna answered, in spite of herself. 'Mr Swenson asked me to come, to set up the books, to meet the officers . . .'

'Lars, oh, Lars can't make it tonight. Or maybe he changed his mind, if he told her, what do you think, Loretta?'

'You know Lars.' She shrugged. 'Well, this will be very nice indeed, cosy, as they say, perfect for an *intimate* group.'

Anna leaned against the wall, seething at lackadaisical Lars and trying not to vent her frustration on Darlene or Loretta.

'So, Darlene, want me to handle the cash box?' The big woman plopped behind the front table.

'Yeah, and the tickets for roast beef or chicken – all set.' She turned to Anna. 'Of course we pay for *your* dinner. That's our way of thanking you for coming.'

'Thank you.' Anna nodded, almost blind with her accumulated irritation.

'I only wish we had done more publicity. You never know. Last month with Leonard Flicker, we had an overflow crowd. I don't know which is more embarrassing, that or this . . .'

'Oh, here's Ernie and Keith. And Adam with Gloria. We may get a little group after all.'

Anna sat down at the far end of a table and counted her breaths. She would have to calm down before she appeared as guest of honour. The writers stood around the front table greeting each other and gossiping. When she felt she was settled enough, she walked over toward Loretta and Darlene, now her old friends. No one seemed to fit the image of Mr Swenson. She stood waiting until Loretta looked up. 'Oh, Ernie, let me introduce you to our guest of honour.'

A thin, blonde, fiftyish woman considered her curiously. 'Anna Lanther. Pleased to make your acquaintance.

I'm Mrs Ernie MacDonald, Chairman of the Writers' Gathering.'

'Happy to meet you,' Anna said. 'Actually, it's "Lanthier".' After an awkward sag of silence she asked, 'What kind of writing do you do?'

'Oh,' Ernie sighed and looked around. 'I haven't written a speck in five years. But history. Natural history. I've published a bird guide and a number of articles.'

A portly man approached and Ernie relaxed. 'Keith, dear.' She took his arm.

'Anna, let me introduce Keith MacDonald, my husband. Keith, this is our guest of honour, Anna Lanthier.'

'Believe that's pronounced "Lanth-e-ay", isn't it, miss?'

'Actually, I don't know if she is a miss or a mrs.'

'"Lanth-e-ay," *is* the French pronunciation, all right, but my family gave up on that years ago. I answer to anything which sounds close.'

'Sense of humour, always nice on a pretty lady.'

Anna smiled and turned to Ernie. 'So members of your group write in a wide variety of fields?'

'Yes,' Ernie perked up. 'Adam writes computer software and articles for *Disk World*. Evelyn does children's books. Edward, Edward's not here yet, but he'll come; he's the life of the party, does freelance travel pieces now that he's retired. Yes, quite a variety we have. The Gathering has been convening for sixty years now; it's a very established group.'

'I see.' Anna smiled and felt as if someone had stripped plastic tape across her mouth.

'Get you a drink, Annie?' offered Keith.

'Thank you. Mineral water would be great.'

'Hitting the hard stuff early, eh?' He looked disappointed.

'Maybe I'll have something stronger after my talk.' She wanted to kick herself for answering him.

'That will be a little while now,' Ernie apologized. 'We don't eat until eight p.m. and then there are some little ceremonies before we open it to you – as the treat of the evening.'

Keith turned away and Anna whispered to Ernie. 'Do

you think I might borrow your comb? I forgot mine. I did just wash my hair this afternoon.' She noticed the panic in her voice. This was the only getaway she could contrive. 'I'd like to freshen up.'

'Of course, dear.' She pulled a small white comb from her evening bag. 'I think the Ladies is just around the corner.'

The rest-room was cramped, with someone smoking in the stall. Anna hated smoke, but she didn't want to stand out in the hall and make herself vulnerable to members of The Gathering. Relax, she told herself. Gather your wits. So they're not fancy writers with important names. Some of them are quite serious. They're decent people and they are honouring your work. The evening will be over soon. You can leave after your talk, slip out the back door. Tell them you have a date with a villanelle tomorrow morning. It will be fine. She ran Ernie's comb through her hair and watched her shoulders relax. Ernie had been sweet about the comb, understanding her need for retreat. It will be fine. Suddenly the stall opened and out walked Beatrice, the bartender, too preoccupied with her cigarette, at first, to notice Anna.

'Oh, it's you,' Beatrice said. 'I told you, Marv's not going to be here tonight.'

'I found what I was looking for, thanks,' said Anna as she entered the stall.

'Well, be careful, honey. Your line of work is risky enough. But we have a banquet of police detectives down the hall.'

Beatrice slammed the bathroom door behind her before Anna understood what she was talking about and burst out laughing. Unable to control herself, she didn't realize that anyone else had walked into the bathroom until she heard Ernie's voice, 'You OK in there? Just thought I'd check that you didn't have nerves or something.'

'No, no.' Anna cleared her throat. 'I'm fine, just fine.'

'Nice to see you smoke too,' Ernie sniffed and lit up a cigarette. 'It's so unfashionable. One feels like a pariah smoking in public, if you know what I mean.'

'Pariah, yes.' Anna finished peeing and warned herself to calm down. Reputation. Remember what Marilyn had said about reputation.

Anna emerged from the stall and handed Ernie the comb. 'Thanks. I'll see you back in there.'

Ernie winked and ducked into the stall. Anna could hear the slow fizzzz of Ernie's cigarette in the toilet bowl.

Keith handed her the mineral water. Mercifully Darlene approached at the same time. 'Now, maybe we can visit. I looked at both your books and they're beautiful. I especially like the cover on *Faces of Sun*.'

'Thank you.' Anna nodded. 'Yes, I like that illustration a lot. And how about you, what do you write?'

'Oh, I've been working on the same project for years. History.'

'Like Ernie? Natural history?'

'No, human history. Actually, it's a history of The Writers' Gathering.'

'Oh!' Anna took a long drink of the mineral water. 'I understand the group is sixty years old.'

'Yes.' Darlene was pleased. 'I guess we have quite a reputation in this area. That's what makes the book challenging. I'm writing about the forties now.'

'I was at Midway, myself,' said Keith. 'Wounded there, so I had to sit out most of the war in Tacoma . . .'

'I should like to introduce myself.' A large, elegant woman approached.

Anna stepped back, then realized she was being addressed directly.

'I am so happy to meet you, Ms Lanthier. I believe we have several friends in common, Ralph Wharton and Antonia Brownell.'

'Yes.' Anna smiled, vaguely remembering the couple from another cocktail party.

'And we have our books side by side on the display table today.' She pointed to a thick novel with a colourful cover. 'I am Vittoria Pucci, author of *Passion's Heritage*, about women in the royal families of Tuscany.'

'Delighted to meet you.' Anna was pleased at the spirit in her reply. Patience, she reminded herself; they're all sincere people.

'So you have heard of *Passion's Heritage*?'

'No, not yet, but I look forward to reading it.' Anna

regretted this immediately. The book must cost at least eighteen dollars.

'I am going on a national tour next week. Ten cities. And I wanted to ask your advice, about clothes and such.'

'Well,' shrugged Anna, 'I wouldn't know. My publisher hasn't sent me as far as Spokane.' Reputation, she reminded herself; that had definitely been the wrong response.

'Yes, well with poetry it's different,' Vittoria responded graciously. 'I know that. Very hard to publish too. I look forward to reading your new book because I admired the first one so much.'

'Thank you,' said Anna.

'It's a shame there aren't more people here,' said Darlene. 'Poetry is a special taste.'

'Yes,' Anna said, staring into her glass and wondering if she shouldn't change her mind and have something more potent.

Vittoria and Keith were comparing European trains.

'Darlene,' Loretta called from the cash box. 'Did you say twenty roast beefs and ten chickens?'

'Excuse me a minute.' Darlene hurried over to her friend.

Anna leaned against the wall and looked at her watch. Only seven-fifteen. Another forty-five minutes of conviviality before dinner. Yes, maybe she would have a beer and a packet of peanuts.

'Ms Lanthier?'

She looked up to meet a tall, red-haired woman and a shorter woman with grey hair. Names, they had names, but Anna couldn't remember any more names just now. They had travelled down from Port Angeles to hear her. No, neither of them wrote. The grey-haired woman called herself a reader and the other woman was a painter. Anna could barely control her urge to hug the reader. They had bought her new book weeks ago and had some particular questions. They could even quote entire lines. Anna was interested in their lives, since she had thought about moving to Port Angeles herself. The painter worked mostly in oils.

She didn't notice her watch again until the red-haired

woman said, 'Looks like it's time to eat,' and pointed to the people seating themselves at tables extending vertically from the large horizontal table at the front of the room.

Anna nodded and wistfully watched them walk off. She waited to be told where to sit. For some reason, the places at the head table were the last to fill. She waited and waited until waiting seemed ridiculous. There were those lovely salads. People were already digging into the bread. Why couldn't she just sit with her friends from Port Angeles? She wasn't meant to speak until after the meal anyway. So, she moved away from the head table over to the women. Vittoria floated forward: 'Do you mind if I join you?'

'No, not at all.' Anna patted the seat next to her own. There was something appealing about Vittoria. Something grand. For instance, she had written all those pages.

Several minutes later, the grey-haired woman nodded to Anna. 'Someone's looking for you.'

Ernie broke into their conversation, 'No, no, this won't do at all.' She put her hands on the back of Anna's chair. 'You must sit at the head table, as guest of honour.'

'But,' Anna could not stop the force of her own reason, 'I'm *happy* here. I'd rather sit here.'

'No, it won't do.' Ernie smiled her conspiratorial smoking smile. 'People want to *see* you. Now, come and bring your salad with you.'

Vittoria protested. The two women from Port Angeles looked disappointed. Anna obeyed, embarrassed to be carrying her salad across the dining-room.

'Oh, the salad!' Ernie said once they were seated. 'It was a joke; you didn't have to bring the salad.'

'Guess I just need practice at being guest of honour,' Anna shrugged.

'Let me introduce myself,' said the man on her left. 'I am William Larkin, this year's Talespinner.'

'Yes.' Ernie leaned over. 'William has won our story contest. You'll be hearing him read later. Before the guest of honour, of course, *you* have the prime spot on the programme.'

'Nice to meet you,' Anna managed. She dug into her

salad. Prime spot, prime ribs; Anna sipped the water and tried to clear her head.

'This is my wife, Anna,' said William. 'Now isn't that funny. I'm surrounded by Annas. But then there's something in the name of Anna that does surround itself.'

Anna found this quite clever until she looked at his wife's face and understood it was a tired joke between them.

'So you're a poet, Anna?'

'Yes.' She noticed too late that Goodwin had cleared away her salad for the next course.

'What's your line, sonnets, ballads?'

Her eyes widened, 'Free verse.'

'Free verse,' he laughed. 'I like that. What most writing is nowadays, I guess. Free. Ha!'

'Now, William, don't forget that money you made off the *Reader's Digest*. Five hundred dollars, wasn't it?'

'Yeah, five hundred dollars for a personal adventure story. They run some poems. Short ones. I imagine they pay for the poems. You write short ones?'

'No, unfortunately not,' she said. 'Hopelessly long ones.'

'William and his wife met at Swingletarians,' Ernie offered.

'Pardon?' Anna asked.

'Swingletarians,' William repeated. 'When I retired from the Navy at forty-five, I decided it was time to find a wife. Anna here had just been widowed. So we dated a while and, actually, tomorrow is our fifth anniversary.'

'Congratulations.'

'My fork, William, did you take my fork?' the other Anna asked.

'No, hon, I don't think so.' He inspected the Anna on his right. 'She only has one fork too.'

'Well, someone took my fork. How can I eat roast beef without a fork. I should have ordered chicken.'

'Hang on, Annabelle, we'll get you another fork. Hey, waiter . . .'

'Is that your name,' Anna felt ridiculously relieved, 'Annabelle?'

'Yes, Mama adored Poe.' She scrutinized Anna as if divining her purloined fork. 'I guess we both appreciate good story-tellers, Mama and me.' She glanced affectionately at William.

'Yes,' nodded Anna, looking nostalgically at the table with Vittoria and the two women from Port Angeles.

The waiter returned to fill their glasses.

Anna wondered if she would explode. The bathroom was her only respite. But could she leave in the middle of a meal like this? Why not? She was the guest of honour; she was bound to be nervous. They would understand. A little neurosis went a long way for the old reputation. 'Excuse me.' She moved behind William and Annabelle to the aisle. 'I'll be right back.'

'Of course, dear.' They studied her with concern.

What if the bartender was in the toilet again? Well, she didn't say she would report her. She just gave a warning. Besides, Anna reminded herself as she tentatively pushed open the lavatory door, she wasn't what the bartender thought. She was the guest of honour. Wasn't she?

It was blissfully empty. Anna entered the stall and sat down with her clothes on. Ludicrous to hide like this. It was going to be fine. They were nice people. She only had to read for an hour. This was good for her reputation. She couldn't wait to talk to Marilyn.

Out at the sink, she held each wrist under the cold stream and splashed water on her flushed face. It was going to be fine. As she walked back into the room, Vittoria nodded encouragingly. She liked Vittoria more and more.

Squeezing behind Annabelle's chair, she stepped on something which flew in the air, hitting her knee. A fork. No point in mentioning it now. Annabelle had finished her ribs.

'Feeling better?' William looked worried.

'Oh, yes, thank you.'

'Butterflies, I've got a few myself.' He patted her shoulder.

'Excuse me,' Ernie interrupted, 'but I need to check some facts with the guest before I introduce her.'

Anna turned.

'Cigarette?' Ernie winked.

'No, thank you.' How could she tell Ernie that she was

allergic to tobacco, when it was the source of their comradeship. 'I, I never smoke before I speak. Bad for the throat.'

'Oh.' Ernie was disappointed, but politely returned the pack to her evening bag.

'Now the details. I'm afraid I didn't have time to get them organized before this. Let's see, you've written two books, which are?'

Anna slowly and politely offered her credits, fighting off depressing memories of job hunting.

'Splendid, now, about your personal life – married, children . . . ?'

The waiter appeared with chocolate cake and lemon ice.

'Lemon ice, please,' Anna said.

'Me too,' Ernie answered resolutely. 'Good for the throat.' Then she regarded her watch with alarm. 'Oh, dear, I better get going. They close at ten, you know.'

Anna checked the wall clock. Nine o'clock. She had prepared to read for an hour, but if William was going to spin tales, she'd have to cut it to half-an-hour. Well, that was probably better anyway.

'Ladies and Gentlemen, I am honoured tonight to chair our meeting and to introduce our guest of honour – which I'll do momentarily. First, as always, we'll go around the room and say what we've been writing this past month. Now don't be shy. Share the success.'

'Well, I'm Edward Whitney and I sold a camping article to *Northwest Life* this month.'

A round of applause.

'I'm George Wilkins and I haven't had anything published this month, but I bought a word processor, so just wait until next month . . .'

More applause.

'Norma Clarendon. Poetry, two poems in our church magazine.'

'Evelyn Peoples . . . Milton Wright . . . Darlene Burnaby . . . Loretta Boyd . . .'

'Gloria Sage. I'm not really a writer. I'm here with my good friend, Adam. However, I aspire to write. I've worked at the post office for ten years and I've always wanted to write about that. So much to say about the various people you meet. And the colourful stamps. Sometimes about the two of them together because of the way people would fight over their favourite stamps if you were running out as we often did because we were a poky little substation. Which isn't to say we didn't have events. Once we got a package from Tasmania, addressed to a gentleman who was never home and would never pick it up. Finally, one day, I'd say months after he received the notice and we really should have returned the parcel, but you figure something comes all the way from Australia – that's where Tasmania is – and you don't want to return it right away. Anyhow, he comes in as casual as you please and says, "I hear you're holding my mother." "Pardon?" I say and he explains that it's his mother's ashes in the box. We've been sharing that dinky little office with a dead woman.' Gloria paused for a sip of wine. 'I know that Adam will say I'm talking too long, but this is an interesting story, don't you think? Anyways, the parcel didn't do any real harm sitting on the back shelf like that. And you know the man was very nice, brought in flowers for me and the other girl who works at the substation, to commemorate his mother's passing, so to speak. Well, those are the things I'd like to write about. Someday . . .'

She was interrupted by Raoul Arnaud who described his two recent articles about acid rain. Next, Maxine Houston said she was just about to submit her first play.

Ernie looked at her watch and the others spoke more quickly. Finally she stood and led a general round of applause. 'Now,' she cleared her throat, 'our Talespinner of the Year, Mr William Larkin.'

William approached the podium enthusiastically. Anna's mind was still reeling from Gloria's story, which she thought had possibilities. Was she losing her grip, or just loosening up?

'I brought my whole repertoire of tales tonight,' he began.

Anna's heart sank.

'But time is getting short and I'm sure you're all as eager as I am to hear our guest of honour.' He nodded hospitably.

Anna found herself blushing. What was going on with her? Why didn't she blow up? First they 'invite' her to the wrong room thirty minutes early. Then no one greets her. Then they treat her like a gatecrasher. This evening would probably induce a five year writer's block. She thought about Annabelle's fork leaping in the air and tried to suppress her hysteria.

'So I'll just read a short ditty that appeared in the *Reader's Digest* . . .'

Anna was engrossed in the story and disappointed when he shrugged at the end, 'That's it.' William nodded shyly at the applause and sat down.

'Now,' Ernie checked her watch with concern, 'last but certainly not least is our guest of honour, ta ta, Anna Lanthier. Ms Lanthier has published two lovely books of poetry with exquisite covers, which are for sale on the back table. I'm sorry we don't have a bigger crowd for her – like the crowd we had last month for Leonard Flicker – but I'm sure we will be a receptive, *intimate* audience. I'm looking forward to hearing her work because I've never read it. On the back of her book, it says, "She represents the best in new women's writing". Because time is short tonight, Ms Lanthier will read for twenty minutes. Now, without further ado, I give you, Anna Lanthier, new woman.'

The applause was warm and loud. Anna noticed that it was more than William Larkin had received and was appalled by her petty ego. She imagined Annabelle glowering.

'I am honoured to be here,' she began. 'I've enjoyed talking to a number of you individually.' She was surprised to detect a particular fondness for Ernie. She smiled to Vittoria, who was sitting forward intently, and to the women from Port Angeles. 'I would like to start with selections from my new book.'

She timed herself carefully.

Ernie looked relieved as well as grateful when she said, 'For my last poem . . .'

The applause was long and wild. Afterwards, Anna was amazed how many people bought books and how kind they were in their detailed responses to her poems.

She noticed Vittoria waiting on the sidelines and tried not to let the woman's intensity curtail her conversations with other people.

The pair from Port Angeles said they would like to organize a reading for her there.

Gloria said she had never really thought about poetry for herself, but she could see ways it might be more suitable for her purposes. She bought three books.

Goodwin winked at her as he wheeled out the centrepiece, 'Good going, much better than the *yawn* they had here last month.'

Finally Vittoria stepped forward, carrying *Passion's Heritage*. 'I wondered if you would agree to a trade – your books for mine. Mine is more expensive, of course, but I would be honoured to trade, myself.'

'Yes,' Anna said, noticing that her breath was not taken away as it would have been at the beginning of the evening. 'Thank you.'

'Thank you.' Vittoria shook her head. '*I savoured every word*.'

When the crowd cleared, Ernie escorted her to the door, where she collected her empty box.

'Thank you so much, Anna. Why, I think this is the best reading we've ever had. I also wanted to say you've been most gracious all evening. Some famous writers find us a little "down-home" for their tastes. But you fit right in.'

Anna nodded thanks, disarmed and a little guilty about her earlier irritability.

'You know I never did find out if you were married or single.'

Anna nodded again and said goodbye. She turned right.

Ernie called out. 'Wrong way, the exit is in that direction.'

'I know,' Anna said. 'I need to visit the Ladies first.'

'Of course, of course,' Ernie agreed, looking around for Keith. 'Nerves. Well, thank you again, dear. And good luck.'

Over. It was *all* over, she thought as she pushed open the bathroom door. The stall was occupied, so she leaned against the sink, her eyes closed, holding her empty box.

The stall door opened and Anna looked up at Beatrice, who was fixed on the box.

'Grapefruits, eh? Hmmm, I've seen some covers in my time, but this is u-nique. Well, you don't have to worry about the cops no more. Gone home. Frankly when they're off duty, they're no different than any men.' She soaped up vigorously under the warning, 'State law requires that all employees wash their hands before returning to work.'

Anna set down the box and pushed into the stall.

'Say,' Beatrice spoke above the hot air dryer. 'You sure this line of work is for you?'

'Some jobs are harder,' Anna volleyed.

'Yeah, well, it's been a long night for both of us. Good luck.' The bartender pushed open the door to the hallway, paused and called in a friendly voice, 'I'll tell Marv you were looking for him.'

'Thanks,' Anna answered automatically, then was caught in a fit of giggles. She heard the door swing shut. And she felt horribly alone.

Anna walked out to the car and tossed the empty box in the back seat. As she started the ignition, she wondered what it would be like to live up in Port Angeles.

– Valentine's Day –

St Valentine, Priest and Martyr
Green, Purple or Red Vestments

Janet woke suddenly. She could tell, even with the blinds closed, that it was early on a cold day. Well, February was unpredictable in San Francisco. And Valentine's Day was unpredictable anywhere. She felt a stab of self-pity about her solitary state and snuggled under the covers. No, she was wide awake. She would make the most of today because she was behind on her taxes and on her tapestry orders. Christ! The Federal Express truck was supposed to collect the last piece for the New York gallery this morning and she hadn't even completed the address form.

She grabbed her robe, filled the kettle and sat at her desk to deal with questions of weight and destination. The form was pleasantly bilingual. She preferred to imagine herself as an *'expediteur'* rather than a 'shipper'. There was some small pleasure in addressing the gallery owner as a 'consignee', which seemed to make them more equal.

The kettle blew. The phone rang.

'Hello, Mom?'

'Oh, Winnie, can you hang on while I get the stove?'

Checking the kitchen clock, she was startled to find her daughter calling at eight a.m. Since going to college Winnie had become a late sleeper.

'Mom, I wondered if I could come and use your computer today.'

'I was planning to do my books on the computer, but I could sort through the files while you use it. I mean if you don't need my help. I'm way behind on taxes. You have an assignment?'

'No. My résumé. Companies are doing on-campus interviews next week. Are you sure it's OK?'

'Yeah, sure.' She closed her eyes. It wouldn't hold her up that much. It might even be nice to have some company. She missed her only child.

Janet finished the form and put the tapestry in a box which she zealously swathed with translucent tape to ensure a safe arrival. After this, there was nothing she could do. She felt as if she were sending it off to war.

She sat at the table with a second cup of coffee, marvelling at how small this looked for six months work. Just another hanging to be put on just another wall.

The phone rang. Her heart sank at the idea of Winnie cancelling. The apartment felt vacant and enormous.

'Janet, dear?'

'Mother, how are you?'

'Fine. I was wondering if Winnie was there?'

'Yes, Mother, she's on her way.' Janet noticed her irritation with Mother who always asked about someone else first when she called – Janet's brother or her daughter or even her ex-husband.

'Yes, I thought she might be. I've left several messages at the dormitory.'

Janet waited. Ever since Mother had been laid off her job, she had been at loose ends, sometimes near the deep end. It was hard to know what to do for her.

'Janet, dear, do you have any plans today?'

'Well, yes, why?'

'I have to be over your way for a hearing test at the hospital and I wonder if we could have coffee – just the two of us.'

'Sure.' She agreed even though Mother had cancelled the last two weekend visits. She missed her job at the department store; her depression was immobilizing. 'I mean I have to get Winnie settled at the computer and the Federal Express truck is coming. But sure, give me a ring when you're finished at the hospital.'

'There's something I need to talk to you about. Something that's eating me up.'

Janet worried. What had she done wrong? Nothing recently. But recently didn't matter. Mother still remembered that Janet had forgotten Mother's Day, 1960.

'I'd like to talk, just the two of us, privately.'

The doorbell rang.

'Hang on a second . . .'

Winnie was more beautiful than ever. Elegantly tall, vivacious, intelligent. Janet had tried unsuccessfully to appreciate the spiked hairdo. Still, she was grateful Winnie hadn't shaved her head like her friends Wendy and Lisa. There was something magnificent about Winnie's combination of mauve hair and yellow sweater. Despite the vibrant colours, the girl looked exhausted.

'Jenny and I went to the city dancing last night. We paid a five dollar cover to get into a good club and the DJ was playing the wimpiest music. Jenny and I like soul. But he was in a time warp or something – playing Pink Floyd! Have you ever heard of anything so weird – oh, oops, I guess you have. Anyway, we stayed there until two a.m. I'm really wiped.'

'Have you had any breakfast?' Janet bit her tongue. She didn't have time to cook. Her accounts were a mess. Winnie had only asked to use the computer.

'Some pretzels on the ride over. You have anything?'

Janet smiled. 'Still like five minute eggs?'

Fixing breakfast for herself and Winnie, she relaxed. She caught a glimpse of herself in the dining-room mirror. What a railing she looked in her sweatshirt and jeans, a figure not much more maternal than Winnie's college friends. This face, though, had its share of wrinkles. Long, straight black hair also revealed her generation. Straight, she didn't like to think of herself as straight.

Winnie talked about her new classes and plans for Easter break. Then she said, 'You know I'm kind of worried about Grandma.'

'Yes?'

'Ever since they closed the store, she's been inviting me to spend time with her. Long periods of time. I went over last weekend for lunch. Then it turned into pinochle and a walk around the neighbourhood.'

Janet nodded.

'And her memory isn't so good. She forgot what game we were playing.'

'Yes,' Janet said. 'I think she needs some kind of routine.'

'That's it.' Winnie gulped the coffee and pulled a face. 'Better get going or I'll wind up unemployed like Grandma.'

Janet followed her daughter into the study. 'The disks are there. Do you know how to turn on the terminal?'

'Well, this is a little different from the one at school.'

Janet's face fell as she looked away from her files.

'How do you centre things?'

An hour later, Winnie was pecking through her résumé. Janet couldn't concentrate on her cancelled cheques; all she could see was Winnie's vitae: Two years lifeguarding; six months waitressing; a year typing insurance forms. Her daughter had grown up. Janet glanced at the young woman squinting at the green screen. Yes, this was her daughter, the two-year-old protegé singing, 'I love you, yeah, yeah, yeah,' backed up by the Beatles in a tacky one-bedroom apartment in Bloomington twenty years ago. Yes, this was her daughter, the sweet punk who wanted to be a 'financial analyst'. This vocation was her father's doing. Since the divorce he had grown more and more conservative and probably introduced Winnie to the most unsavoury assortment of stockbrokers and lawyers. Well, it was Winnie's life. After all, she, herself, was hardly the successful suburban matron her own mother hoped she had raised. You don't raise children any more than you raise chickens. You simply supply the feed and trust and they grow up. Janet returned to her books. Although she hated tax time, she was lucky to be making her living from her art. She was lucky in many ways.

'Mom, does this mean the end of the page? Is my résumé too long? Everyone says you have to get it on one page.'

The phone rang.

'Oh, Mother,' Janet sighed, 'the Federal Express

truck hasn't arrived yet. Let me see if Winnie can handle it . . . Yes, it's OK, Mother. I'll pick you up in five minutes.'

Pulling out of the driveway, Janet noticed a truck striped in patriotic colours at the end of the street. At first she was puzzled that Federal Express would have another customer in her obscure neighbourhood. She really should stop cultivating her eccentricity and learn more about the neighbours. She waited a moment to see if the truck were about to move. Ridiculous anxiety: a financial analyst was capable of handing a package to a truck driver. For some reason she suddenly recalled girls exchanging valentines in her third grade class. Her favourite one was from Cindy, made with a border of real lace.

Mother stood, small and frail, in front of the hospital. Janet aimed for objectivity. Martha Frederickson was a handsome woman in her early seventies with grey hair and delicate features. She claimed her ground with the confidence of someone who had worked all her life and had raised two kids alone. As always she was wearing complimentary muted colours, dark, low-heeled shoes and a matching handbag.

Janet honked and waved broadly, hoping for a smile. Martha looked lost. Janet summoned the strength to find her. The older woman nodded and laboriously climbed into the car. She began to talk immediately.

'I thought it was Thursday. The eye doctor's nurse called and said they had to change the appointment until one o'clock because they were running late. That was fine with me. They have a lot of patients. But I got here and realized that this was Friday, not Thursday. I'll just have to call and tell them I slept through the appointment. I don't like to lie, but it's the only thing I can do.'

'Mother, just relax and put on your seat belt.'

'Oh, yes, dear. I believe in seat belts.'

Janet admired her mother's abiding faith in things technological despite a life of disappointment in the modern world.

When they turned onto Janet's street, the truck was

idling in front of the apartment building. Had Winnie got confused? Had she, herself, filled out the form wrong? In an uncharacteristically daring automotive manoeuvre, Janet pulled her car across the path of the truck and jumped out. The truck driver looked up, startled.

'My daughter was handling the package. Is everything OK?'

'Just fine, ma'am.' The driver grinned down at her.

'Thank you.' Janet smiled foolishly. It took all her willpower not to instruct the driver to handle the package carefully.

A car honked from behind.

'You're blocking the road, dear,' Martha called out the window, gripping her seat belt.

'Yes. Sorry.' Janet waved to the car behind. She reversed into her own driveway.

Janet ran upstairs and stuck her head in the study, 'Grandma's here, if you want to say hello.'

Winnie smiled conspiratorially. 'Just to say hello, OK? I really have to finish.'

Janet paused in the kitchen doorway to admire her mother and daughter, joking with each other on the couch. Winnie really was a sweet young woman; Mother was coming alive. She was nervous about what Mother needed to discuss.

'Your brother makes a good cup of coffee too.' Martha warmed her hands on the hot mug and talked about her son. He had invited her to New York the following month.

'That sounds nice,' Janet encouraged. 'You deserve a vacation.' She thought about the St Valentine's Day Massacre, wondering vaguely whether it had taken place in Chicago or New York.

'I'm afraid I have a long holiday ahead of me. Where would I find another job at my age . . . ?'

'Mom. Mom.' Winnie was shouting from the study. 'Can you help me with the margins?'

Janet didn't want to desert Martha, just as she was embarking on her long vacation. 'Here, did you see these pictures of Carmel? I keep meaning to put them in a photo album, but . . .'

'Organization was never your greatest skill,' Martha smiled as she accepted the photographs.

Janet helped Winnie finish the résumé and showed her how to print it. She returned to the living-room to find her mother staring blankly out the window. What an old woman she looked today. Perhaps this was the consequence of being left alone for younger people with louder demands.

Winnie rushed in. 'Are you sure this is going to reduce OK? I should have used the computer at school.'

Martha regarded her granddaughter as if the girl were speaking Arabic.

Janet, caught between Winnie's anxiety and Mother's astonishment, sat down heavily on the chair and said she was sure everything would work out fine.

'Can I leave my books here while I go to the xerox shop?'

Mi casa es su casa.'

Martha concentrated on the photos, trying to match up images with people in the living-room.

As the door banged after Winnie, Janet realized she was starving.

'How about some lunch, Mother? I got crab to celebrate finishing my tapestry. There's plenty for two.' She hoped, guiltily, that they would finish eating before Winnie returned from the copy shop. If you were stranded in the desert without enough food, would you feed your mother or your daughter first? She shook her head which contained a mind so often given to pointless ethical dilemmas.

The phone rang.

Janet switched on the answering machine to hear the accountant ask for her books which were now a week overdue. Janet turned down the volume and let her talk into the tape.

As she fixed the coffee, she mused about creating a robot to deal with Mother like her tape machine handled business. There were so many of Mother's needs she could not meet.

Finally seated in the front room, Janet could wait no longer. 'Mother, Winnie may be back any time. While we have a minute to ourselves, will you tell me what you needed to talk about?'

Martha looked blank.

'Remember, on the phone you said you needed to talk about something that was "eating you up"?'

'Oh,' Martha frowned. 'We've already discussed it, dear. In the car. The memory problem. It's quite frightening.' She sounded reluctant to go into it again.

'Yes,' Janet said softly, giving Martha time to continue if she wanted.

'While you were in the kitchen,' Martha's voice grew stronger, 'I was reading the newspaper here. An article about St Valentine. Did you know that he was a Roman priest who ministered during the persecution of Claudius II. He was martyred under Aurelian, in 270.'

'No.' Janet smiled. 'I didn't know that.'

'Well, well.' Martha turned to the door. 'Look who's coming.'

Winnie burst in, carrying a large stack of beige paper. 'It went fine. The guy was really cute. He showed me how to centre it. And he gave me a special deal. He said your computer had good contrast – that it was ideal for a résumé.'

Janet hugged her daughter and felt unreasonably proud of her computer.

'I'll just get my binder.' Winnie read her watch. 'I may be able to do an hour at the library if I hurry.'

Martha was staring into the coffee cup.

Winnie kissed her mother on the cheek. 'Oh, Grandma, can I give you a lift to the bus-stop?'

Martha looked at Janet.

'No,' Janet answered. 'I'll take Grandma.'

'OK.' Winnie looked obliged. 'Gotta rush. Bye, Mom. Bye, Grandma.'

The door slammed on the suddenly small, stuffy house. Martha was staring into her cup.

'I have to go shopping, Mother. Would you like to go with me – on the way to the bus?'

'Yes.' Martha perked up. 'I'd love that. Remember when you were little and we used to go shopping?'

Afternoon was cast in the same heavy grey as the morning. Janet hated this waiting-room weather. San Francisco architecture had been drawn by people with sun in mind. On bright days, the white and yellow and pale blue houses reflected heat and light. But on cold, grim days the pastel edifices seemed to fade into oblivion. She longed for New York's tall brick buildings which resisted dreary weather, which seemed to impose character into grey days.

'I really like that little café.'

'Which café, Mother?'

'You know, the one where we had pea soup, or was it lentil soup?'

'No, I don't remember. Where was it?'

'In the Mission. No, maybe not, maybe it was up on Union.'

Janet was looking for a parking space, a pursuit which Mother, who did not drive, never took seriously.

'What are we shopping for?' Martha asked as they walked across the street.

'A Valentine's present.'

They stopped at a window featuring bright red sweaters.

'Nice cardigan,' Martha observed.

'Yes.' Janet was delighted. 'Let me get it for you for Valentine's Day.'

'No.' Martha shook her head vociferously. 'I was thinking of you. Let me get it for you.'

They walked on in search of Martha's favourite kind of dark chocolate. Finally, Jane found the right candy and a novel she thought her mother would enjoy.

The next shop had a sale on sweat-pants. Janet thought this might break through her laziness and get her to exercise class. 'Mother, do you mind if I pop in here a second?'

The sweat-pants fitted and as they left the shop Martha took Janet's arm. 'Let me get them for you for Valentine's Day.'

'OK.' Janet smiled. They had been, after all, on sale. She noticed that her mother was flagging.

'How about some coffee?' Janet thought how young she felt when she was with Martha and how old she felt when she was with Winnie. What was her real age? Would Winnie be caught between her mother and daughter? Did financial analysts have daughters?

They sat in the café, reminiscing about family vacations. Next to them, an old woman left her purse on the table, wandering over to gossip with the cashier. Janet and Martha turned to each other in dismay. 'Someone should tell her not to leave her purse.' Janet heard her mother, or herself, say.

They finished their coffee in silence.

'Well, it's been a long day,' sighed Martha. 'I should be on my way.'

'Sure, Mother.' Janet was pleased by how much Martha had brightened over the afternoon. As they drove to the bus-stop she told herself that, once she got settled with retirement activities, everything would be fine. Briefly she considered how Mother had forgotten to pay for the sweat-pants. But she didn't want to bring it up, lest it revive her panic about memory.

'Do you mind if I take the book *next* time? It's rather heavy to carry with all this.'

'No.' Janet shook her head, wishing she had insisted on the red sweater. Maybe Mother felt intimidated by the book. And she had always looked great in red.

It was dark by the time Janet arrived home. She wished daylight savings time functioned all year long. Carrying a cup of coffee into the study, she was heartened to see a red light pulsing on her answering machine. Two calls. She sat on the rug, sipped the coffee and listened. Oh, yes, the accountant asking about her late books. Winnie calling to say thanks and to wish her a Happy Valentine's Day.

Maybe she'd try on the sweat-pants and do some exercises to remove the kinks. Opening the bag, she found money scattered on top of the pants. Had she dropped her change in the bag like this? No, she counted fifty dollars; this wasn't her change. Of course, *Mother* had done this. Her Valentine. Janet slumped at her desk, surveying the money and the sweat-pants and the Federal Express receipt. She didn't know whether to laugh or cry. Just like that time in high school when she received a gorgeous red satin heart without a signature.

– Objectivity, She Said –

'John Doe, San Francisco School Board member, is on trial for the murder of a 17-year-old black prostitute,' said KCBS *Radio News.*

*

The phone woke me this morning. Carla. 'Did you hear about the rape by the Campanile?' she asked.

I did not need this before nine o'clock in the morning.

'It was still daylight,' Carla said. 'She was walking alone. He grabbed her can of Halt and sprayed it in her eyes. Then he shoved her in a van, one of those ugly modern ones with a thick carpet.'

What the carpet had to do with the story, I did not know, but I was glad Carla told me. I would watch out for carpeted vans more than I did already.

'He made her suck him off,' Carla said, 'raped her repeatedly and then . . .'

'Did he kill her?' I needed to know.

'She made it back to campus by nine p.m. to tell the police.'

Just yesterday after class I almost went up to the Campanile terrace to sit in the late sun. I was tired from teaching for three hours. And I was nostalgic. In another age, when I was a student, I used to neck with my fiancé by the Campanile. But yesterday I felt too tired for reliving memories. So I went home. Home to my apartment where I locked the doors securely.

'And the day before yesterday,' Carla was still talking.

'Oh, yes,' I said, because it's not as though I could go back to sleep after hearing such a story.

'There was another rape,' she said, 'up by International House.'

I wonder about the late 1930s in Europe, about whether the Jews phoned each other like this. Did they wake each other with clipped warnings? Did they tell each other to get away?

'John Doe is on trial for the murder of an Oakland prostitute,' said the KRON *evening news.*

*

But how do we get away?
 I was jogging at a park near my house. Ho Chi Minh Park, we named it in the 1960s before we learned how long the revolution might take.
 'Hot stuff,' called the leering man who looked like a used teenager under his long, blond hair.
 'Hot stuff,' he murmured before taking another swig from the sherry bottle. Sherry at eight a.m. Sherry in this neighbourhood park next to the junior high school which had seemed like a safe place to jog.
 'Hot stuff,' he said, despite the fact that I was wearing baggy pants and a sweatshirt.
 I tried to ignore him.
 'Get her, boy,' he said to his big dog. 'Get her.'
 His Boxer loped towards me. I remembered another oversized Boxer dog who masturbated himself against me when I was a fifth grader. So I jogged on home and locked the doors securely.

'Oakland prostitute,' said KNBR. *'Black prostitute,' said* KGO. *Usually they left out the 17-year-old part. The lawyers were having trouble finding a jury.*

*

Tonight I visited my friend Maggie who is a tough woman. She lives in a 'bad neighbourhood' because she is poor.
 'I don't mind having bars on the windows,' she said. 'Don't notice them anymore. But this door bothers me. You can't get in or out without a key. The fire department would slap a fine on me in two minutes flat. But they can't get in here either.'

'John Doe is on trial for the shooting of a prostitute . . .' a student read the newspaper article aloud.

'Objectivity,' I asked my class. 'How is the notion of objectivity in today's media related to the nineteenth century concept of logical positivism?'

'It was still daylight,' Carla said. *'She was walking alone.'*

*

I told my mother I went to a pornography conference.

My mother stiffened. She already disagrees with 85 per cent of my life. She said coolly, 'I don't like pornography.'

'Neither do I,' I said.

'I think that pornography incites rape,' my mother said flatly.

I considered the fact that she works in an all-night coffee shop where she sees both porn and violence.

'I think you're right,' I answered. But she wasn't interested in the sociological research proving the correlation. Some women do not need statistical evidence.

'John Doe faces his second trial for the shooting of an Oakland prostitute,' said the man on the tube. *'The first trial ended in a hung jury.'*

*

I saw a television series on Marie Curie. It was inspirational to watch her perseverance, to see her working in her laboratory until very, very late at night.

(This reminded me of the rush of dedication, fascination and hope I used to feel when I stayed at the library until three a.m., studying. Then one night a policeman caught me leaving the library.

'How are you getting home?' he demanded.

'Walking,' I said.

'You looking to get raped?' he asked.

'No,' I answered briskly, 'just looking to pass my class.'

I was angry. He was admonishing me. Accusing me. But the powers of my patriarchal logic acknowledged that he

was right. No more necking by the Campanile. No more walking home alone at night.
Now thirteen years later as a teacher on the same campus, I know when to leave my office. I go home at dark. I smile at the policeman. I am a good girl.)
If Madame Curie returned to the Sorbonne today, would she need to stay as late? Would she be able to stay as late?

A woman was found dead in the trunk of her car. A seventy-two-year-old woman. The first murder since the town was incorporated in 1971. Who? Where? I asked my students. The facts, I said, put all your facts in the lead.
My class was discussing the mass magazine market.
'Six out of ten of the best-selling news-stand monthlies are men's entertainment magazines,' said one student. She showed a *Penthouse* cartoon where a rape victim is calling, 'Encore'.
Several men in the class giggled.
A woman got angry. 'That cartoon implies that women *like* getting raped,' she said.
'Well,' said one man in all seriousness. 'Don't *some* of them enjoy it?'
He felt the wrath of seventeen women, few of them self-declared feminists.
'But,' he persisted in a softer, incredulous voice, 'don't *some* of them enjoy it *some*times?'

'The Fremont rapist has raped forty women, but luckily,' according to KPIX, *'no one has been injured.'*

*

I went to London to work last summer. I stayed with friends in a house on Gloucester Drive.
'Gloucester Drive,' said the taxi driver, raising his eyebrows in surprise and then driving on because cabbies, like priests have heard a lot of stories.
Gloucester Drive, my friends had written, to prepare me for the raised eyebrows, is in a red light district. Not a proper red light district with madames and limousines, just

a working-class neighbourhood in Hackney where women on the dole turn a few tricks to keep their kids fed.

Gloucester Drive, I learned, was a tricky street to cross. You had to *look out* for *cars*, but you could not *look at* the *drivers* or they would stop. Gloucester Drive was always crawling with businessmen on their lunch breaks.

It took me a week of practice before I got across the street safely, without having one of the prowlers stop.

Worse things might happen, of course. I learned this during my fifth week there. Walking home alone, I sensed a man following me. I moved out on the street and he hugged my heels. I turned around and shouted at him to go away. He just stood there. I walked faster. So did he. Then I ran, flinging open our gate, rushing up the steps and ringing the bell as I fumbled for the keys. He just hung on the gate, watching. Deborah opened the door and as we walked into the hallway, I breathlessly told her my story.

'Happens all the time,' she said, handing me a glass of burgundy.

We walked into the dining-room where a group of women were sitting around a table, drinking and laughing. And I wondered if we were all fools.

– *All Those Dead Horses* –

Cecilia fished the lime from her Perrier and squeezed until she realized she was simply exercising her fingers. Michael was ten minutes late. She picked the dry cuticle on her index finger and returned to her list. Two magazine editors tomorrow and a final visit with her agent who was about as forthcoming as her therapist. Then the red eye flight back to Portland. It would be good to be back home. Sometimes when she came to New York, she wondered if she were a fraud. She didn't feel like a writer here. Michael was one of the few New York authors with whom she had any personal contact – and although that was limited to lunch or a drink every nine months when she came to the city, she felt she did know him. She had been a little surprised by his choice of this glitzy tavern. Perhaps she was getting stodgy and provincial in Portland. She always enjoyed seeing him.

Michael rushed down the street – a little late – five minutes at most. They had agreed to meet in one of those paté and wine bars in Soho. The afternoon was almost gone and the streets were slick with rain. He smiled at the thought of meeting Cecilia; he just wished she had given him more notice.

He had arranged to leave work early and meet her for an hour before his dinner date – his old room-mate, Phil, was in town, fund-raising for his campaign. Only thirty-four and already shaking up Congress.

A bus roared, then idled, blocking the crosswalk. He walked behind it, careful not to get too close to the exhaust. He was maybe fifteen minutes late, but she'd have brought something to read.

Michael pushed through the crowd on Seventh Avenue, thinking how crazy it was to feel competitive with his room-mate. They were in different fields. He, himself, had also done well – a senior magazine editor and author of a definitive book on Fitzgerald. Four publishers had asked him for his next manuscript. He was being only slightly coy in refusing to show a draft, wanting to complete the book on his own before getting an editor involved.

As he turned the final corner, he tried to conjure Cecilia's face. Round, open, flushed with determination. She was an unusual friend. One of those forthright Western women – from Portland or Seattle. Portland, he was almost sure. They had met two or three years before at a party with mutual friends, somewhere in the Village.

She saw him first because her eyes were used to the light. His blond hair was shorter than last year, perhaps a little curlier. He was boyishly gangly at six feet. During one lunch they determined that they were the same age, she just a few weeks older.

He caught her broad, Western wave and immediately felt cheered. The visit would do him good. It would give him an un-neurotic perspective and prepare him to face Phil tonight.

'Martini.' He signalled the waitress before he sat down. Only forty-five minutes left and he wanted to make the most of it.

They smiled as he slid into the booth. Nothing sexual, she noticed with relief. Just friends.

Nothing manipulative, he observed, thinking again, that he might take up that offer to do a biography of John Muir and go West after all. Maybe she'd introduce him to other Western writers. It would be a good change of scene.

'Get you another?' the waitress asked as she served Michael's drink.

'No thanks. But another lime would be nice.'

The short, dark waitress nodded as if she were actually shaking her head and saying, 'This isn't a grocery store, lady.' Before Cecilia had time to feel hyper-sensitive, she heard Michael's voice.

'So how's the trip been?' He smiled at her, thinking how he liked her hair long like this. She reminded him faintly of Joan Baez.

'Fine,' she said, pausing to feel something she might

communicate. But it was hard. Coming to New York was like being at the dentist. She came because she knew she should. You got lost as a writer if you didn't keep up contacts with people East of the Hudson. She never knew what the trip would bring and she felt drugged with anxiety most of the time. If she always came hoping it wouldn't hurt so much, she always left grateful she had survived. Of course she would feel some nervousness in any strange city. She was too hard on New York. She loved the city's vitality. There were certain people, like Michael, who gave her hope. Good people and good writers. She was delighted when their chance meeting at a party in Brooklyn had blossomed into a friendship. Well, sort of a friendship. She had been disappointed that he hadn't written to her about her last novel. The publisher had sworn he was sent a copy. But perhaps he was waiting until they met in person.

He regarded her with concern. What was this pensive expression? Did she want something from him? Outsiders sometimes thought that if you had an editing job you had New York publishing under control. They didn't realize how cut-throat it was here. How many of them could take the pressure? How many could stand a Manhattan winter for that matter?

She smiled. 'I really liked your essay last month. I thought you captured the prep school very well – and the complexity of being a student in a place where your father was principal.'

'Oh, yes?' He was pleased because she was, after all, a novelist. And her books were quite well received. 'I wish my father had liked it.'

'You were very complimentary.' She was surprised his father could have been offended.

'Well, yes, I suppose I just expected an "A+". He liked it well enough on the whole. But the cafeteria scene, he said I could have left out the food throwing.'

The waitress brought her quarter lime in a cut-glass bowl.

'*You* seem to be flourishing.' He was eager to bring her out, to hear about her life, which was so much more relaxed and sane than his here.

'My third novel will be published in October,' she said,

amazed, herself, to hear these words and a little frightened of them. Third novel, she cringed, why did she have to remind him? Of course he knew; of course he took her seriously. She picked up the lime and squeezed it tightly.

'And the previous one, that's done well?'

'Yes,' she said, holding back news of the paperback sale to hear his reaction.

He knew he should admit he hadn't read it, that he'd been too busy. She'd understand. But he was a coward. He turned for the waitress and signalled for another martini. He resolved to read the book this weekend and write her a note. Now, he fumbled for an exit. 'And your parents, what did they think of it?'

Her surprise at the question concealed her disappointment at his lack of response. Perhaps he hated her writing. Well, there was nothing she could do about that.

'My parents don't read,' she said. 'English, that is. They emigrated from Calabria when they were in their teens. I mean they can read street signs and tin cans. But most of the reading they do – and it's quite occasional – is in an Italo-American newspaper.' When she told this story she was always caught between the embarrassment her parents' foreignness caused her as a child and the pride their story brought her as an adult.

'What did they do?' he asked reflexively. Perhaps the novel had been about Italian immigrants and he should know all this from having read the book.

'They still do – cleaning,' she said, amused at how chic it had suddenly become to have working-class parents.

'But how, I mean, how did you get from there to here?'

The waitress brought the martini and observed her with arch enquiry.

'Yes, another, please,' said Cecilia. 'With . . .'

'More lime,' smiled the young woman, who seemed to be loosening up a bit.

'Well, it took some doing.' She was glad she could say that to him.

He nodded respectfully.

'What about your new book?' she asked. 'I don't even know what it's about.'

'Would you believe – about a young man enduring prep school in the 1970s.'

She nodded, thinking she would enjoy reading it.

'I've also got a novel in the drawer.' Instantly he regretted the self-exposure. 'I guess everyone has a novel in the drawer.'

She shrugged. It was true. So many people had told her about their secret novels that she sometimes wished she had picked a more remote line of work – such as astrophysics.

'My great-grandparents,' he floundered, 'you know they were immigrants too. County Clare. My nanny was a seamstress and her husband was a labourer – a builder.'

'Oh, yes?' This was all going a little too fast. 'You'll put them in the book too?'

'No,' he answered, confused at first. 'I just mention it to say how much I learned from my family, through my mother. And to say we're all immigrants in this country.'

'Even the Eskimos crossed the Bering Straight.' She didn't know if she intended to be sarcastic.

He looked at his watch.

Cecilia told herself not to be defensive. When she talked about her family people often found a grandparent or lost uncle who were also working-class. Sometimes they would settle for a bankrupt cousin. They spoke as if in complicity. But Cecilia knew they didn't understand what it was like to have moved from a home where there were no books or records into their intellectual milieu. If Michael had had more time, she would talk about this. He was a thoughtful man.

She could see from the silver digits on his watch that they only had half-an-hour left. New Yorkers said they 'only had half-an-hour' with the urgency of dying people.

Embarrassed, he looked absently around the table for the bill.

Cecilia sipped her water and tried to regain perspective. 'Sometimes I feel so isolated in Portland,' she began.

He looked at her with concern. Not her usual vibrant self. Irrationally, he was hoping she did not plan to move to New York.

'I wonder,' she continued, 'if you might introduce me to some writers when I next visit.'

'Sure, if that's what you want. Frankly, New York writers are no great shakes. I get much more from listening to you.' He knew he didn't sound convincing, but it was true. Usually she was full of energy and optimism.

'I'm not looking for inspiration,' she said, resenting that she, the provincial, was the one explaining strategies.

'Oh, contacts, yes, I see your point. It's true I met Ira at Columbia and Clement in my last job. The contacts here can, no doubt, be useful, but,' and he could hardly maintain an even tone, 'you're not going to *move* here are you?' This sounded terrible, but he was never articulate when pressed for time.

The waitress served their drinks and Michael, forgetting his feminist instincts, quickly paid the cheque. Cecilia felt as if she were making some kind of deal. He would pay for the Perrier and introduce her to his friends if she would stay in Portland.

'I have no intention of moving,' she began.

'Well, of course, of course.' He wondered why he was such a grudge. It would be easy enough to meet at a restaurant and introduce her to a few people. Why hadn't he thought of it before? 'Let me know about your next trip and I'll plan an evening.'

This tension spent, the silence between them was cavernous. Cecilia felt she should apologize, but she knew she shouldn't. She wondered how they would get through the rest of the visit.

'Did you read about the IRA explosion in London?' he asked. It had been bothering him all day.

'Hyde Park, yes,' she nodded, thinking of the soldiers killed, her fears of war, his family in County Clare.

'All those dead horses,' he shook his head. 'I haven't been able to get them out of my mind. All those dead horses.'

Cecilia was speechless. She tried to conjure a different topic, however she knew if she opened her mouth she would cry and the tears wouldn't be for anything as significant as the Irish troubles.

Michael was baffled by her distress. Still, there was really no time to go into it. He was almost late to meet his room-mate. One of these days . . . He slipped on his coat and began to fumble a farewell.

She knew she should leave with him. She didn't want to reveal that she had no evening plan. But she was tired and had used up all her discretion for the day. She tried humour instead as she extended her hand. 'Come back any time.'

He frowned, then grinned, then squeezed her hand tightly. 'Great to see you.' As he hurried out the door and hailed a taxi he thought how genuine he felt. And hey, a cab right away. Yes, he had been right to make time for her.

Cecilia stared into her glass wondering if she had been a fool to maintain the friendship when he turned up late to their occasional meetings, didn't read her books and grew paranoid at the notion of her being in New York permanently. She did like his work. She knew it was important to make friends with other writers. She found herself squeezing the lime into an empty glass and caught the waitress's eye.

'Another Perrier?'

'No, Scotch,' Cecilia sighed. 'Straight up.'

She wondered how often her parents had felt at sea like this, learning too late, because of language and cultural differences, that a friendship wasn't going to work out. And she wondered how long it would take her to find the courage to make another friend in New York.

'Say.' The waitress smiled as she served Cecilia's Scotch. 'I'm going off shift now and I wondered . . . ?'

'Oh, I have the money right here,' Cecilia said, fighting the apology in her voice – how was she to know it was the end of her shift?

'No.' The young woman laughed. 'I mean I couldn't help hearing parts of your conversation with Joe Go-getter there. I see you're alone from out of town.'

Cecilia kept her eyes on the table, thinking this was a very unlikely beginning or ending to a story.

The waitress continued, 'I'm interested in writing myself and, well, I wondered if you'd like to schmooze a bit over some spaghetti? There's a great place around the corner, where the drinks are half the price.'

Cecilia sipped the Scotch. 'Why not,' she grinned, 'I haven't had a good schmooze in six days.'

II

– Transfer –
– A Novella –

I
– One of the Family –

The man came to dinner bringing wine. I remember because no one brought wine. Chocolates. Flowers. Whiskey, maybe. But my parents never drank wine and the Japanese glasses were dusty.

'Ellen,' Mom whispered, 'wash the wine glasses and quickly set them out on the table while *they*'re watching TV.'

The guest's name was Martin Andropolous, my father's friend, and therefore an accomplished man because my irascible father exposed his intelligence to few. Martin had gone to college and worked in the same company as Dad. 'Two old soldiers,' my father had explained. Martin had done his duty in Korea whereas Dad had been all around the world. Too many times, he was quick to say.

Martin first came to dinner forty years ago, when I was ten and he was twenty-five. I remember him sitting on the edge of the couch, pretending to watch the baseball game with Dad and my brother Terry. He seemed too large and dramatic for our fading brocade couch. His black hair needed a trim; the melancholy hazel eyes squinted against the TV glare and his clothes were baggy. He looked as if he were in a perpetual hurry. When Mom finally announced dinner, he acted relieved, yet shy in approaching the table.

'What a lovely centrepiece.' He reached over to touch one of the shiny gourds my mother had collected. She was always creating seasonal decorations which my father called 'clutter'.

Mom beamed. Terry looked at the ceiling. Dad cleared his throat. After this, dinner was uneventful. I guess the adults drank wine.

Later, Martin asked Terry and me if we knew any games. We chose a word game Mom had invented called 'Speculation' and I won. Terry, quick to bore in defeat, declared, 'What a stupid game. Words. Women love words.' Martin shrugged good-naturedly. My brother joined Dad watching the second part of a Giants' double header. Mom had left to wash the dishes. Martin won the next round of Speculation and I didn't mind at all.

He seemed comfortable in the dining-room. It was my favourite place in the house. I loved the large picture window and the tall china cabinet. This was the only room my father hadn't panelled in wood. Since he quit the army he was always busy with home improvements or with the TV. Because my boudoir was done in dark brown wood and tucked at the end of the house, I liked to sit in the pale green room reading while the rest of the family watched television in the adjacent parlour. I was glad Martin shared my taste.

Once the door closed on our guest, Mom exclaimed, 'Such a nice man. What is his last name?'

'Greek. He's tall for a Greek,' Dad answered. 'They're Catholic, too, the Greeks.'

'Orthodox.' I began to relate our religion lesson about ancient schisms.

'Catholic,' Dad said and we all went to bed.

The next week he brought chocolate. A baseball magazine for my brother. *A Tale of Two Cities* for me. After dinner, he helped with my homework. Nobody had ever helped with my homework. When I would ask Mom, she shook her head to say she thought the nuns expected too much of us. Dad said he didn't understand sentence diagrams. I thought my parents were unfair. My best friend Mandy got help from her mother and father who were lawyers. So it wasn't cheating to ask questions at home. Martin turned out to be a whizz at diagrams.

'No family,' Dad explained to Mom and me after Martin left. 'Died in some tenement fire back East. Nice young guy. We should take him in.'

Mom nodded over her shoulder, pleased with Dad's concern, yet a little wary. She was always a little wary of my father.

Martin came almost every Sunday after that. He would watch sports with Dad and Terry before supper and help me with my homework afterwards.

My grades took off the next year. Mom and Dad seemed unnerved to have an honour roll student in the house. Dad issued vague warnings about staying out of trouble like his independent sister Jeanette hadn't done. My brother and I moved further apart as I grew too uppity to be the Cowboy's Indian. Mom was mildly pleased with my success, yet worried I would stray out of reach. Don't spend so many afternoons in the library, she told me. We lived in San Francisco, after all, not New York, where she grew up. In San Francisco you could play outside all year long. She explained I was too serious for a little girl.

I left the book on the coffee table intentionally. As Martin walked into the living-room, he did a double take.

'Portrait of the artist, are you enjoying it?' He tried, too late, to conceal his surprise.

'If you mean, do I understand it,' I said, 'the answer is yes. I'm reading *Ulysses* next!'

'Quite a different story, you know.' He faced my indignation squarely. 'Longer.'

'I've got a lot of time.'

'I guess so.'

'Soup's on,' Mom called.

Martin and I sat at opposite ends of the table. Supper was unusually quiet. Afterwards, once he had gone off bowling with Dad, I considered how Martin fit into my life. He was the understanding father I had always wanted; the companionable older brother. That was more than enough, I told myself.

On my thirteenth birthday I had a slumber party. Mandy, Susan, Maggie and Angela arrived at six p.m. carrying sleeping bags and pastel overnight cases containing my presents and their night-gowns. Dad had taken Terry fishing. Maggie, at least, seemed disappointed that my brother was away.

Mom was terrific. She set out the pizza and pop, then

wheeled the television into her bedroom. Angela had just got Bruce's class ring, so we talked about going steady, about whether Sister Madeline would let her wear his basketball sweater to class. Frankly, I thought she was a little young, but I listened politely. Mandy called Angela silly. She also had read *Portrait of the Artist* and was planning to go to college.

Two hours into the party, I knocked on Mom's door because she said we could have the TV to watch '77 Sunset Strip'. After that, Angela wanted to see a Doris Day movie. I was hoping we could play some word games.

When the doorbell rang, Mom answered it.

'For you, Ellen,' she called.

My first thought was, oh, no, Sara McKinstry crashing the party. I flushed, hurrying away from my curious friends.

'For you, Ellen,' my mother repeated, as surprised as I by the bouquet of white roses.

My hands shook as I opened the card. 'Happiest of Birthdays to a lovely young lady. From an admirer.'

'Isn't that nice?' Mom said, her voice betraying the slightest query. 'An . . . admirer?'

'Oh, Mom,' I handed her the flowers quickly, hoping she might hide them in the garage until the girls left the next day. 'It's Martin. It's his idea of a joke.'

My stomach was pitching from pizza, chocolate and the sweet fragrance of too many roses.

'Does seem a bit extravagant.' Mom shook her head as if she were as unsettled as I.

'It *is* my birthday,' I bristled.

'Yes, but he's a grown man. And you're . . .'

'Thirteen,' I said in spite of myself because soon the commercial would come on and the girls would look for me. 'It's a special birthday. I'm not a little kid any more.' I watched the worry take over her face. 'We're friends, Mother.' I sighed and glanced into the living-room at the four young girls. Class rings and basketball sweaters seemed pathetically petty. Yet I yearned for that kind of venial turmoil. 'Martin does admire me. We enjoy talking, discussing books, in case you haven't noticed.'

'Perhaps I haven't noticed enough.' She held the roses behind her. Then she brightened, recovering the appropriate lines. 'He's such a nice man, one of the family, really.'

I kissed her cheek, pretending she understood and accepted it all. I realized my thirteenth birthday was more momentous than I had imagined, for this was the first time I had ever dismissed my mother.

The girls were engrossed in the programme. Maggie had a crush on Ephraim Zimbalist Jr.

'Who sent the flowers?' asked Angela.

'An admirer,' I slipped, then bit my lip.

'Who's that?' Maggie perked up.

'Probably that old guy they invite on Sundays,' Angela answered in an unpleasant voice.

'He's not *old*,' I said. 'Just because he isn't oozing zits like your Bruce the Younger.'

'*Him*, really, Ellen? Martin sent the flowers?'

I couldn't tell if Susan were conciliatory or awed.

'White stands for loyalty,' put in Mandy, pretending to be only slightly distracted from the television.

'What does it mean?' Maggie demanded.

For weeks I tried not to think about it. I was ashamed of my weird crush on Martin. It was one thing for me to imagine kissing him and quite another for him to . . . send flowers. That's all he did, I told myself, send flowers as a surprise for a little girl's birthday.

Sure, he had plenty of *real* dates. He had told me about them – women he took to movies and concerts. That's why he always came on Sundays. Saturday nights were booked up.

My interest in rollerskating was as passionate as it was sudden. Susan was delighted to have me enrol in her Sunday afternoon class. Mom was happy to see me out from behind the books, getting some healthy exercise, even if it did mean missing Sunday dinner.

Two months passed before I saw Martin to thank him for

the flowers. By then it seemed too late. I had almost convinced myself that they had come from another admirer.

II
The Second Bouquet

This time he brought a woman to dinner. Ronda was a typist at their company. I first met her when I went to the office with Dad. The thin blonde woman was very busy but she treated me like a human being. Before Martin got me interested in books, I planned to grow up and be a thin, blonde secretary.

When Mom had said, 'Martin's bringing a friend to dinner, Sunday,' I thought she meant another one of his buddies from Korea. I was disappointed because I had just finished reading *The Winter of our Discontent*, which he had given me for my sixteenth birthday. I considered it a far more appropriate gift than the thirteen roses. (He had never admitted to being the secret admirer and I had never asked him.) I had looked forward to our usual talk before dinner while Dad and Terry watched bowling. So with some pique I decided to skip dinner to study with Mandy.

When I returned from the library that night Mom said I would *have* to stay home the following Sunday. Martin was bringing Ronda back to meet me.
　'Why does he want to do that?' I pouted. 'I've known her a hundred years. Anyway, what would I have in common with an older woman like that?'
　'Martin,' smirked my mature brother.
　I shrugged, refusing to acknowledge that my feelings for Martin were visible to anyone in the family.
　'He wants to make sure you approve,' Mom said soothingly. I realized it was from her that I inherited my talent for denial.
　It had been six years since he first entered the house, teasing my father, flattering my mother, showing me that I had possibilities no one else in the family imagined. Six years of serious discussions and books and little presents.

When he left at ten on Sunday nights, he always seemed to be looking over his shoulder to see if I were catching up.

I was. I had gone from 'F's' in math to College Prep, from class recluse to editor of the paper. I had lost the pudge that always made summer a dreaded revelation. My pimples and blackheads had nearly cleared up. I was still a little awkward, haunted by the notion that I was going to be 'found out' posturing as a smart person. But my history teacher had written 'Very promising' across the last report card. Why, I had almost finished high school. Alive. After college, it would only be another five or six years until . . . I never finished the sentence, never consciously formulated the thought because I knew I would destroy it. I didn't dare let him know how I felt. Sometimes I missed Sunday dinner so he wouldn't take me for granted.

And now he would be bringing Ronda.

That week before their second visit was a marathon of self-flagellation. How could I think a thirty-one-year-old man would be interested in a high-school girl? Why did I believe he would wait for me to grow up? Because he said so? I remembered the first year when he seemed to open a bright light on my life. We had such a good time, joking and sparring. That Halloween I eagerly modelled my costume. Mom and Dad were baffled, but he recognized me right away. 'Cleopatra,' he laughed. 'When you grow up, we'll sail the Nile together.' Of course there were other intimations over the years – the books, the damn white roses.

By Sunday I was furious. Mom refused once again to let me go to the library.

'You study too much. God gave us Sunday to relax.'

I thought I would stay in my room with Kerouac, for I now found Steinbeck bland and folksy. Mom wouldn't permit that either. My father still hadn't recovered from the time I brought *America, America* to Candlestick Park and read it all the way through a harrowing baseball game. Mom and Dad agreed on less and less nowadays, but I knew that neither would abide by my rudeness.

Since it was too late to develop typhoid fever, I decided to attend dinner as a participant-observer. I was planning to become a psychologist and everything would be useful experience. How did lovers behave in public? Would the man or the woman be more nervous? Martin, apparently, was certain of *his* catch. I had overheard Dad tell Mom that Martin had actually interviewed Ronda's friends. He wasn't a man to take chances. Mom was horrified, but I thought it made sense; you couldn't be too careful about emotional commitments. I kept reminding myself that the evening would be interesting and that as a social scientist I needed to practise detachment. When Mom saw me in my new black skirt and sweater, she began to protest and then thought the better of it.

They arrived on time – Ronda's influence, I surmised, for Martin was usually late, having forgotten something at the last minute.

Today he hadn't forgotten a thing. He brought flowers for Mom, Scotch for Dad, pie for dessert. At least he didn't say, 'For the children.'

Martin looked more comfortable than usual. He had an almost stylish haircut and a new striped shirt.

Ronda seemed stiff. She looked heavier as well as older than I recalled. But then I had been a child when I last saw her. The wrinkles around her eyes were exaggerated by midnight blue mascara. Her arms sagged above the elbows. I suspected she was at least thirty-five.

'Ronda, Ellen, you remember each other?' Martin was casual.

'Yes,' she grinned, 'but you've grown a lot since our last encounter.'

'So have you,' I observed neutrally.

'I suppose so,' she laughed and looked, suddenly, at ease.

I felt terrible. Martin would be appalled with me. I hated her all the more for taking it so well. She was more astute than I had reckoned.

'Perhaps I'll see if Miriam needs help,' Ronda turned to Martin.

He nodded and asked me, 'So what did you think of the Steinbeck?' This was the same keenness with which he first approached my fifth grade sentence diagrams. 'It's my favourite of his books.'

'A little staid.' I stared at my fingernails. Maybe I had overdone it, frosting the white over the coral like this. 'I couldn't finish it actually. I've been reading a new author lately.'

'Oh, yes?' He recovered from my shot with an easy amusement I resented. 'One of the wild writers, eh? Kesey or Kerouac?'

'The latter . . . if you call imagination "wild".'

'No,' he grinned, 'I guess imagination, like kindness, is something one has to cultivate.'

'Hey, Martin,' my father called. 'Leave the kitchen to the girls for once. Come watch the game with us.' Dad considered Ronda the perfect addition to our extended family, just the puzzle piece to tip Martin back into place with the boys.

I stared at Martin defiantly.

His answer was quick. 'No, I'll see if I can confuse the cooks today.' He turned to the kitchen, smiling. I couldn't bear to be with them as Mom chatted and fussed over the vegetables. I knew that going back to Kerouac would seem petulant. So I called to Dad, 'What's the score?' and sauntered into the living-room.

Mom served roast beef with mashed potatoes, my favourite, which we could only afford on special occasions. She arranged the seating so Dad and Terry were next to each other. This was just as well because they were completely preoccupied with Donleavy's split in the eighth frame.

Mom asked Ronda about their wedding plans. She offered advice about the cake and champagne. I hadn't seen her this animated in months. Martin and I ate, our eyes fixed on the spring wildflowers in the centrepiece.

Noticing the silence, Ronda turned to me, 'Martin tells me you're reading Kerouac now.'

I stared at her incredulously.

She smiled patiently.

I felt myself smiling back. 'He's great. You've read him?'

'One of my favourite writers.' She nodded. 'I'd love to know what you think.'

My snide response dissolved instantly, perhaps because

I knew it was useless. Everything was useless. I was sixteen. Martin had used his imagination to be kind to me. We were all growing older.

III
– *Moving On Out* –

Martin and Ronda visited us our first September in Long Beach. It was a hot, humid week and Ronda, who was pregnant, spent most of her time on the *chaise longue* in our backyard. Dad promised to build a swimming-pool there some day. We had moved to the Garden of Eden.

Dad had jumped at the chance of a transfer to the Los Angeles office, where the pace would be easy and the sun constant. Mom supported him, promising warm surf and proximity to Hollywood. They had been arguing more than usual since the move but they did agree that Southern California was nirvana. After a week, I decided they were severely deluded. All I could see were oil cisterns and blonde girls who seemed smarter and prettier than I. I longed for my motley group of San Francisco friends. I was about to start college. Alone. My brother had been drafted.

Within an hour of his arrival, Martin assessed the general despair. He tried to patch things up between my parents. What an important part of our family he had become over the years. I was pleased with myself for recovering from the silly crush and for developing a genuine fondness for Ronda. Martin cajoled Dad when he became drunk and bad tempered. He flattered Mom about her cooking and decorating. He praised my parents to each other. That first summer of exile I was too distracted by my own loneliness to try to help my parents.

Martin invited me for a walk on the beach. The shore was so much tamer here than in the north. You could get a magnificent tan lying on the sand. What was wrong with me? Was I too caught up in childish nostalgia about San Francisco and guilt about my parents' bickering? Why couldn't an eighteen-year-old girl enjoy Eden? I wondered how old Eve was when she insisted on the apple.

'How're things going?' he asked when we reached the water.

'OK,' I said grudgingly.

'Aren't you excited about college?'

The sun caught shards of red in his hair, which was hopelessly tousled although the day was windless.

I sighed, 'Maybe if I were going to Berkeley. But Dad says there are too many hippies. And Mom says it's too far away. They think college is impractical.'

'You'll love it once you get started. UCLA's got to be more fun than Trenton State.' He shrugged.

'Trenton State!' I laughed. 'I thought you went to Fordham.'

'I transferred. Once you're in you can always transfer. Like your Dad in his job.'

'Guess so.' We walked in silence. I knew I should ask him about his life, about Ronda, about his incipient fatherhood. But I couldn't. It took all my courage just to keep from crying. We must have walked a couple of miles without speaking. On the way back to the house, we talked about names for the baby. If it were a boy, they were going to name him 'Jim', after my father; if it were a girl, 'Sherry', after Ronda's dead sister. I was relieved he hadn't said 'Ellen'. I was having enough trouble maintaining my identity. As we parked the car, he said quietly, 'Keep in touch.'

Forget about keeping in touch, I wanted to hold on for dear life.

They were all wrong.

I hated school. UCLA was so homogeneous I felt as if I were attending a dairy. The girls in my class came from Beverly Hills or Palos Verde and their parents were either in 'the industry' or in one of the helping professions such as law or insurance. Maybe Mom was right. Maybe a secretarial course would have been more appropriate. Maybe I wasn't smart enough or blonde enough to be in college. I spent a lot of time at home.

I hated our new house. I missed damp San Francisco cosiness, even the panelled walls. Here we had lots of windows – which looked out on frantic palm trees, a sea of smog and many other glass houses crowded into our 'residential community'. The windows would have been all right if we overlooked the ocean, but here glass provided more exposure than access.

I still don't know why they schedule finals just after New Year's. Appropriately inquisitional torture. By mid-January I was pretty strung out – spinning from family Christmas hostilities; wound up from the diet pills I was gulping to reduce after holiday meals; panicked about not fitting in at school. To make me relax, Dad gave me the Darvon left over from his stomach operation. It had the opposite effect. How did I pass History, English, French and Cultural Anthropology? I also passed into a scary outerzone in which I felt certain I was about to be wildly violent. I would fixate on swinging objects and believe I was being hypnotized to burn down the library or kill my parents.

Was I angry at anyone? the campus doctor asked. 'No,' I answered, astonished. At no one. Only at myself. He took me off the diet pills, prescribed a heavy dose of valium and placed me in the student hospital. Mom and Dad were desperate with worry and visited every day. They had known I wasn't meant for college. Dad cancelled several trips to San Diego, anxious to bring me home.

Come June, they promised, we would take a family vacation in San Francisco. We would go to the wharf and the marina and visit old friends. We would stay with Martin and Ronda.

June came. I remember reading a biography of Oliver Wendell Holmes in the back seat of the Pontiac as Dad sped north on Highway I. Mom kept turning around to make sure I was OK. They argued endlessly – about which road to take, about where to stop for lunch, about how fast we should be driving. All the while, Holmes' mature family discussed the US Constitution at their breakfast table. Mom and Dad agreed to stop in San Luis Obispo for the night, but they couldn't settle on a motel. She wanted a room with a bath, not a shower. He insisted on getting a room with a view. I forget the motel. I remember that we had chicken-in-the-basket for dinner.

Ronda was feeding the baby when we arrived. Sherry

looked like a cross between Martin and Ronda. I wondered why it didn't bother me. I had been off valium for a month. Perhaps I really had outgrown my childhood crush.

It was an ideal San Francisco week. Cool, foggy mornings led to bright afternoons. I went hiking with my best friend Mandy and shopping with Angela. Most days, however, I hung around the house with Mom and Ronda and the baby. One afternoon Martin and I took a walk at Half Moon Bay. The last night of our visit, my high school friends joined us for a barbecue in the garden.

Life seemed to fit together again. Martin's lemon tree dropped yellow globes. His lettuce patch was crowded with romaine and red leaf and chard. Squash was erupting into huge, sensual flowers. Late evening light held us securely in an open summer palm.

Two weeks after we returned to Long Beach, Dad ran away with a secretary from the San Diego office.

IV
Driving Lesson

Martin moved to LA the same summer Dad ran away.

I was working at Woolworths and going to summer school at UCLA. My brother Terry was on furlough, waiting to go to Vietnam.

Dad's plan was to leave on a Friday – as he often did on these sales trips – then to have Mom tell us on Monday that he wouldn't be coming back home this time.

Mom put her foot down, saying it was one thing to make the mistake of unqualified loyalty during marriage. She wasn't fool enough to behave that way through a divorce. He would have to tell the children himself.

I remember sitting by the picture window in the livingroom, staring at a pink house down the street. Dad had a beer in his hand as he paced back and forth across the parquet floor. He was sorry, he said, but the marriage just wasn't working.

My brother tried to reason with him. Dad reasoned back. In the end, Terry was too preoccupied with the army to worry much about anything else.

I screamed and cried it wasn't fair, no he couldn't leave, he had a family, how could he even think about it?

My father looked stunned. (The next day I saw this same stunned look on a dog hit while threading his way through the traffic.) Dad said he was sorry. Very sorry. Then he and my brother went to a tavern.

The worst possible thing had happened and it seemed like a familiar film. Dad was always leaving – for six month stretches when I was little and, once he got a shore job, for weeks at a time. Now he had made a complete break. You're supposed to be relieved when you survive the worst thing, however, I was petrified.

Three days later Terry left for the war.

During the first few weeks I was too busy taking care of

Mom to feel much. She was so numb with shock that she walked into the walls and the furniture. Then grief came with weeks of sobbing. Then silence. We would sit up by the fire until late at night. A fire in July? I asked stupidly. For company, she said. She would fall asleep at three or four a.m. Sometimes the house got so hot I worried the windows would pop out. We took long walks on the beach. We went to a lot of movies.

One Saturday I lay in the backyard alone, trying to study for my Jane Austen class. The *chaise* lounged near the spot where Dad had promised to build a pool and I realized our yard was too small for a swimming-pool. Jane Austen seemed so elegantly controlled and remote. I decided it would have been easier if Dad had died. At least there wouldn't have been so many false promises. I wondered whether it was him I missed – for surely when he was home, he had one eye on the TV and one eye on his beer. Maybe it was the 'idea' of having a father that I missed. My friend Mandy was probably right about the myth of the nuclear family. This was not the best moment to read Jane Austen. Maybe I wasn't objective enough to be an academic.

About this time Martin moved to Los Angeles. He came very much because Dad had left. The company needed to replace my father after he transferred to the San Diego office. Martin arrived ahead of his family – leaving Ronda to sell their San Francisco home while he looked for a place in LA. Given the market, it could take him three or four months to find a house. It seemed natural for Martin to move in with us for there was plenty of room.

Martin looked pretty much the same as when I last had seen him. The dark hair whispered across his moon face. He never had learned to dress fashionably although Ronda had found him a couple of classy suits. He had put on a little weight and looked healthier. He wasn't handsome, exactly, rather *compelling*. He attended so closely. And what did he see? Of course I had changed in the nine years since we first met. Even in the last month I had grown taller and fuller. I still had my father's big, brown eyes; my mother's fair skin and her slight hesitation in speech.

He cheered Mom up considerably. Hospitality forced her to talk. Gradually she returned to her old self – telling corny jokes and taking pride in the house. We had Sunday dinners again: a different style of chicken each week as well as a surprise dessert supplied by Martin. Then we would read Terry's letters from Vietnam. We talked about Civil Rights and cultural events. This wasn't exactly Oliver Wendell Holmes, but it was a civilized 'family'. None of us admitted how we missed the TV static in the background.

After dinner each week, Martin gave me a driving lesson. I was a disgrace, he said, a nineteen-year-old college student who didn't know how to drive.

There wasn't anything else to do that summer; I had no other company. My few school friends were even more outsiders than I: a Brooklyn Jew who had returned to New York for the summer; a female forestry major who had gone off to safeguard Wyoming; a black sociologist who was cooling down Watts. None of them wrote; neither did I.

Martin would drive up to Hillridge Mall, talking rapidly about Africa or Flaubert or something blessedly distant from my torments about Dad.

'So I bet you don't like Darcy,' he teased as we pulled into the empty lot.

'How did you know?' I asked, distracted by the silent order of white lines on the black macadam. It reminded me of a cemetery organized by the cold order of useless bodies. Dad had taken us shopping at this mall last Christmas.

'Because you don't believe in compromise,' he said.

In response to what, I couldn't remember.

The next Sunday was one of those clear days which, even then, were becoming rare in Southern California. Saturday's rain and wind had nudged the smog over the hills. I was quiet during dinner. All day I had been thinking about my father and what had drawn him south. Just as his promises to us slipped behind our reality, his reality had fallen behind his own dreams. Perhaps the West Coast was a dangerous land after all, a place where unsuspecting people tripped over the edge. Perhaps that was the point of building a swimming-pool, so the ocean didn't lure you off the cliff.

We practised parallel parking and my stomach knotted tighter and tighter. This was a complete act of faith – as inexplicable as algebra. I had done OK with geometry – where the curves were clearly charted on paper. But algebra, which depended on memorization of formulae hidden behind coded letters, was always vaguely frightening. The algebra teacher had chided me for asking too many questions and this only reinforced my belief that neither she nor Euclid could be trusted.

'But you'll need to know parallel parking if you drive downtown.'

It seemed so much easier to take the bus. Anyway, I supported mass transportation for political reasons.

We practised for half-an-hour before Martin relented. 'Maybe it's like typing was for you. Remember you were all thumbs for months and then one day you just did it. Maybe it's an issue of trust – in the instructor; in yourself.'

He opened his door and suggested a walk.

I was touched that he remembered my typing struggles. He had known me almost half my life.

'Or an issue of boredom.' I shrugged nonchalantly. 'Why make a project out of it? When I get my licence, I'll drive around the block until I can find a real parking space.'

By this time we were walking to the edge of the lot.

'Graceful entrances and exits count for something,' he smiled.

I blinked at the sheen of sunlight on the hill of silver icepant. We could see the harbour and beyond it, miles across the Pacific.

'See that ship down there? It's like the one I took to Korea.'

I tried not to think about my father's trips to Japan.

'Gorgeous day.' He breathed deeply.

His arm was on my shoulders. I could smell a trace of sweat from beneath his deodorant. I knew I should inch away. He was a married man. Married to a woman I liked. He had been taken into our house as a friend. Yet I couldn't move. Instead, I made myself as small as possible, concentrating on the nature of compromise and trust.

A moment later he stepped back. Stretching his arms toward the sky, he declared, 'It's so rare you have a clear day like this.'

V

– The New House –

'Gotta date?' asked my room-mate, Gloria. 'You look real neat.'

'Yes,' I nodded nervously. I knew I was lucky to have Gloria as a room-mate compared to a lot of the bubbleheads in the dorm. I also knew I wasn't her ideal confidante. We seemed to get along best on minimal interaction. I was scared that second year in college, too scared to admit it.

I didn't want to visit Martin's new house. I had a midterm the next morning. I especially didn't want to go to the movies first. But he seemed so eager and he had been very kind to me. He said he'd pick me up at six p.m. I still hadn't got my driver's licence.

I had mixed feelings about Martin finding a house. Certainly I was happy for him. The arduous real estate negotiations made me want to postpone the adult world a little longer. Growing up, which had once meant freedom, now was turning into what Mom had always described as 'complex'. Who would have thought she could be deserted after all those years? Well, everyone had *thought* about it, but who could have *believed* it? You couldn't go on living if you believed in such possibilities. Or perhaps that's what adults did.

As much as I was happy for Martin, I was sorry that Mom would lose her roomer – especially since I was living at the dorm this year. The new house also meant that Ronda and little Sherry would be moving down. I would see less of him. But that was fair enough. He must miss his wife and daughter. I had my whole life ahead of me.

'Who's the date with?' Gloria persisted politely. She was changing into warmer clothes for the library.

'Just an old friend of the family.' I hated the cold, dismissive tone of my voice, but I didn't want to get into a discussion about how I had once had a childhood crush on my father's friend who was now my good buddy. 'Not a real date.'

'OK.' She smiled and collected her books. 'Have a great time.'

After she left I combed my hair in front of the mirror. I finally understood what girls meant when they said I had nice skin. My complexion was smooth and I never had to wear rouge. The buzzer rang. I wondered as I anxiously rushed to the door – then back again for my purse – whether Martin had ever seen this pink and green dress.

The double bill was the perfect balance for me – 'The Pawnbroker' and 'The Umbrellas of Cherbourg'. Something deep and relevant; something sophisticated and charming. My nervousness eventually dissolved.

At the intermission we discussed World War II, the Holocaust, Vietnam. Martin quickly switched the topic from Vietnam. While he loved to argue, lately he just cut off the Vietnam arguments with, 'I fought in Korea', or 'Wait till your brother comes home'. He said girls couldn't really understand war.

'Well,' he spoke into the void. 'I thought I was too old for a double bill. But I wouldn't want to go home after "The Pawnbroker" and I've heard this next film is good.'

It was *so* elegant. I had been hearing the theme music on the radio for months. Catherine Deneuve was exquisite. A smart blond. Perhaps I had underestimated Gloria. Martin was wearing a little too much Aqua Velva. Did I know him well enough to mention it? His arm rested casually on the back of my seat, touching my shoulders occasionally. I couldn't imagine what I had been worried about. I felt terribly lucky. Martin was better than a brother or a father or a boyfriend. He was a constant presence. He understood me in ways my brother never could. He would never leave me as Dad had done. He was crying at the end of the film.

I had forgotten about the next day's exam by the time Martin was driving us to Malibu. A beach house, he explained to me now. Somehow I had pictured him tucked snugly into the well-lit streets of a new housing development or living in one of those old Spanish places, with weathered adobe and a red-tiled roof. He was taken aback, because, he said, this is what he had been looking for all along. Since Ronda's father died, they had a little money and wanted to invest in a nice place. Yes, I reminded myself, Martin had married up. There were things besides Vietnam we couldn't discuss. Of course it made perfect sense for him to settle on the beach.

The night was afire with stars and surprisingly chilly. I scolded myself for not bringing a shawl, but I hadn't considered the beach. Not wanting him to see me shiver, I rushed toward the white house, exclaiming over everything – the gorgeous jacaranda, the cute shutters.

Catherine Deneuve would have been comfortable here with the wall-to-wall carpeting in the halls, the sunken living-room, the Italian tiles in the bathroom. Sherry's bedroom was at the back, facing what Martin promised would soon be the garden, but which tonight was a vast darkness. Across the hall was their bedroom, brightened by moonlight and overlooking the ocean.

My tears seeped out. It was ridiculous to feel jealous. I had my whole life ahead of me. I walked to the French doors to escape Martin's view.

'Here, I'll turn on the lamp,' he said. 'I'll show you the built-in closets.'

'No, no,' I tried to sound less urgent. 'You'll just shut off the moonlight that way.'

I wanted to tell him to go, to leave me alone, but it was his house – their house. Why had he brought me here – as torture? No, I reminded myself, this was Martin. He was better than a boyfriend or a father or a brother. He was Martin. I was crying and shaking. I felt as if my flesh had been peeled away. It was more than wanting to be alone. I wanted to be. I wanted to feel supported by my skeleton and contained by my skin. He walked over and put that supportive arm around my shoulders. I was furious.

'You OK?'

'Sure, why?' Now I needed him to name my pain, to name his feelings, which could not be so different from mine, simply better concealed.

'I don't know,' he was maddeningly soothing, 'but why don't we go into the kitchen for a drink?'

I tensed, knowing he could easily transmute my anxiety into mid-term jitters once we were under the bright lights of his modular kitchen.

'The drive back to school is so long,' I heard myself saying. It seemed as if the earth revolved two or three times before I could utter the next sentence. 'Then you'll just have to come back here. Why don't I stay the night?'

I could feel his breath. I wasn't cold any more. A soft, warm light was waking me. I felt woozy; also wired. I was hungry and thrilled and thoroughly astonished by his response.

'Some hot chocolate should do the trick.' His arm lifted, light as the wing of an imaginary bird. 'That will be good for both of us.'

I don't remember how I got to the kitchen. There we were, sitting at the round arborite table facing the avocado refrigerator talking about Rod Steiger and my mother's new typing job and my major in International Relations.

We managed to ride safely from Malibu to Westwood despite the drivers racing alongside us, despite the feelings racing through my body. I wanted to grab the steering wheel and swerve us into the freeway divider. We would both go together in one sharp, brutal pain. Ronda and Mom would be called to the hospital. They would console each other with the report that death had been instantaneous.

When we passed the sign for the university, I opened my mouth. I had to ask.

'So I guess I wasn't tempting?'

He didn't answer for a long time. I imagined that he didn't hear me or that he didn't understand. I sweated fury and humiliation. Finally he said softly, 'Too tempting.'

I could see a light in the fourth floor corner room and I knew Gloria was waiting up, worried. I looked at my watch, not surprised to find it was one a.m. You can't take in a double feature, a new home and a life's worth of questions without spending time.

He pulled over to the curb and started to open his door.

'Don't get out,' I spoke lightly. 'I'll be fine and you've got an early morning.'

'OK.' He sounded tired, resigned.

It gave me satisfaction to think of him as ageing.

'Listen,' he handed me a twenty dollar bill, 'I know it's tough working and going to school. Take this – I just want to know you're OK.'

I was horrified. What if one of my friends walked by and saw this old guy handing me money? Why was he doing this? Had I provided the appropriate pleasure for his evening? Was he trying to buy off his conscience? For what? He could afford the twenty dollars, I knew that much.

'No,' I replied as calmly as I could. (Often since then I've wished I had taken the money. First of all, he was right that I was struggling to pay the bills. And I know now that the best people can do for one another is to stem the suffering. Accepting the money would have done that a little – for each of us.) 'No,' I repeated as I left the car. 'Thanks for the movies.'

I walked away abruptly, knowing another word from either of us would shatter me. I prayed that Gloria would leave the light on just five more minutes.

VI
– *Dear Martin and Ronda* –

Dear Martin and Ronda,

Thank you for your friendship. I want you to know how much I value that. Dinner last night was delicious. I still can't believe we were sitting in your living-room watching men walk on the moon. What's next? I enjoyed our talk afterward. You have such a good life together – a very fine family. I hope to find that one day myself.

Love

Ellen

VII
– *Ever After* –

I knew you were supposed to feel nervous before your wedding, but I was floating. Mom fretted endlessly. Terry smoked a lot of pot. My father was absent. He did send fifty dollars. Fifty dollars and Martin. He asked his old friend to give me away.

Truthfully, I didn't want anyone giving me away. Still, this gesture would involve Martin in the ceremony and I did consider him one of the family so I took it in my stride. What if I had once had an adolescent crush on him? We could both forget that in the wash of years. Family friend. It was a significant bond. I was sorry we hadn't seen each other much since Ronda sold their old house and joined him in Los Angeles. But a wife and daughter kept you busy. I was absorbed at college. And then I met Evan.

I took everything in my stride until the morning of the wedding when I dropped an elegant Beleek vase that Evan's Aunt Meg sent us. I took that in my stride and decided I must be crazy because the damn thing cost at least two hundred dollars.

Mom swept up the shamrock slivers and said Aunt Meg would never know the difference. After swallowing two Compoz tablets, I pretended to be an adult. I concentrated on packing my modest trousseau. Mom showed me how to keep the negligé from wrinkling by using tissue paper.

The doorbell rang.

'Evan,' my brother called from his chair in front of the TV.

'No,' I whispered to Evan through a crack in the door. 'It's bad luck for you to see me before the wedding.'

We first met at the library. I worked behind the desk and Evan came to check out a book.

'Oh, *The Aeneid*,' I said. 'Are you in Johnson's class?'

'Yes,' he smiled. 'I've noticed you there. I liked your comment yesterday about grace.'

I stared at him. He was the smart guy in the front row who had corrected Professor Johnson during the second week. I looked closely at his tweed jacket and jeans. His tall, thin good looks were made less intimidating by his wire-rimmed glasses, repaired on one side by a bandaid.

'When do you get off work?'

'Ten o'clock,' I said, ignoring my plan to study with Gloria.

'How about meeting Virgil and me at Driscoll's for coffee?'

We fell in love the first month. Gloria forgave me when she heard it was true love. She was a much better roommate than I deserved.

Evan and I decided to wait until graduation before we married. We were both sensible people, who believed that you should be twenty-one to marry. Something warned me to wait. How could I trust Evan's love? Maybe being abandoned was a genetic tendency I could watch for.

He was a kind, gentle, studious man. He was everything my family wasn't. He took me to galleries and taught me to listen to classical music. He told me about living in Paris while his father taught at the Sorbonne. His kind, gentle, studious parents took me in. His mother was a high school counsellor and his father, a famous professor. They never flaunted their success or looked down on me. They inquired about my classes and encouraged me to apply to graduate school.

Mom tried to like Evan. She invited us to dinner on Sundays, exclaiming how nice it was to have another man around the house. Evan was polite and helpful, but he wasn't the authoritative voice Dad – or even Martin – had been. He could talk about modernism and alienation, yet when it came to the 'real things' of the world – the Domino Theory, the assassinations, baseball – he didn't think he had an original opinion. Terry didn't try to understand him. He had been even more distracted than usual since he returned from the war. Mom mistook Evan's modesty for otherworldliness. After the first few meals, she made excuses to leave the table early and work on her afghan. Still, she was happy that I was happy, even when I announced that we had each received a fellowship to London and that we would be leaving for England after the honeymoon.

'Graduate school, what are you going to do with that, after four years of college?'

I expected that from Terry or my father or even Mom. But this was Martin talking. On the phone. We kept missing each other in person. Actually, he had never met Evan. I'd have to introduce them at the wedding.

Martin drove me to the church. He was in one of those quiet moods which came on him more frequently as he got older. I could have used a compliment or a little reassurance. I loved the daring gown I had borrowed from Evan's sister, although it was a little tight across the bust. At a stoplight, he asked about my seat belt, worried I would crush the expensive satin. 'Are you OK?' His voice quavered, as if suddenly realizing the fragility of his passenger or himself. Then he fell silent until we reached the church.

St Agnes' wasn't the prettiest chapel, but it was cosy and their hall was cheap. Evan wasn't a Catholic, so we had a brief service rather than a Nuptial Mass. Evan's family wanted to help with the expenses, but Mom insisted on taking care of everything. It was a simple reception with hors d'oeuvres. Mom spent all her vacation money on the champagne. What I remember most was the receiving line: our friends coming through with smiles and hugs and congratulations as if we had actually *accomplished* something.

Martin was speaking to Evan. 'Be sure to take care of her.' Martin tried to sound hardy.

'Oh, she can take care of herself,' Evan answered confidently.

I couldn't decide how I felt about that.

VIII
– *Paprika and Toothpaste* –

Evan had been right; I could take care of myself. Four years after the wedding, I had a teaching post in London and a flat of my own off the Finchley Road. The hardest part of the divorce was telling my family. Even that was tolerable. Mom didn't scold; she simply despaired that I would ever be happy. My brother was moderate in his 'I-told-you-so's'. I never did hear back from Dad. During Christmas week I got a package from Martin. 'Happy Holidays from an old family friend. Here's something to keep you company.' A copy of *Fear of Flying* and *The Tales of Mula Nasrudin*.

That spring I returned to Los Angeles for a visit. To organize my life. To have a holiday. To take a break from the pace of London. To see Mom. To do some research, I finally rationalized when a trans-Atlantic trip still felt too self-indulgent.

Three days into my visit I awoke to hear the phone ringing. Ten a.m. Mom had obviously left for work. I couldn't seem to shake the jetlag. The ringing continued, just like the phones in England. The telephone was the first thing I noticed about returning home. Americans expected you to answer by the fourth ring. In London no one answered before the tenth ring. Perhaps someone from the university was calling. I stumbled out of bed.

'Ellen? Is that you, Ellen?'

His accent was broad. He spoke so slowly. And frankly, I didn't know the answer to his question. Which Ellen did he want? I was a grown woman, tipping into my late twenties. A divorcee. A professor. Yet hearing his voice, I was ten years old again.

'Yes. Martin! Hello.'

'You OK?'

Again, the voice was as broad as the tourists who talked so loudly in the Courtald Gallery. My hero was just another middle-aged American. Middle-aged. He must be over forty by now.

'Yes, just some congestion.' I cleared my throat and dried my eyes. 'From the flight. I'm still all stuffed up.'

'Paprika should take care of that. How about we go to the Hungarian Castle for lunch?'

How about we go to . . . ? Had he always talked in those constructions?

'Well, I have to go to Evan's mother's house at four, to clear away some books I left there,' I spoke absently, curious about my reluctance.

'Even Hungarians finish lunch by four o'clock.'

His laugh was so familiar that I almost started to cry again.

'Lunch sounds lovely,' I managed. 'What time?'

'I'll pick you up at noon,' he answered. 'And did you know you have an English accent?'

He still wore too much aftershave. He was remarkably unchanged – slim and just a touch of grey. I tried to consider him through the eyes of little Ellen. When I realized his own daughter must be ten by now, I stopped. He was very glad to see me – kissing me once on each cheek and then on the lips. First we went to the bar where we had a couple of martinis while waiting for our table. Martinis – it was such an adventure after drowning in lager for four years – and I didn't even start to notice the effect until I sipped the wine at lunch.

Martin had reserved a window table. He'd had a corsage of white roses set at my place. This was so unlike the welcome I had received when Mom met me on the Airporter bus, exhausted from her job and worried about my brother's new baby, who had a kidney problem. Mom was also worried about me – about why I was choosing to stay over in that damp, god-forsaken country now that I could come home. I still had a home here, she kept saying in a voice she meant to be reassuring.

'London is wonderfully cosmopolitan,' Martin smiled. 'Do you get to much theatre?'

'I like fringe theatre best. But I do go to the National

occasionally.' This conversation was such a relief. Martin had always understood. His accent was beginning to soften. I got carried away in my detailed cultural comparison. He listened attentively and asked questions. I was, after all, his protégé. I wouldn't have gone to London if it hadn't been for Martin, for I wouldn't have made the honour roll and applied to college and moved into the dorm and got a job at the library where I met Evan. He was proud of me – proud of those things about which my mother could only be fearful. I tried to make the best of it for him today – to appear the glamorous, young intellectual flourishing in Europe.

'You really are extraordinary,' he sighed.

I flushed with pleasure.

'Beautiful. Successful. Full of possibility . . .'

I could only bear so much.

'How are Ronda and Sherry?' My voice betrayed a penitential edge. 'Did you bring pictures?'

He shook his head indifferently. 'Sherry's fine. She's ten now, you know?'

'And brilliant in school?'

'She seems more interested in sports. Gymnastics.'

'Oh, I watched that on the Olympics. They didn't teach it when I took PE.' I was grateful for all distinctions between little Sherry and little Ellen. 'Gymnastics are very graceful.'

Martin nodded. He seemed distracted. Perhaps he had simply drunk too much wine.

I sipped the ice water. My teeth hurt, giving me the satisfaction of feeling English. Ice water seemed so eccentrically American.

'And Ronda?' I reminded myself how much I respected his wife. 'How is she?'

'Fine. Fine. Gone back to work. Very active in different community groups. Everyone's fine.'

As if sensing the danger of our intimacy, the waiter appeared with entrées. Martin seemed to be having some problems at work, but he shrugged them off as 'mid-life slump'. The conversation shifted to my mother's health, my brother's family and my father, who no one ever seemed to hear from.

I didn't usually eat desserts, but the tray of gooey cakes was tempting. I checked my watch. Two-thirty. 'Don't you have to get back to work?'

'No, no, I'm fine,' he said.

So we had dessert and coffee and brandy. Then Martin took my hand. 'Do you remember that night when you and I were alone in the new house in Malibu?'

Stiffening, I concentrated on his awkward American idioms. I thought of little Sherry. Of Ronda, who had always been kind to me. Still, I was flooded with the ache from that night in the beach house and with the hollowness I had felt recently in London.

My face was crimson.

He squeezed my hand.

'Too bad we didn't meet at a different time in our lives.' I smiled sadly.

'But we have. We've met at all different times in our lives.' He smiled back.

Withdrawing my hand, I looked at my watch. 'Three o'clock. I really have to go. Got to pick up something at Mom's to bring Evan's mother.' It was agonizing to say no, especially because I didn't know what I was saying no to.

'I can swing by your Mom's apartment.'

I should have taken the bus, I knew. But it was so comforting to be with Martin. As we pulled up to the curb, he said, 'I'll come in with you.'

'Don't bother. Mom's at the office. I'll just be a second.'

'I'd like to. I want to brush my teeth.'

I stared at him. 'You carry a toothbrush?'

He nodded, 'Scout's honour.'

'No, Martin.' I couldn't muffle the alarm in my voice. 'I'll just be a second.' I dashed into the building.

Once I shut the door, I was in a panic about what to pretend I was bringing Evan's mother. The Persian pillow caught my eye. Evan had given it to me before we were married, explaining that his Uncle Thurman had captured it in World War I. That would make a suitable peace offering to Mrs Revson for storing my books all these years. And I could place it in the front seat between Martin and me.

Before leaving, I dashed to my suitcase for some chewing-gum.

Martin accepted a stick and chewed it slowly. He seemed older than he had in the restaurant. Worn down, perhaps, from the alcohol. I wished I had been less self-absorbed over lunch and asked him more about his tensions at work. We didn't exchange a word until we entered Beverly Hills. Two blocks from Evan's house, he pulled down a side street.

'Martin, it's that way.'

He stopped the car and faced me directly. 'I've got to ask. Why didn't you want me to brush my teeth?'

I started to smile, grateful he was making a joke of it. Then I looked more closely. He was frowning. I unwrapped a stick of gum for myself.

'You didn't want to be alone in the apartment with me, did you?'

The voice was hard, as if he were a stranger arguing about an automobile collision.

'That's right,' I answered. The gum was dry and brittle.

'You know I think I made a mistake that night in Malibu.'

It was silly to feel trapped. Here in broad daylight in the middle of Beverly Hills. I could *walk* to Evan's house from here.

'No, *I* did,' I heard myself say. 'I shouldn't have tempted you – us.'

'It would have been good if I had initiated you.'

I blinked. I tried to hear love, even passion.

'I would have done it carefully, lovingly. Then maybe you wouldn't have had to marry that Evan fellow.'

I wanted to protest that I didn't *have* to marry Evan. I wanted to say I hadn't needed an initiation. But we weren't having a conversation.

'Of course we're both adults now.' He was staring straight ahead at the generous lawn of a white-columned mansion. 'There's nothing stopping us now.'

'Except good sense.'

He raised a shaggy eyebrow.

'Martin, we have a friendship. A long friendship. We're

family to each other. We don't want to destroy that because of sexual feelings.'

He turned the key in his ignition and skidded around the corner, driving furiously to Evan's house which, I was surprised, he remembered from years before.

'Thanks for lunch,' I said as I got out. I was going to suggest that he and Ronda come to Mom's for dinner before I returned to London.

'You're still so young.' He shook his head fondly.

'No.' I kissed his cheek. 'Neither still nor young.'

IX
– Just Out of Reach –

'Hello, Ellen, this is Martin.'

I was half asleep when Verity handed me the phone on one of those frozen English mornings that make you resent anyone who wakens you. Why was Martin Campbell calling from Glasgow at this hour – Christ, six a.m.? No, *not* Martin Campbell. Strange American voice. Martin.

'Oh, Martin. Hello. Where are you?'

'Somewhere called the Clifton. A skyscraper downtown.'

'Downtown?' I asked groggily. Verity looked annoyed for it was one thing to be dragged out of bed for an emergency, but this was ridiculous. She snuggled under the covers, her arms around my waist.

'Yes. I don't think I'm very far from you.'

I tried to collect myself. This was not the best week for old friends from the States. My job was on the line and I was getting flack from the immigration people for being arrested at a recent health cuts demo.

'London,' I said. Verity pulled a pillow over her head. 'You're in London?'

'Yes,' he sounded more confident. 'This is a sudden trip. The company signed a contract with the Swedes and they've sent me. Pretty cosmopolitan, huh?'

'The Swedes?'

'I'm on my way to Sweden. But I managed to square away a couple of days in London. So we could spend some time together.'

I looked at my watch. Tuesday. I had to teach today. Tomorrow was a big faculty meeting. Tomorrow night Verity and I were celebrating our second anniversary. 'How about supper tonight?' I asked.

'I was hoping . . .'

'I've got to work today.' I noticed petulance in my voice. He never believed I had grown up. I wasn't sure just how much I wanted to tell him about this adult life. 'But I could meet you by seven.'

'Twelve hours alone in the big city.' He whistled. 'Well, I'll find something to do. Maybe sleep. Maybe tomorrow you can take me to a cathedral. Your mother would like that.'

'I guess she would. How about meeting at a wine bar I know near there; it's called . . .'

'A "wine bar"? You've started to talk like them again, you know. Hey, why don't you come up to the hotel. By then I'll have found us a decent place to eat.'

Up to the hotel, I sighed, remembering my last visit to the States. Well, that was over five years ago. What was I worried about? All those wonderful Sunday family dinners certainly overshadowed a botched seduction. I had almost forgotten it. I should be hospitable and meet him at the hotel. He was a stranger in the city.

'Sure. The Clifton at seven.' I agreed. 'Looking forward to it.'

I hung up the phone and sank beneath the covers.

'Your friend Martin from home?' Verity asked.

'How did you know?'

'You used to talk about him all the time.'

'I did?'

I wanted to wear slacks, but I would be coming straight from class. Surveying the closet, I picked my darkest outfit. Then I decided I was obsessing. Just wear what you were planning to wear, I told myself. The blue dress. So what if you look good in it. This was just a visit from an *old* friend. When was I going to relax?

I had never entered the Clifton, or any of the other skyscraper hotels in London. As I ascended in the glass-enclosed elevator, I thought about my brother's last phone call when he coyly referred to Martin's business being bad but his 'affairs' going well. I tried to shrug it off; lots of couples had open marriages. It was none of my business. But I was so angry at Terry that I hadn't written back for months. Now I wondered if Martin were in London to play the lascivious businessman? I sighed nervously.

Yes, it was Martin, a very grey Martin. For a moment I lost my breath. Why did I care so much about his appearance?

'Ellen, you look lovely,' he exclaimed, leaning forward to kiss my cheek.

I knew I should have worn the slacks. 'Great to see you,' I said, surprised how true this was. I was caught by the light in those hazel eyes and by the kindness of his smile. How much I owed him. What a steady friend he had been.

'Come on in,' he took my hand. I smelled the reassuring Aqua Velva.

The room was small and compact: table by the window; chest of drawers; double bed; bathroom. He opened a tiny refrigerator.

'Oh, isn't that cute,' I laughed before I had time to critique the hotel's individualistic excesses.

Inside were a dozen miniature bottles of liquor.

'What can I get you?'

I stood near the door, 'Oh, nothing. Why don't I take you to an authentic London wine bar?' I asked desperately. 'Remember that bottle of wine you brought the first time you visited the family? Pinot Noir.'

'Well, I'm not so sure they'd have my label. I've become a California wine snob.' He fixed himself a double martini. 'How about it?' he asked. 'You used to go for these.'

'No thanks.'

'A man can't drink alone.'

He frowned and handed me a glass wrapped in a sanitary plastic cover. I was beginning to feel like Alice in Wonderland.

'So how's your life here?' he asked.

I wanted to tell him about Verity, but it seemed wiser to wait until we had exchanged a few words. 'My job is fine. Teaching is hectic this time of year. But I love London. I wish you were staying longer. I'd take you to the theatre.'

'Might come through again on my way back from Sweden.' He sipped his drink.

'How're Ronda and Sherry?'

'Sherry's fine. She's going to secretarial school, you know. A cute girl. Good kid.'

'And Ronda?' I had grown past my grudging respect for her into a genuine appreciation. Ronda was bright and independent, definitely Martin's equal. And she had been very attentive to my mother since I moved to London.

'Ronda's fine.' He finished his drink and stood. 'So where's this city you're going to show me?'

We walked for an hour. This was the easiest way to see London and the easiest way to chat. Or to listen. Martin talked continually about the 'deal', about his firm teetering into bankruptcy, about his alternate plans if the deal fell through. Occasionally he would turn and squeeze my arm, saying how thrilling, yet unreal, it was to be together in London.

We stopped at a Southbank cafeteria, my favourite place to take visitors. (It saddened and relieved me to think of Martin as 'a visitor'.) The food was reasonable and the view of the Thames was glorious. It took me ten minutes to convince Martin I could pay for my own meal. Then I wondered why I had been so ardent. British salaries were paltry and I might not have even a British salary much longer. We found a seat by the window and I pointed down the river to the bridges and historical buildings.

'How is Ronda?' I tried once more, vaguely alarmed that he hadn't answered the first time.

'Fine. Finer than ever, actually.'

'Oh, yes?'

She's working in a fancy dress shop in Belair. It's a drain on us financially, completely screws up the taxes, but it's what she wants. Feels that she *has* to work. Still, it makes no sense.'

'Maybe it makes sense to her.'

'Listen, I'm not against women improving themselves. I would have understood if she had gone to college. Or learned a skill. But selling dresses?'

'People have to wear clothes.'

'You wouldn't approve of this extravagant gear.' He sipped the wine. 'Frivolous.'

I thought how Verity teased me about being overly rational – about how I had no appreciation of the 'kinesthetic intelligence' of the creatively dressed.

'You'd be surprised,' I laughed. 'I'm much more accepting. I've been practising.'

'You needed practise.' He grinned.

The colour rose up my neck, whether because of the familiarity or the admonition, I couldn't tell. Changing the topic, I enquired, 'Have you seen Mom lately?'

'She came to dinner on Easter,' Martin answered, watching a tourist boat churn down the Thames.

'She seems to like the new apartment.'

'Yes.' He yawned. 'Speaking of which, how do you live here? In a flat or a bed-sit? I always imagined that in a flat you can lie down to sleep whereas in a bed-sit you have to sit up all night. "Bed-sit", I love that word.'

'I live with a woman named Verity,' I rushed to speak before I lost my nerve. 'We're very happy . . .'

He blushed, or did I imagine it? 'Verity. I would expect you to be happy with the truth.'

'You don't understand, Verity and I . . .'

'Oh, I always understood,' he smiled ruefully, 'that you'd never stop searching until you found the truth.' He rose and walked to the counter for another carafe of Pinot Noir.

Martin was smiling as he returned. He stood for a moment, extending his glass in a toast. I was too far away to clink glasses. I stood to tap his glass with mine, but by then he was drinking. We had always been like this. Just out of reach.

X
– Wake –

I almost missed Dad's funeral. Snow grounded my plane at Heathrow for twenty hours. A few years ago I would have given up at this juncture, declaring it stupid to travel six thousand miles and find him already underground. But Verity once more urged me beyond my dogged rationality.

So, weary and dizzy with jetlag, I arrived in a cab at the church after everyone was seated. I dumped my suitcase in the vestibule and settled into a back pew. It took me a moment to get my bearings. The organ sounded off-key, but since it wasn't 'The Star Spangled Banner', my father wouldn't have noticed. The only time he listened to music was when the National Anthem played before a ball game.

My brother and I agreed we would be the head pallbearers. When I phoned from London about the delay, Terry said he would find a replacement. I hadn't expected it to be Martin.

I didn't even know Martin was still talking to my father. Few people were, at the end. Dad had told me Martin refused to support him in a company dispute. Martin had told me Dad was lying outrageously. Since I corresponded only intermittently from London, it was easy to ignore the dispute. But come to think of it, Martin was always around, the true friend-of-the-family. Hadn't he given me away at my wedding?

Today he seemed more like a ghost than my father did, perhaps because his spectre was so visible. I had once known him well. Now, at sixty-five, his hair was thinning. He seemed five inches shorter. I could hear him wheezing under the coffin's weight. Did they keep spare coffins behind the altar in case one of the pallbearers collapsed? I realized I was furious at this ghost, maybe angrier than I had ever been with my father.

Concentrate on the Mass, I told myself. This is your father's requiem. He helped give you life. He helped raise you. This is your last chance with him. This is your father. On top of the coffin was a gorgeous wreath of white roses.

'Eternal rest give to them, O, Lord; and let perpetual light shine upon them.'

I wondered if any of us had been in church for years. I doubted that my father or brother had. Martin's daughter Sherry was probably married in a church. My own wedding – thirty years ago – was the last time I had genuflected. Why were we here? Despite our private rebellions, perhaps we all hoped for prayers at the end.

The pews were virtually empty. I knew I should move farther up and sit with Dad's second wife Susanna and her sister. But I was exhausted and the back row felt safe.

The pallbearers sat together. Martin was by far the oldest, and in spite of his stoop, the tallest. Six men in black suits. I'd bet he had never carried another man, dead or alive.

'The just shall be in everlasting remembrance . . .'

I tried to shut out the prayers. I recalled gruesome saint legends from catechism class – about people who were buried alive. The priests knew this because when the bodies were dug up, scratch marks were found inside the coffins. If the scratch marks were discovered in a saint's coffin, canonization was revoked because the person might have despaired at the last moment. 'Why do they tell children such gory stories?' Mom asked. 'To get them to contribute more to the offertory plate,' Dad chuckled. But I could tell he believed the stories too. I wonder what he believed now. I wonder what he regretted about his life and what gratified him.

I wondered the same about Martin. I had known the man forty years – or had not known him forty years. At first he had been my guardian angel. Then he was a nervous young husband to someone else. (Yes, there was Ronda, sitting by the left aisle. She was a handsome woman, well-dressed and self-assured.) Then he was an ageing man looking over his shoulder at how he had missed me. We had never stood on equal ground. Here I was – fifty years old – and still I had not come to peace about Martin. I felt glad he was here today.

What would Mom be feeling now? I would go to her

apartment right after the burial. She would need comfort as much as she would resist it. What did she care for this man who had deserted her in the middle of her years? At least she had the satisfaction of knowing that her own life had flourished after the desertion and Dad's had gone downhill. From what Terry said, Dad's last years were spent at a bar on the San Diego docks.

Martin would never have behaved like my father. He stuck with his wife despite Ronda's success in the dress trade and his own business failure. Terry said he had a small real estate office in Venice. Martin was a decent, good man. Why did I feel betrayed by him?

'And they who have done good shall come forth unto the resurrection of life . . .'

I liked this rummage sale sort of church – baroque carvings, abstract statues, utilitarian indoor-outdoor carpeting and ornate tapestries. I recalled attending Mass in my St Benedict's uniform. How smart and regimented my classmates were then and how random this crew seemed to be. You can't predict the guests at your funeral.

In fact I couldn't identify the other dozen people. Men who Dad had met in San Diego, perhaps. Or was that Colonel James? Yes. Good thing this was a solemn occasion, I couldn't imagine us all talking to one another. Suddenly, I felt a twinge. Wasn't the family supposed to invite everyone over afterwards? For drinks and plates of home-made food? I hadn't even considered this in my rush to leave work in London. Who would do it with his children living out of town and his wife here from San Diego just for the funeral? (My father *would* insist on being buried in a Los Angeles plot he had bought years before. Never a penny wasted.) Staring at Susanna, I remembered her sister lived nearby in San Bernadino. The reception must be at her house.

'Let the holy standard-bearer Michael bring them into that holy light which Thou didst promise of old to Abraham and to his seed.'

Martin hosted the gathering. Of course, his place was much closer to the cemetery than San Bernadino. I drove with

Terry, trying to concentrate on the memory of Dad's coffin being lowered into the earth and not get tangled in my ridiculous fear of returning to Martin's house in Malibu.

He greeted me with a big hug, still slightly winded. He was an ageing man, I told myself, who had learned to compromise wisely. And I was a stoutish older woman who still tried to barge through walls. Still, there was something between us and he seemed to be feeling it too as he guided me into the living-room.

Ronda was serving quiche and salad to Colonel James and his wife. She waved to me, at once the gracious hostess and reliable friend. She had been so kind to my mother and to me; I was humiliated by my pang of jealousy.

Susanna sat with her sister by the window, staring out at the waves. It was a warm, smoggy day. I longed for the chill of London, for some sensation to release me from the soporific Southern California depression.

Martin handed me a glass of Pinot Noir.

'You remembered.' I declared, in spite of myself.

'Yes,' he smiled, clinking my glass.

I sat down, totally depleted from the plane delay and the journey and the funeral and the afternoon ahead of us. He talked about Dad with unsentimental affection. I had never been able to figure out the friendship between the two men. Was it a rivalry, based on mutual admiration? They were so different. Perhaps that was the point. After all, Martin and I were different. And as the years passed, inevitably I had to admit the parallels between myself and my father. I listened, grateful for the familiarity of his voice.

'Your father was an original.' Martin smiled. 'Had his own ideas and followed them, no matter what.'

I remembered Martin's first visit to our house – him standing there with a bottle of wine that was so much not the thing to bring to our meat-and-potatoes household. He had won *this* over my father. He had toasted him at his funeral.

'I remember when he wangled that transfer to the San Diego office . . .'

I watched the sunlight cross his cat's eyes and knew that Martin was just hiding inside this old man. Pretty soon he would ask if I wanted to practise my parallel parking. I mused sadly about his getting older. Then I reminded myself everyone changed. We moved on to our own lives. After all, I no longer worried about moral scrutiny in James Joyce or stayed up late with my homework. Well, in a sense I was doing the latter every time I prepared a lecture in London. And here was Martin, still in the *middle* of my family. We had all changed; we hadn't changed at all. What a silly, drugged conundrum. I tried to waken by introducing a new character.

'How's Sherry?'

'I've got two grandsons now!' Martin seemed as surprised as I.

'I realized Sherry had kids, but it never occurred to me that that made you a grandfather!' I laughed.

'Dearest Ellen, always believing in eternal youth.'

'What's that supposed to mean?' I was dismayed to find myself on the verge of crying. But tears were normal; this was Dad's funeral. Relax, relax. I ached for Verity.

'Never resting, always sizing up the next door.'

I tried to shrug it off, but I was irritated that he had found me, that he had always known where to find me.

We talked about my job, British elections, the possibility of spending a sabbatical year here in California before Mom died. Before Mom died. One minute, time stretched to infinity. Suddenly, we had to race against deadlines.

Martin said he could locate Verity and me a beach cottage for a reasonable rent. Just let him know when we were coming.

I sat with Susanna a while. Then I talked with Ronda, the jealousy of an hour ago replaced by a more comfortable fondness. Terry and I nodded to each other, knowing it was time to go to Mother's. While he retrieved my jacket, I stood by the French doors overlooking the water. We had moved to California for this warm surf, which, like Dad, was always coming and going.

I felt something – Martin's arm – on my shoulder. I didn't acknowledge it, but kept staring into the ocean, lost in reverie. We had drifted apart years ago. We had completely different values and politics and lives. Terry and I didn't have much in common, but we were family. Martin was . . . just a friend. And friends disappear.

Maybe he was more than that. I could feel the heat rise to my neck and turned more directly toward the sea so he wouldn't notice. Maybe we had loved each other too much. Or maybe we loved the possibilities in ourselves which were provoked by the other. One day we would talk about this. I turned to pat the hand on my shoulder and discovered I was alone. Martin sat in an armchair across the room, smiling at me.

III

– Away –

– Worms and Women Have Spun –
– Magic –

Silk threads stream like sunlight against the hard-clanking metal machine. She perches on a moving chair, delicately capturing strands onto wooden spools. Her fingers are as graceful as those of a Beijing Opera star.

Outside, beneath high blue sky, they are building another factory wing. Outside, past a gold sign declaring monthly quotas, one sister carries bricks, another slaps mortar. They prepare for more rooms of colour and clank and silk.

A white cotton baker's cap covers her short black hair. Tucked near the rim are seven strands of silver. This hair is silver, not grey, and shinier than anything spun in Suzhou. She first found the silver in her photograph, one of twelve, on the model worker poster.

Outside her daughter sings in the nursery. There she boards for five days at a time with other workers' children. Down the slide she streams, sleek as satin. Clapping her hands, she squeals high. It is hard for a mother to hear so far away. It is hard to hear at all after a week of screeching spools.

Inside from the outside, come tourist women to flash cameras and take notes in little books. A dozen foreigners talk quick as thread as if she could not understand – or hear. They point and stare at her white hat, rice-sack apron, flowered blouse and black shoes. She trains her attention on the silk and soon they disappear.

Outside they return, burdened by bags of clothing from the factory shop. Worms and women have spun magic in Suzhou since the Tang Dynasty. Marco Polo, himself, made several trips here from the outside.

Pressing the foot lever, she zips to the end of the turquoise row. She supervises blue quivering into green into scarves, drapes, dresses, robes. For Marco Polo's followers. For flashing ladies to wear outside to the Beijing Opera.

Or inside out, like so many reversible robes bound for Paris. Four thousand years on the Silk Route, Suzhou now boasts sturdy new wings. Meanwhile, she imagines her daughter's bright laughter. Stealthily, she tucks the silver threads beneath her white cotton cap.

– *Uncommon Ground* –

In front of us an African priest was being greeted with chants and drums. 'From my village,' he explained as we waited in the airport queue.

'Great music,' I said, reckoning for the first time how far we had travelled.

'*Salama.*' The priest nodded before being engulfed by his congregation.

A Kenyan immigration officer assiduously checked all the details on Billy's passport. I looked out to find Arthur leaning against a ledge, reading his watch.

I spotted Arthur first although it was Billy with whom he had attended Oxford ten years before. Tall, lean, tanned Arthur was quite a contrast to his old American class-mate, who had grown chunky and more easy-going over the past decade.

Billy had devised the bright idea of visiting Arthur and Eleanor before I travelled down to Tanzania on my magazine assignment. Billy was accompanying me for two weeks of my three months in Africa. He considered it a good chance for a holiday and a last effort to patch together our flagging relationship. While I refused to feel nervous about travelling, I was grateful for company at the beginning of my long journey. Initially I protested against visiting his British friend, now a businessman managing a branch plant in Nairobi, but Billy convinced me that I should see as many sides of Africa as possible.

When we reached Arthur's cream-coloured Ford sedan, he turned to us. 'Now, Alice and Billy, this isn't America. Be sure to lock the car doors. So the Kaffirs don't get you.'

Neither of us laughed.

He probably dismissed our silence as exhaustion. 'Ten hours late. Not so bad. Sometimes that flight is two days late. Different sense of time here. Perhaps we'll leave the "sense" out of it.'

Time was hard to gauge. I should have been tired, however my body felt shocked into action, radiating energy.

Billy put a hand on my shoulder – admonition, not affection. 'Wait until we're alone.' His fingers tapped on my shoulder.

'You've got some explaining to do,' my left eyebrow responded.

'You two probably just want to rest,' Arthur said. 'That's it. Sit back and enjoy. He switched on his tapedeck: 'Michele, Ma Belle . . .'

Eleanor greeted us at the door. 'Welcome, Alice and Billy . . .'

Arthur boomed forward carrying a suitcase under each arm and shouting, 'Woman, don't answer the bloody door! How many times have I told you to have Jonathan do it? Who knows who it could be? Haven't there been enough *incidents* in the neighbourhood?'

'Jonathan is in the garden,' she managed before he cut her off.

'What the hell are we paying these Kaffirs for anyway, dammit.'

My face must have revealed my astonishment and anger, because I felt Billy's familiar shoulder tap.

Turning towards Eleanor, I discovered her hostility directed not at Arthur, but at Billy and me. She looked through us with cool, green eyes. Why had I succumbed to Billy's nostalgia about 'good old Arthur'? I could be in a quiet hotel now.

'Let me show you to your room.' Eleanor's recovery was seamless.

Delicate, lithe, blonde woman. Thirtyish, like me, but that was all that was 'like me'. Here we were, worlds apart in a world apart, the travelling expatriate theatre.

I tried to concentrate as her crisp voice informed us, '. . . the bathroom . . . towels on your bed . . . rest before dinner . . . cocktails in the front room . . .'

Billy and I flopped on the bed. We knew each other well

enough to understand that there would be time for argument later, after a nap. Whether this was the end of our two year relationship or a fight about how to behave among imperialists, it would wait until we were coherent again.

When Billy felt me stirring, he said in a wide-awake voice, 'Can't predict how a guy will change after college.'

'No,' I said foggily, confused as any native New Yorker might be by the purple glare of Jacaranda and the screeches of Sykes monkeys in the avocado tree outside our window.

Then, like a hangover, Arthur's image filled my skull. I felt more self-contempt than I had experienced since Little Rock. I had flown to Africa to write about women cooperating in Ujamaa villages. How could I stay in this bigot's house and eat his food? Detachment, I reminded myself. A good writer needs to meet all kinds of people. But somewhere behind that professional curiosity and my mother's warning about forbearance, even for the intolerant, I felt caught in unwitting complicity with Arthur.

'Alice, you've got to remember, the English love to act eccentric,' Billy reflected. 'And dramatic. Like saying "Kaffir." Only white South Africans say "Kaffir", right? It was all a show this afternoon.'

'Good show.' I tried to dismiss Arthur ironically, for I was relying on a brief rest in Kenya before my assignment. I did want to see flamingos and zebras and blazing skies. I had always hoped to come to East Africa. After all, the human race was born here. I admired Nyerere's African socialism. I was a great fan of Lessing and Dinesen. And didn't I deserve a vacation? Maybe I could write something about Arthur himself – portrait of the arch neocolonial?

The show continued over supper, escalating with a second bottle of wine. At first I tried to draw out Eleanor, but she deflected every question. Arthur was a magnet for attention as his provocative rhetoric shifted from 'mud-thick bureaucracy' and 'adventuring journalists' to 'the necessity of funding anti-communist mercenaries'.

I argued back, 'But the soldiers fighting Samora Machel are pawns of Pretoria.'

'And Machel's men are Soviet pawns,' Arthur retorted.

'They're not all men. And . . .' I began.

'Just shows women can be drugged by communism too.'

I sighed, aware that he wasn't debating seriously, but rather inciting me and thoroughly enjoying his visiting dupe. His diatribe became all of such a boring piece that my attention was drawn to the details of their tasteful 1930s furniture and to Eleanor again.

She sat straight and elegant in the Eames chair, careful to keep our plates and glasses filled. Why did she seem a generation older than I? Eleanor held her eyes on the thin crust of *pommes au gratin* when Arthur spoke of bureaucracy. She whispered to Jonathan for more butter during Arthur's journalist lecture. She folded her napkin neatly as Arthur held forth against communists. It was almost as if she were listening to another voice. Was it her fifth form headmistresses or the priest at Evensong or some promise to herself made long ago? I ached to talk with her and considered times when the two of us might escape for a chat.

Eleanor never seemed to agree with Arthur. Nor did she exactly disagree. Her face was set in imperturbable graciousness. I perceived slight flickers of discomfort when Billy or I spoke up. Perhaps she was reacting as much to our American accents as to our dissenting opinions. I looked forward to the next morning when Arthur returned to his office and we all went shopping.

The shopping began with shoes for Billy. Just like him not to buy them at Macy's. We poked around stores in search of sneakers. Eleanor apologized for the high prices in these modern shops, refraining from asking Billy why he hadn't brought his Western goods from New York. After an hour Billy found some affordable shoes from Poland. Comfortable in the new sneakers, he grinned with such unselfconscious pleasure that I was filled with affection. Eleanor and I exchanged indulgent smiles.

Life grew more interesting as we entered a section where more of the Africans shopped. The noise was louder; the colours brighter; the market altogether more alive. I coveted the brilliant khangas and kitenges, but I was too shy to approach the vendor and ask how to wear the bright lengths of fabric. Maybe tomorrow.

'*Jambo,*' Eleanor greeted the merchants. 'Hello.'

'*Jambo,*' they returned.

We visited an old rope maker in a dusty shop. Eleanor poked around in search of a brass samovar.

The market was crowded with people of all ages and sizes. Mothers carried babies on their backs and baskets of food on their heads. The stalls offered spices and nuts and buttons and laundry detergent. The aroma of succulent samosas mingled with the sharp scents of fresh cloves and lemon grass.

This felt like Africa, the Africa of my fantasies. I resisted returning to Eleanor's posh Kensington mansion perched high above Nairobi like an international jetliner lounge. I looked at the vendors looking at us – assembling us as parts of one predictable puzzle. Our differing passports and politics didn't matter to them. We fit together neatly. Not far from the market, we passed a settlement of shanties, where many of the merchants lived.

Back at the compound, Billy and I politely declined tea. I was more polite during those few days than I had been in the twenty years since my fourth grade Christian courtesy courses. I wanted to be quiet a while, absorbing this day resplendent with new sounds and textures. I lay down, dozing straight into a dream that I was, indeed, in Africa.

A rap on the door. 'All right, you lazy buggers.'

I glanced at Billy, who was still asleep. What should I say to Arthur? 'Come in'? 'Go to hell'? Behind him, I could hear Eleanor whispering, 'Shhh.' This simply provoked him further.

'Got the Kaffir disease, have you, lazy bums?'

Billy turned to me, blinking in confusion.

'Your eccentric monologuist,' I said.

'Shhh,' I heard Eleanor whisper.

As I washed and dressed, I wondered if I weren't making Arthur the foil. Was he simply an exaggerated symbol of my own privilege, a convenient target of my guilt and discomfort? He must have positive qualities. Billy had promised a sharp wit and a lively intellect. Perhaps they were just beneath the surface.

By the time we arrived for cocktails, Arthur was absorbed in the wireless, his feet on a leopard skin ottoman.

Eleanor entered the room with a tray of drinks. She moved with modest majesty, in a long, loose, tie-dyed dress. On the outside she was very much the gracious hostess, but I imagined her legs twitching inside the dress, her heart pounding fast. She had remembered what we drank the previous evening. Scotch with one ice for me and bourbon with two cubes for Billy.

The BBC occupied the parlour. 'Accident on a motorway near Leeds . . . Trouble in the Kuwait government . . . Seventy-ninth birthday of Sir . . .'

No hint of wit or intellect.

How long could this go on? Abruptly bereft of polite pretensions, I fumed to myself, What did this parlour have to do with Africa? Why didn't I have any Black friends to visit here? Did all colonials behave like this? Were we colonials? I counted the days on my fingers: one, two, five days until we caught the bus to Tanzania. (Now that Arthur had warned us to fly – 'No telling what diseases you'll contract on a common coach' – I was determined to take that bus.) Five days of silence was impossible. So it slipped out. 'Why did you come to Africa?' I asked.

Billy was seated too far away to tap my shoulder. As he was formulating a properly discreet glance, Eleanor answered. I was surprised and then ashamed of my surprise.

'My idea at first,' she said. 'I was studying politics. My speciality was East African economy. When the time came for Arthur's posting with the company, we requested Kenya.'

'Hmmmm,' Arthur seemed about to speak, but he sipped his drink and nodded back to the soccer news. 'Manchester United . . .'

'So that's what we got,' she said with a definitiveness that closed the conversation.

I didn't pursue it, whether out of social courtesy or bewilderment or sympathy for Eleanor, I didn't know.

Sympathy, was the word sympathy? Regardless, this is one of my regrets about that week. Several times in the company of our men, I passed up the opportunity to talk, waiting for a more private moment.

Camping in the Masai Mara, Billy had promised me. He spoke of fresh air on the great, open plain. In addition to elephants, giraffes and lions, we saw a fair amount of Eleanor, Arthur and their Welsh friends, Phillip and Penny. The expedition was nothing like I had imagined.

We unpacked cots, pillows, egg mayonnaise, brandy, radio, tables, chairs. Eleanor and Penny had prepared an elegant array of diversions. Arthur had insisted that we set up camp in a remote area, miles from the 'tourist' tents.

The first afternoon, I sat at a card table, under a large tree as Eleanor and Penny washed in the river below camp.

'Some crocs mooning about, but it's safe enough if you keep a lookout,' Eleanor reported.

'Really?' My eyes widened. 'Crocodiles?' No, I decided immediately they were teasing the gringa. I started to laugh.

'Really,' Eleanor and Penny nodded. 'Crocodiles.'

'Well, I don't much feel like a bath.' I shrugged. So I stayed at the table, pretending to be Martha Gellhorn. Did she pray that lions wouldn't wander through camp while Ernest Hemingway was off on safari? So much for my snide judgement of Eleanor as fragile handmaiden.

In general, I had a tough time with the essentials. After I had spent ten hours desperate to piss and incapable of relaxing my muscles, Billy had suggested that I distract myself by reciting something. So I had tried Hail Marys and was halfway through the rosary before I found sweet relief.

I kept hoping to get to know Eleanor better. But with Penny along, it was even more of a public school social than it had been the previous week. Chat about families, past and future. I would have suggested a walk, but we could hardly leave Penny alone. Were there really crocodiles in that river?

When the men returned from drinking beer at Governor's Camp, we consumed a hearty lunch of pâté and roast chicken and potato salad. We retreated to our tents until dusk when it was time to take a run to see game.

African Hawk Eagle. Grey Kingfisher. Rhino. Giraffe. Wart Hog. Vulture eating from a zebra carcass. I remembered how I had had to get up at five a.m. to take a raft down the Snake River in Wyoming just to see a couple of Osprey. Here was a glorious profusion of nature five hundred yards from camp. The broad blue sky stretched endlessly across a plain that was perfectly flat except for the occasional lacy tree and thorny bush. But it was the animals which captured our imaginations: Playful vervets. Astonishingly powerful baboons. (How had they become the butt of jokes? Human intimidation, most likely.) Processions of dignified wildebeest. From the safety of our car we watched a very fat lion waddle under a tree. He lowered himself, delicately delivering his stomach to the stubbled ground. I don't think he would have moved if I had pierced his ears. Never had I felt this happy and tranquil. Even the vulture seemed to fit.

That evening the menu was beef stroganoff and burgundy. Lots of Johnny Walker afterward. I faded quickly. As Billy entered our tent, Arthur reported that last week another remote camp had been invaded by elephant. What were we going to do with that information? There had been enough Johnny Walker so that I didn't care.

The noise came about three a.m. I thought I heard a box, something, falling in front of the tent where Eleanor and Arthur slept. Wind, I guessed. 'Elephant,' Billy bolted forward.

Shouting. Arthur's voice. 'Bloody Kaffirs.'

'What –' Billy and I stuck out our heads '– is going on?' we asked in unison.

'Probably some nigger puberty rite,' Arthur declared furiously. 'And poaching by the visitors. We'll teach them.'

'Stealing?' asked Penny. 'What's missing?'

'The panga for one thing,' said Arthur, referring to the knife that he had stuck with authority into the tree stump.

'And the blue wash basin,' mused Eleanor.

'And my shoes,' moaned Phillip.

'And,' shouted Arthur, 'just as I thought, the *bleeding brandy*. They've made off with a whole bottle of Courvoissier VSOP.'

'Oh,' Phillip tried to laugh, 'I can see it now – a tipsy Masai kid drunkenly weaving around the plain wearing my size twelve hiking boots, swinging the panga and singing, "God Save The Queen".'

'Well, we'll show them,' said Arthur. 'Come along, Phillip. And, Billy, you guard the camp. Take care of the women.'

Fierce Arthur struck off into the bush, with reluctant Phillip shuffling behind in sandals. Penny protested that he would get hurt without proper shoes, then threw up her hands and returned to the tent. Eleanor watched until the men were out of sight. She glanced at Billy and me, sitting by the dead fire and sipping Johnny Walker. Was I right in perceiving a brief movement towards us? She licked her lower lip absently and returned to her tent. After another drink, Billy and I also went to bed.

Fifteen minutes passed. Half-an-hour. Occasionally Billy looked out in ritualistic survey. He alternated between exasperation with his old friend's machismo and concern for his safety. The night grew still, with not so much as a dream of elephants. Then, abruptly, we heard Arthur shouting, 'Billy! Billy, man, where are you?'

Sheepishly, Billy ducked out of our tent. I followed, shivering, but relieved that they hadn't managed to stir up any trouble. Eleanor and Penny observed mutely, heads poking from their canvas shells.

'Billy, Billy, man,' Arthur was still shouting. It was hard to tell whether he was angrier at Billy or at his Masai marauders.

Disgusted, Arthur ripped into his tent, almost knocking down Eleanor. He emerged with a pistol, 'This ought to rouse them.'

'Oh, Arthur.' Eleanor's voice came the closest to protest I ever heard.

'Just to scare them. Don't worry. I won't shoot anyone.'

She stared him down, refraining from being more disloyal publicly.

'It's dark,' I said. 'Don't be a fool.'

Eleanor regarded me with a mixture of gratitude and resentment.

Arthur turned towards me with the pistol.

'Don't point that thing at her,' Billy demanded.

'Don't point it at anything,' I yelled. 'Put it away.'

Arthur regarded and disregarded me.

'Come along, Phillip,' he called. Then he repeated his lines from the previous act more forcefully, 'Billy, you guard the camp.' He pointed with his pistol to the chair by the dead campfire.

Billy and I waited outside. Now fully conscious of our camp's isolation neither of us were able to sleep. What idiots, we said, to go tripping into the darkness where just this evening we had seen wild animals. Phillip with no shoes. And Arthur with a gun! What were we doing in this 1950s re-run? We were stranded. There was only one car.

Gunshots slapped in the distance. I prayed no one, nothing, was hurt.' . . . Now and at the hour of our death-Amen-Hail Mary, full of grace . . .' I recalled the tranquil scene at dusk. The memory shattered like a stained-glass window, beyond repair, the plain strewn with shards of colour.

Another gunshot.

No screams.

Silence.

'What's *she* doing out here?' Arthur yelled before we could see him. He strolled into range of the lantern, empty-handed except for the pistol. Phillip followed, limping and exhausted.

'Guarding the camp,' I said. 'I hear there's a maniac loose with a gun on the plain.'

Eleanor called from the tent. 'Arthur, thank God you're back. Come in here this minute.'

Arthur surveyed the camp – the chest with tomorrow's lunch, the rack of dishes, the crate of wine. His face held an even satisfaction, as if to say, 'At least we protected the rest of it.'

In fact, he said, 'That ought to hold them for tonight.'

Dawn came within the hour. We made ready to leave camp a day early. As Billy and I were folding our cots, Arthur stumbled over. His eyes were red and his skin blotchy. 'That incident last night,' he cleared his throat. 'Let's forget it, shall we? Damned government prohibits these pistols. Although, as you can see, we need them for self-protection. So let's just forget anything happened, OK? No one hurt after all. Bad for the company, should this sort of thing leak out, if you know what I mean.'

The following morning Eleanor drove Billy and me to the bus station. No one mentioned the safari. Eleanor was bright, cheerful and newly inquisitive about my work. Why the change in mood? Because everyone had developed a solidarity during the ordeal? Because Arthur had been subdued for a few days? Because all along she, too, had been hoping for that private moment which never materialized?

'I want to hear how all your interviews go,' she said. 'Will you come through Nairobi on your way back to the States?'

Perhaps to save each of us, Billy interjected. 'I'll be back in Nairobi in two weeks. You are expecting me?'

'Of course . . .' said Eleanor. A sharp sound interrupted her. Like a gunshot. The bus backfired once again as it rolled to a stop. She blurted, 'The coach. This is a miracle. Spot on time.'

She helped with the bags. There was an instant, as she handed up the last satchel, that I wondered if she might climb aboard.

But the hand she could have placed on the railing to hoist herself up, she threw high in the air, waving.

'*Kwaheri*,' she called. 'Goodbye.'

'*Salama*,' I said.

After we squeezed into our seats, Billy tried several conversations – apologies and explanations about his old friend Arthur. But I was quiet for the next sixty kilometres, staring out the window in search of Africa.

Instead, I saw Eleanor behind every avocado tree and kopje. I recalled a story she told about a friend whose husband was stationed in the Serengeti. After several years in isolation, the woman managed to have an old piano transported to the outpost. And every afternoon she played Mozart concertos to ward away the madness.

– *Deutschmarks and –*
– Venetian Blinds –

Eva Feldman sat by the window which overlooked Primrose Hill, which would have overlooked Primrose Hill if she opened her blinds. But the council had placed George IV Senior Citizens' Residence three yards too close to Regents Park Road. The traffic noise and filth would be unbearable without the Venetian blinds. When the architects won their award for innovation and grace, the judges didn't consider that if Mrs Eva Feldman opened her front window during the day, she would have to spend all her time dusting and she wouldn't be able to hear herself think. Not that she did much thinking. She kept that down to a minimum because so much thinking, at least at her age, was remembering.

Albert, rest his soul, would have offered 'Time heals', or one of his other good maxims. Her husband had been very comforting when he was alert (which wasn't every day because he had survived the war with certain scars). Eva had managed not to think about Albert except at night when she indulged in a bedtime conversation and on Fridays when she set a place for him, as he had told her to do that last night at the hospital. 'Go home and light the candles for Shabbas,' he whispered. They had telephoned an hour later, just as she had sat down to the chicken (you can always have something nice, if you try, even on a pension. Well, it was true that she did have the allowance from the German government. They sent a personal note on watermarked stationery when her cheque was late). She had just sat down to the dinner and a little cherry wine when the hospital rang to say Albert had died. The end to his wounds from the camps. At seventy-five, who wouldn't get tired of fighting? Tonight Eva sat alone as she had for ten years, since 1964, at the folded-up table next to the window.

A good table – solid oak – a gift from Manny when they

were setting up a flat after the war. She hadn't seen Manny for twenty years now, not since his furniture business got big and he moved to Bradford with Esther. A pity because they had been such good friends and the best majong partners. It didn't really bear thinking about. Eva hadn't thought two sentences about Manny in twenty years. Why start now? The table was well-placed, to catch the park light through the blinds. She used to read here all evening long until last spring when her eyes gave out. Not such a loss. What was there to read any more? *The Daily Mirror* was always saying the same old thing about the Battenbergs (that was the Windsors' real name, German, when you thought about it. Not many people did). So who cared that Princess Anne bought a new racehorse? Sometimes Eva had sat at the table reading letters from her sister Sara in Kilburn. Sara lived only two miles away, but she was arthritic and couldn't come to visit any more, not being able to afford a chauffeur like the Queen Mother. (No, mustn't be catty. Eva had a soft spot for the old Queen because of her war work.) But lately – maybe Sara's eyes had gone too – she had stopped writing. The housing officer kept promising to find them a flat to share, but it took time. Occasionally the thought crossed Eva's mind that Sara had died. However Mrs Levy down the hall kept close watch on the obituaries in *The Jewish Chronicle*. Besides, *they* would have told her.

She was not completely sure who *they* were. Yet they always seemed to be around. The home help, the meals-on-wheels lady, the community leisure officer (that was a good one. Eva wasn't going to let him into her head or her purse. Aside from anything else, he could well be a poofter), the doctor, the house warden (they could have picked a kinder term; still, no one thought nowadays), the physiotherapist, the young Jewish Wives Volunteer. Surely one of *them* would have told her if Sara had died.

When the door buzzer sounded, Eva didn't know quite what she was thinking about. Seven-thirty, Tuesday night. Who could that be? None of them came on a Tuesday night. She regretted it the moment she pressed the button. What a fool. A senile old fool. It might be a burglar or one of those children who were responsible – so who else – for all this vandalism. Eva Feldman, you are a foolish old woman. How did Albert put up with you? (Perhaps there were some times during the day when she allowed a memory of him. But not often. No good to coddle herself.) Now what had she done? Careless old woman. Eva cringed as she heard the eager knock on her door.

'Yes, who is it?' she shouted.

'My name is Ruth Marks. I'm from the Senior Citizen's . . .'

Eva pulled her greeny-blue nylon housecoat around her white slip. It was a clean slip, nothing to be ashamed of. She did her laundry every week by hand. You couldn't trust the machines even *if* you could afford them. Did her own sheets that way too, washed and ironed every week. The home help, who saw a lot of unmade beds, said Eva's flat was the cleanest in George IV House. She patted her bouffant hair-do and opened the door.

Marks. Blonde Marks. Pretty blue eyes, skinny features, rich clothes. German Marks? She wore a clean, dainty, waisted blouse. Also those sloppy blue jeans you saw on everyone – from the community leisure officer (well, what could you tell from him?), down to the young hoodlums. But Eva knew she should be grateful that God wasn't punishing her foolishness. He had only sent this . . .

'Ruth Marks.' She extended her ringed hand. 'And I'm from the Senior Citizen's Welfare Association.' Eva Goldman hated the kindness in Ruth Marks' voice. She gave a worn, dignified smile drawing her hand away from the girl and towards the table by the window. Sunset would come in an hour and she wondered whether this girl with the German name would leave her to enjoy it in peace. It didn't really bear thinking about. If she left, she left. But first to find out why she came.

'Is it about Sara?' Eva sat with a thud before the girl had a chance to smooth the long blouse under her toosh and sit down herself. Funny how she should keep such gracefulness even in the ragged trousers.

The girl smiled sweetly. Then she repeated loudly, as if

volume would penetrate senility. 'My name is Ruth Marks.' She raised her voice further. Perhaps she thought Eva was deaf just because she was almost blind. 'I dropped by to see if you needed anything, Mrs Feldman?'

Needed anything? No, of course it wasn't about Sara. Eva regarded the girl closely. Seventeen or eighteen at most. About the age of her own grandchildren if God had chosen to grant her any. Yes, she had lost five children in Germany. Eva started to talk about them as she hadn't in years. Well, you had to be hospitable and the girl asked. David had been studying law – head of his class at Cologne. And Aaron had been a pianist – they knew, even as a baby, those fingers.

The girl seemed genuinely interested. She didn't fidget. Most of them began to fidget after ten or fifteen minutes. She asked careful questions. She was nice. She didn't even seem to have a reason for being here. That was the pleasant part. For ten years now, Eva Feldman had had good reasons for people to visit her. She received every help she needed. The doctor did all that was possible for her eczema. The physiotherapist took her every week to a clinic for the stiff hip. To tell the truth, those electric machines in the water scared her, but therapy made a change and they always gave you a cup of tea and biscuits afterwards.

'Oh, what am I thinking about?' Eva rose to her feet. 'Here you are sitting all this time with nothing in front of you. Such hospitality! Tea? Or is it coffee? I baked honeycakes just this morning.' No thank you, said the girl. She had to go. She didn't have a lamp for her bicycle and it was growing dark. Eva sat down heavily, lost in her thoughts. She rides her bicycle on the city streets? This was the first time Eva Feldman had ever thought of these cyclists as people. They were loonies – crazier than she was – zooming in and out of traffic lanes when she couldn't even walk on the pavement, when she couldn't even open her window.

A terrible idea struck her. Even if this beautiful Dresden doll wasn't smashed on the Euston Road, what guarantee was there that Eva would ever see her again. Such a fool.

Albert, how had he put up with her? What problem did Ruth Marks come to solve and did she think she had already solved it? In one visit? Perhaps there was still time to catch her. What about Sara?

'My sister, Sara,' Eva said, sickening at her own obsequiousness. (Shame, for using poor Sara like this.) 'Could you find out if she is well? It's been six months since I've heard, you know, and she only lives in Kilburn.'

'Of course, Mrs Feldman. I was going to ask if I could drop by next Tuesday for another visit. Is that OK? Sometime between six-thirty and seven?'

Eva was too grateful to respond, too ashamed for having put on her housecoat so early in the evening.

'If that's OK?' said the girl, sweeping her blondeness into an orange beret. 'I should go. I'd like to get home before dark.'

Eva's excitement about the next visit was soon lost in mortification over her behaviour. So what had she asked the poor girl about herself, her family, her boyfriends? Then again, why trust this strange girl? Who's to know she's not from the English welfare, investigating foreign names on the pension rolls? Who's to know where she's from and why she should care about Eva Feldman, Senior Citizen?

When Ruth Marks returned the following Tuesday night, she didn't ask Eva any probing questions. She informed her that her sister, who was in good health, promised to write. This time Eva had the presence of mind to enquire after the girl. She *was* just a girl, nineteen, studying for a year abroad. Abroad? How had she failed to notice the girl's accent? American, of course. From somewhere in Dakota. Her grandparents had come from Europe – from Venice – she told Eva, and from Munich, she said more quickly. Ruth had always wanted to come back. Actually, she said, you're a lot like my grandmother, the same colour jerseys and everything. Jerseys? Oh, yes, the dress. Eva was glad she had put on the good dress. And when she had listened long enough to the girl, she talked about the children again. Ruth had brought a bicycle lamp so she could stay later. She would have to leave by nine-fifteen because she had an early class in the morning. An intelligent girl, thought Eva, as she pressed an apple on her at the door.

Afterwards, Eva again felt ashamed. So what did the little blondie care about five Jewish children she never would have known, even if they hadn't been killed before she was born. If Eva had had the biggest hopes for the boys, it was Rosa, Marlene and Emma she loved the most – their black hair roped back like the silk coiffures of their Japanese dolls. She had passed on to them her embroidery, red cheeks and good sense. Lately, she was thinking about them more than Albert ever allowed. He would forgive her, though, when she talked with him in bed that night.

Eva Feldman began to look forward to Tuesday nights. Cautiously. The girl seemed to enjoy trying her desserts. As for herself, Eva always liked playing hostess ('What good is it to have if you can't share?' Albert would say), especially to a foreign visitor. Tonight it was strudel – and a little wine to celebrate the holidays.

'Yes, I'm very excited about Christmas,' said Ruth. 'We get two weeks off school.'

'So you're going home?' Eva swallowed the cherry sweetness and thought it good even to share with a rich American girl. 'To see your family in Biltmont?' By now she had seen pictures of the girl's big family on the South Dakota ranch.

'No, some of the other kids are going home, but I thought I might as well stay. I mean it's not as though I come to Europe every year. There's so much I want to see. Some of us, my friends Mikey, Lynda, Larry and I, are going to wander around Germany and Italy. Mainly Italy. Mainly Venice.'

'And *how* are you going? Not like this, I hope?' she thrust her thumb in the air.

The girl laughed and rotated Eva's finger in a ninety-degrees.

'No, we're renting a car.'

Eva smiled, but she would not relinquish her worries. 'Where will you stay in Germany?' Despite their conversations about the war, Eva bet that Rhineland castles and chocolate forests was all the girl expected.

'Munich, for my grandfather,' said Ruth, 'and Berlin to do some research for my history class.'

'Berlin.' The old woman sighed. 'Have I told you about when we lived in Berlin?' She did not really care. They had spent enough talk on the girl tonight. 'We had a shop in Berlin, furs and fine cloth coats – Scottish cashmere. Just Albert and me, so of course I chose all the stock.' She had already explained Albert's particular sensibilities. He was a refined man, from a cultured family. He brought in grand friends from the galleries, was devoted to the children and never so much as glanced at silk stockings unless they were in the shops, her size and colour. However, he had no head for business. It was a good store – one of those comfortable places where people came to gossip, to ask advice, to borrow a few marks. 'Eva Feldman,' they always said, 'if you're in trouble, there's always Eva Feldman.' It was a good family business where the children came in after school to help out or to study in the back room. But the best parts, shameful mother that she was, were the times she and Albert went away on fur-buying expeditions. 'Just the two of us in the car – through the snow to Warsaw and Leningrad where he was born.'

A week later, the girl sent a postcard of frosty canals, saying she was looking forward to seeing Eva in six days.

The next Tuesday, they picked up as if there had been no interruption. 'They were wonderful, those journeys. Fierce winds and huge snow drifts. But we would always pack a good bottle of Vodka and some thick beef sandwiches. I remember Leningrad in the January of 1929 – such a different place from when I went with my family as a girl. Still poverty, still beggars at St Issac's, but not such desperation. That's one thing you can say for the Communists.'

The girl seemed surprised by her politics. Eva explained that the Nazis persecuted the Communists too. The girl murmured something about capitalism and oppression. She said she belonged to one of those alphabet groups and that it would be interesting to talk issues sometime.

Yes, sometime. First Eva would tell her about their expedition down the Neva, about Moscow and the Metropole. She hadn't thought about it in years, the seal-skin hats and the matryoshkas she brought back for her daughters.

Occasionally after the girl left, Eva wondered how much longer she would stay. Was she boring her? She scolded herself again and again for being so self-centred. Still what did she know about this American student? What she would do when she grew up? What kind of husband she wanted? This talk tonight was the first Eva had heard of her 'revolution'. And what was this Senior Citizen's Welfare? She hadn't signed up for anything. Don't let anyone mistake it. Eva Feldman did not apply for charity. However, when Eva did try to be sociable it was as if the girl didn't understand her questions. She said she didn't want any kind of husband. Relationships were non-nuclear nowadays, she said. Open marriage, bisexuality, collective, cooperative, communal. Community. She used that word – community – a lot to explain what Eva did not understand. So for several nights they began earnestly to discuss nowadays, only to move to Eva's life in pre-war Germany or post-war England. They never talked about the war itself.

Sometimes the girl would bring chocolates. She didn't know about Eva's allergy. And because Eva had not told her the first time, she could not tell her the next time or the next. So Eva always put these sweets in the kitchen until the morning when she took them to poor Mrs Levy down the hall. She had told the girl that Mrs Levy was the only person she could talk to on the whole council estate. The other people weren't her type, hanging out as they did at pubs and such. 'Common, if you know what I mean,' Eva said. The girl nodded. But Eva bet the girl reckoned everyone on the estate was a member of the oppressed. Perhaps that's why she came each week, to recruit for the revolution. Sometimes it occurred to Eva that the girl just might feel an affection for her, the way she did for the girl. She didn't think about that very often. She always gave the girl an orange or an apple as she left.

One April evening, the girl did not come. Eva was prepared for this possibility. She told herself not to worry almost before she began. Perhaps the girl had exams or a trip to the country. If Eva had learned anything over the years, it was not to depend.

When Ruth came the next Tuesday, she brought flowers – to celebrate May Day. So it was. Yes, the previous week had been exams. The end of school. Remember, Ruth asked, she had said she would be leaving May 3. Eva did not remember, but she didn't credit her memory with much any more. Ruth was going back to Biltmont and then to a summer job on an Indian reservation. She would write.

An old woman knows tricks with her eyes. People could not always tell what was going on behind the cataracts.

'For how long?' asked Eva after what might have been a big silence.

'Well, I'll be away for at least a year. But when I finish college, I want to come back to Europe for grad school. Will you write to me?'

'Yes, of course, dear,' said Eva. She gave the girl two oranges for the long journey.

The following week Eva received a postcard from the girl, full of the glory of the Black Hills and exclamations about how she would miss their talks. She asked Eva to write soon, but forgot to add her address. There was another card in the post, from the Senior Citizen's Welfare Association, saying they had received notification that someone should visit her. Unfortunately, they explained, it was difficult to get volunteers during the summer holidays.

Eva was not angry with Ruth Marks, no. Nor with the Senior Citizen's Whatchamacallit. What had they done? With herself she was angry, yes. She never should have answered that buzzer. 'Foolish old woman. It could have been vandals or burglars or even worse.' She shut up. She wasn't going to start talking to herself. Enough regret. Albert had taught her long ago not to regret.

That evening Eva started early on the preparations for Shabbas. She put new candles in the holders and laid out the lace cloth. She opened the blinds a bit because the sunsets were getting particularly nice again. Time heals, even when there isn't much time left. Albert was such a sensitive, refined man. And she was always such a foolish woman.

– *The Giants Haven't Won –*
– a Pennant Since '62 –

'Hey, chicks, welcome to Fès!' called the dark, skinny boy, his hands clasped behind his back in mock respect. 'You want a nice, clean hotel?' He watched them lift rucksacks from the dust-streamed bus and shouted, 'Cheap hotel. Good price.'

The two young women consulted each other as if they were choosing a movie back in Sydney. But their fatigue reminded them that they were in Morocco, hunched under packs of dirty laundry wrapped around heavy Berber souvenirs. Vivian and Lindsey, friends since school, had made a striking team these last six months on the road. Dark, thin Lindsey carried the common sense and fair, petite Vivian watched for romance of one sort or another.

The Arab kid kept his distance. And he grinned at the short woman with long blonde pigtails.

Vivian frowned back. She whispered to her dour friend, 'He's prepared for any kind of tourist, this kid. Look at the combination of baseball cap and *djellaba*.'

Lindsey flicked the sweat off her sunglasses, 'You know these "local guides"; they up the hotel rates three or four dirhams.'

Both women knew they were too exhausted to slog around in search of a cheap bed. The ride down from the Rif mountains had been rough. Across the aisle, three pregnant Arab women had vomited into rusty tin cans all the way to Fès.

'Ah, OK,' said Lindsey. 'I don't imagine that American bloke from the bus knows any budget places.'

Vivian waved a friendly, almost wistful goodbye to the American man in the amber necklace who was yanking the arm of his irritable five-year-old son.

'We'll catch you later,' Vivian called, although she knew Lindsey wouldn't approve of her infatuation.

The Arab kid was already walking towards the *medina*.

'Come this way.' He looked back at them. 'You two girls Yankees?'

'Just as obnoxious as all of them,' Lindsey said as she shook her head.

'No, there's something special about him,' considered Vivian. 'For one thing – that silly black and orange hat.'

Lindsey tapped his shoulder. 'Something you'll have to get straight is that we're *not* Americans. And in the 1970s women are not called "girls".'

He said he should have known. They were too bronzed for Americans. And they had orange Levi tags rather than red Levi tags. Still, they were big women. 'Aussies?' he guessed.

'Right, mate,' said Vivian. 'Now on to this luxury hotel for six dirhams.'

Australians were great people, he said. But he happened to like Americans best, especially the ones from Frisco. He explained that he wasn't like the other boys. He didn't want money from them. He just wanted to practise his English. Someday he was going to America and, he added politely, to Australia on the way. To prove he wasn't the average rip-off kid, he would let them register by themselves at the Hotel Belle Vue. No commission accepted. If they wanted to see the *medina*, he would meet them at the city gate, the Bab Bou Jeloud at four o'clock, OK?

He smiled as he saw them walking towards the ancient gate. Of course they would turn up.

'*Bonjour encore!*' said the lanky woman with the short, dark hair. '*Je m'appelle Lindsey et elle s'appelle Vivian. Comment vous appellez vous?*'

'Willie,' he said. 'Let's speak English, OK?'

Vivian looked sceptical. 'Willie. That's a crazy name for Morocco . . .' She dropped the question as he led them into the *suk*, for she needed all her concentration to navigate around the swarming market.

'It's best to visit the *medina* in the morning,' he told them later, as they sat over mint tea in the dark café. Lindsey preferred the tables out in the sun, but Willie explained that the sidewalk seats cost more. And they *were* travellers, not tourists, right? Leave it to him. He would show them the real Fès.

They exchanged vital statistics. The women were twenty-five, secretaries from Sydney in south-east Australia. They had been on the road for six months and were headed for temporary jobs in London. Maybe they would do the Middle East on the way home. He was sixteen, only a child, keen on languages and geography. But he still had a lot of the Koran to learn before he could specialize at the *lycée*.

'What am I going to do when I grow up?' Willie repeated the familiar question. 'I usually answer that by looking very serious and saying, 'medicine'. Most visitors like that. They are disturbed by the blindness they see in Morocco. Did you know that sixty per cent of our people have eye problems? I didn't know myself, until a lady from Milpitas, California told me.'

Willie shrugged, apparently uninterested in his old game of bait-the-tourists today. He wanted to ask more about America. 'Did you visit Frisco? Did you see a Giants game?'

'Sorry, friend.' Lindsey shook her head. 'What kind of game do the Giants play, anyway?'

'Baseball, I'd say.' Vivian pointed to his cap. 'Are they your team, Willie?'

He told them all about San Francisco, baseball and the Giants. They sat talking in the café for hours. As the streets quietened and darkened, the smell of *harira* steamed up from the kettles. They ordered huge bowls of the vegetable soup with fresh bread for their supper.

He explained that the old days were the best – with Willie McCovey, Willie Kirkland and Willie Mays, the greatest all-round player of them all. He liked to think it was Mays he was named after. His father had been batboy for the Giants when . . .

His father, yes, everyone always found this the most interesting part of the story. Actually Willie had never seen him. It was one of those vacations when six weeks after the man goes home the woman discovers she's pregnant. The man had written letters for a long time, sent small financial subsidies and baseball cards for his son.

Willie pulled out a creased bubble gum card showing

Mays hitting the record run-batted-in. His mother, Fatima, taught him to read English on these cards. They would sit upstairs in Grandmother's house and talk about going to see a Giants game with Dad and eating hotdogs with sauerkraut. Then after a few years, the Giants went downhill, trading Davenport and a couple of others. The letters stopped. Mother found a Westernized pharmacist from Rabat who didn't mind about the boy. And she wouldn't let Willie talk about the Giants or Frisco any more. That's when he started going out to meet the tourists. At first he had a crazy idea that he would greet his father coming off one of the buses. Now that he was older, he knew he'd have to find his own way to America.

In the Hotel Belle Vue, as their socks and bikini knickers were drying over the bedposts, the two women sat in their night-gowns and talked. Vivian was idly counting their dirhams and their stamps.

'The story is too complex for a sixteen-year-old to make up,' said Lindsey as she brushed her shiny auburn hair. 'But then he is a whizz kid.'

Vivian looked up at her pseudo cynical friend. 'Where would a Moroccan boy dig up an eight-year-old bubble gum card of Willie Mays?' she asked. 'Poor, gutsy . . .'

'Hooooold on, Vivian,' said Lindsey, flinging the brush on a rickety, rattan chair. 'What can you do? Just remember that bratty little boy on the bus, the son of your "American friend". We don't need a kid hanging around our holiday and you can't do anything for Willie.'

The next morning they saw the American and his child sitting on the sidewalk of an outdoor café. The tall man was intently writing in his spiral pad while his distracted son engaged in eager genocide on the local fly population.

'Hi there,' called Vivian.

'Oh, hello.' The balding head was raised to reveal mirror sunglasses and a pale face.

Lindsey, leery of Vivian's easy flirtations, quickly appropriated the chair next to the professor. He had to be a professor. His workshirt and jeans were too faded for a doctor or a barrister; his hello was too demure for a hippie capitalist or a journalist.

He nodded for the waiter to bring two Perriers.

'So what are you scribbling?' Vivian asked.

The small boy regarded the women resentfully. Lindsey guessed that ladies were always distracting Daddy, making him stop for another mint tea or glass of fizzy water.

'Nothing much,' he said. 'I'm doing a study of Berber traces in Arab urban society. I teach.' He lowered his voice modestly, 'Cultural anthropology at Stanford.'

He turned to his son, 'Ohhhh, Ed.' He wiped up the milk and said with great patience. 'Here, have another Freshette. I thought you liked warm milk.'

'It's sour, Mike.' Ed pouted. 'And you promised we could see the donkeys after you wrote for an hour.'

'So I did.' Mike's contrition was genuine. 'It's hard when two people travel together,' he said, addressing no one in particular. 'Different interests. Different priorities.'

The two women nodded politely.

'His mother,' Mike continued, 'is hiking in the Rockies with some women friends. I thought this would be a good chance to return to Morocco and get to know my son.'

The boy listened reluctantly.

'Ed and I were thinking of going off to the ruins in Moulay Idriss,' said Mike. 'Do either of you know where to get the bus?'

'Up in the New Town,' said Vivian.

'We had a car,' said Mike, 'until a truck kicked up a rock, smashing the windshield. But there are compensations. We'll see more of the people by taking the bus.'

Vivian wanted to go along, but she couldn't interpret Lindsey's withdrawal behind closed eyes as she soaked up the sun. Was her friend missing the cue or ignoring it? Maybe this fellow *was* somewhat facile. Still, he had bought their drinks with that earnest American generosity.

Finally Mike suggested, 'Would you care to join us? Moulay Idriss has some terrific donkeys.' He smiled at Ed, 'And,' he nodded to Lindsey, 'some excellent *suks* for shopping.'

'You've been to Morocco before?' asked Lindsey, stalling for time.

'Hasn't everybody?' He smiled. When she did not smile back, he added quickly, 'Yes, some years ago. I was the Young Man In Search of Himself. There are a lot of versions. *Siddhartha* was my favourite. Hesse was sort of my spiritual teacher then.'

'Can women find themselves in Moulay Idriss too?' asked Vivian. 'What do you say, Lindsey?'

'Well, that Moroccan kid said he wouldn't get out of school until late,' Lindsey said grudgingly. 'I suppose it's OK.'

The ancient bus took twenty minutes to start. Meanwhile Mike ran across the road and bought a large bag of oranges.

'Incredibly cheap prices – eighty francs a kilo,' said Mike, as he peeled off a segment for Ed. 'I feel like an imperialist no matter what I'm doing.'

By now the small bus was crowded and the other passengers were curious about the Western touring party. The women peeked surreptitiously through black and brown veils, their gossip hushed in polyester. Four young men in T-shirts stared and snickered. When the old Volvo bus sputtered, jostling forward, the rear window vibrated like gelatin.

'God, I hope we make it there and back,' said Mike. 'Years ago, I wouldn't have worried, but with Ed . . .'

'Just remember that there are more of them than us,' said Lindsey, wondering what her friend saw in this man. 'And their lives aren't worth any less than ours.'

Mike frowned. 'I agree with that, cognitively. But there's something inside me that assumes they have a racial resistance to tragedy . . .'

The oleanders, mustard and blue bells of the Plain de Said momentarily obscured their conversation. This was the fertile North Africa of Arabesque fantasy. And they were going to Moulay Idriss, the Roman ruins, the Imperial City.

Mike broke the reverie. 'This difference in the value of life hit me during the Flood of '68.'

Vivian and Lindsey shook their heads.

He seemed relieved. 'It's easy to forget, isn't it? Well, I remember because I lost some friends.' He looked out the window, as though he might be trying to hold back tears. 'It was the first item on the CBS Evening News – this massive flood in and around Fès, four hundred people wiped out. My first reaction was no reaction. Floods, famine, it's all part of life in India or Ethiopia or wherever. Maybe I couldn't deal with the scale; maybe I couldn't handle my privileged safety. Anyway, it took a conscious effort to stop and remember my *friends*.'

'People you met when you were here before?' Vivian asked.

'In a way, yes.' He regarded his son carefully. 'A long story, actually.'

Mike was wrong about the *suks* in Moulay Idriss. They were small and spare. Lindsey wasn't surprised. She had already dismissed the day as a loss. He was Vivian's indulgence. As Mike said, different interests, different priorities.

'The last time I was here,' Mike pointed his lens up the hillside, 'it was the end of *Ramadan* and these hills were covered with white Berber tents, like storks sunning themselves.' He seemed glad to talk about it now that Lindsey – out of distraction or boredom – had wandered off with Ed. 'It was my last week with Fatima. I always intended to come back. I wrote, every week at first, then after a time . . . well, after a few years, that flood happened.'

Vivian nodded for him to continue. She was impressed with his candour; flabbergasted at the sudden intimacy.

'It was all so sudden,' he said, laying the camera beside him on the grass. 'I hadn't intended a commitment. I just . . . There was this child, you see. It got complicated. I had just wanted a rest before graduate school. I did manage to scrape together a monthly subsidy.'

'And you never came back to Morocco because of those memories?' asked Vivian.

'Yeah,' said Mike, looking away, 'like the day my package was returned. I never knew what to send the kid. I wasn't into comics or cowboys when I was young. My heroes were baseball players. Anyway, I'll never forget when I got back that package – full colour team photographs – "addressee deceased".'

At the hotel that night, Vivian told Lindsey the rest of the story. At first Lindsey wouldn't believe the connection, but she had to admit that Mike's dates matched Willie's.

'Anyway, so what if it's true?' she demanded. 'What's it got to do with us, Vivian? It's time to be moving on. Too bloody hot here. This is worse than Brisbane. Besides, we agreed to avoid cities.'

'We can't just leave it like this,' said Vivian. She knew Lindsey's indifference was an act. 'I mean Willie will be devastated to find that Mike is his unheroic father.'

'To say nothing of Ed being his brother,' Lindsey winced.

'Seriously, Lindsey, what gives Willie a chance, what makes him different from the other kids in this place is his hope that a man will ride in one day with a coach full of Giants.'

Lindsey was intractable. 'What can you do?' she flared, admiring her friend's compassion as much as she resisted her romanticism. 'You can't change other people's lives or cultures or economies. Willie and Mike are just two more people outside the bus window. You can pull down the shade or close your eyes or turn away. But you can't change the bloody scene.'

'Well, at least we can be careful they don't meet through us,' said Vivian.

'Fine with me,' shrugged Lindsey, 'I won't miss the great white professor's company.'

When they met Willie the next day, they steered him away from the neighbourhood where Mike was staying. Walking more rapidly than Willie liked, towards the city outskirts, they heard a broad 'Hello there!' Turning, they saw Mike and Ed sitting at another outdoor café.

Spotting Willie's cap, Mike laughed, 'Hey, you like American baseball, kid?'

Lindsey looked at her friend, frowning helplessly. Vivian whispered a warning to Lindsey not to use Willie's name in front of Mike.

Meanwhile, Willie offered a winning smile as he invited Mike and Ed to join their tour of the Old Town.

The five of them trailed around the market looking for a green and brown hassock for Mike's office.

'I like to create an informal atmosphere for seminars,' Mike explained, 'to break down this cult of the expert. We're each an expert on something. Why look at this kid here . . .'

A loud crash interrupted him. They all rushed over to the dark side of the boutique where Ed had been amusing himself with the brass framed mirrors. The old shopkeeper flashed on the ceiling bulb, revealing walls of *ancien* silver, shelves of pewter kettles and a floor of splintered glass. He threw up his arms.

'*Les glaces,*' moaned the old man. '*Les glaces, elles sont très chères, monsieur.*'

'OK, keep your shirt on,' cried Mike nervously. 'Let's see if the child is all right.'

Vivian turned to the merchant, '*Un moment, s'il vous plaît. Nous vous payerons.*'

'He's OK,' said Lindsey. 'Just needs some fresh air. Whadya say, Ed, how about a sprint around the gardens?'

The two men confronted each other over the value of mirrors: the Arab reluctant to lose access to the American Express card and the Westerner determined not to be cheated. Willie negotiated a compromise. Then he advised Mike about a less commercial place down the road.

Vivian stayed with them, between them, asking more and more desperate questions about the similarities between American and African deserts, the differences between Canadian and Australian tourists – anything to keep them apart. However, Willie finally managed to squeeze in.

'So Mike,' said Willie, trying to sound casual. 'You come from my favourite city. Tell me what the weather's like now in Frisco.'

Mike laughed kindly, 'The first thing I'll tell you is not to call it Frisco,' he said. 'The natives say "San Fran-cis-co".'

'Ah, the *Medersa*,' Vivian interrupted. 'They say the *Medersa* is the best part of the *medina*. I've got to get some pictures.'

They had to climb three dozen flights of the cloister to satisfy her light metre. She made them examine each cell of the *Medersa* carefully for shape and size and anything that might distract them from each other. As Vivian turned to get a final photograph of the fountain, Willie wedged between her and Mike.

'What are the Giants' chances for a pennant this year?' Willie asked. 'I heard a couple of weeks ago that they were only two games out of first.'

'They were, the bastards,' Mike's face turned red, 'but since then they lost three in a row to the Dodgers. Completely blew it. Say, how do you know so much about baseball?'

'Hey, hey, Mike,' called Vivian pointing to a shop across from the *Medersa*. 'What do you think of that hassock there? Isn't it just what you wanted?' Anxiously, she avoided Willie's eyes.

Mike was delighted with the shop. Not only were the prices lower, but everyone was offered a cup of mint tea. The merchant, who didn't speak English or French, sat and smiled while his wife set the pot and cups before them. The Arab man watched, fascinated, as Mike popped out a contact lens and cleaned it. Then the merchant ceremoniously prepared the tea, pouring it out of the pot and back again three times before serving them.

'You see,' Mike said, 'this is what I try to communicate to my students. The integration of life, the society of the workplace. The last time I was here . . .'

'When was that, Mike?' asked Willie.

Vivian stood up abruptly. 'Oh, here, Mike, how about a hat to keep the sun out of your eyes?'

Mike ignored her and turned to the boy. 'A long time ago,' he answered. 'Before you were born. I had just graduated from college.'

Willie nodded happily. Vivian sat down and Mike turned to her as the most likely person to catch the subtleties of his narrative. 'The first week I was here, I met this Moroccan girl – they *were* called "girls" then – and I started travelling around with her. It was very unusual, but she was quite Westernized, quite unusual, herself.'

Vivian sipped the thickly sweet tea and gripped herself for another banal change of subject. 'I'll never be able to have mint sauce again without thinking of this place.'

Mike resumed singlemindedly. 'Anyway, the girl taught me a lot about the country, and a lot about myself. I decided to go home and send for her,' he bowed his head. 'I had just enough money.'

Oblivious to the shopkeeper and the boy, Mike was talking to Vivian. She was too nervous to hear him. She watched Willie's eyes shift from acute surprise to assumed naïvety.

'The pregnancy was hard to handle, hearing about it right in the middle of finals. Somehow I moved in with Joyce – the lady who's currently hiking in the Rockies – but I still wrote to Fatima.'

Mike noticed a slight movement in Willie's face and turned to him amiably. 'I wonder if you knew Fatima?' he asked. 'She died in the flood of '68, but her family might still be around.'

Willie stared at Mike, then at his own feet, then at Vivian as though he were waiting for her to translate.

'Fatima is a common name,' Vivian said at last. 'I even know a Portuguese woman in Sydney whose name is Fatima.'

'Yes,' said Willie uncomfortably, 'it is very common.'

'What time did we say we'd meet Lindsey and Ed?' Vivian asked suddenly.

'Lord, you're right,' said Mike. 'It's almost eight o'clock. Ed'll have a real tantrum. Let's get this wrapped up.'

He bought two hassocks and thanked the man for the tea. They waved congenially to the woman at the back of the shop who was clearing away the hospitality.

'Now I hope Lindsey can find that *tagine* restaurant,' said Mike as they stepped into the black *medina*.

It was Mike who couldn't find the café.

'Too dark,' he said. 'It's confusing in the dark.' He nodded to the boy, 'Do you think you could jar my memory a bit, old man?'

'Sure,' Willie said neutrally. 'I used to live nearby.'

The shops in the *medina* never seemed to close or open,

thought Vivian. They were always crowded – when she padded down from her pension at eight-thirty in the morning and when she went up to bed at ten p.m. Now she paused at the spice *suk*, asking Willie to evaluate the vibrant orange on the brass scales. She wanted to buy some paprika, but Lindsey would say that she was nuts, that she had nowhere to cook, that they'd get stopped by the border drug squad. They passed another stall, where Woolworth' scarves and nylon night-gowns hung in an open doorway.

'Just look at this flimsy, gaudy sweat-shop stuff,' said Mike. 'The Moroccans buy our cheap consumer durables and we buy their silver bracelets. Incredible the way we romanticize each other's cultures.' He turned to Willie. 'We never did talk about the Giants. Did you know they haven't won a pennant since 1962?'

'If they hadn't traded Cepeda,' said Willie, brightening again, 'their hitting strength would have been first rate.'

'I don't know,' mused Mike. 'He was pretty much of an old horse.'

'But look what he did for St Louis,' offered Willie.

'Naw, he was worn out,' said Mike. 'I know what I'm talking about. I was a batboy for the Giants when I was your age.'

Willie remained silent.

'Listen,' said Mike. 'I didn't mean to hurt your feelings. Baseball is a kind of science. When I get back to San Francisco – you remember that: San Fran-cis-co – I'll send you some sports magazines. Maybe a few of those cards with players' photographs.'

'No,' said Willie. 'No thank you. The mail is very unreliable.' His idiom faltered and his voice sounded stiff. 'It is most generous.'

Mike whispered to Vivian, 'Damn Arab kids. Sometimes they turn off just like that. What the hell can you do?'

At the door to the small café stood a tall man, his face creased with a stubborn frown. He was explaining in sign language that there was no room. Mike stepped past him and peered anxiously for Lindsey and Ed. Willie presented their problem to the proprietor and they were quickly guided to their friends, sitting at a corner table.

'I must admit,' said Mike, swallowing a chunk of carrot and dipping his bread into the lamb sauce, 'I've never tasted anything as good as Moroccan *tagine*. But, Ed, that doesn't mean you have to advertize it all over your shirt!'

Ed pursed his lips with half-hearted petulance.

'He's had a tough day,' said Lindsey, gulping a glass of Moroccan white wine. 'He threw up after lunch.'

'Threw up?' Mike was alarmed. 'Oh, it must have been those peaches. You'll never live up to your namesake this way.'

'Edward Kennedy?' Willie asked proudly.

'Lord.' Mike laughed. 'Preserve us from fuzzy liberals. No.'

'Edmund Hilary,' guessed Lindsey. 'You always wanted to climb mountains, right?'

'How did you know?' Mike asked incredulously.

Before she could answer, Edmund Hilary Larsen retched and turned paler than the Himalayan snow.

'Say, this looks serious,' said Mike. 'Maybe we should get a doctor.'

Willie scrutinized the boy. 'Have you had diarrhoea?'

Lindsey nodded wearily. 'He's been running to the toilet all afternoon, when he wasn't wearing me out running around the gardens.'

'What did he eat yesterday?' asked Willie.

Silence followed until Mike realized that he was the one being asked.

'The watermelon,' he said finally, 'the damn watermelon.'

'Yes,' Willie nodded, 'it is very bad for visitors to eat watermelon here. It grows in overflow areas from the city.'

Mike stood up irritably, 'I'll run over to the *farmacie* and get some entrovioform.'

'No, no,' said Willie, startling everyone with his urgency.

Everyone except Vivian, who, remembering Willie's mother, suggested, 'Why don't *I* go? It's just across the way and I need some aspirin.'

'You won't get what you want in this country,' Mike said as he rocked Ed in his arms.

Willie interrupted with deliberate calm, 'I have seen

many people with this problem. I have a friend at the *farmacie* and can get medicine for free. I will be back soon.'

Mike watched Willie walk out to the street and then looked down at the child in his arms. At last he spoke, 'The kindness of these people,' he shook his head. 'I don't even know the kid's name.'

'How about "The Lone Ranger"?' Lindsey snapped.

Mike forced a smile.

Vivian couldn't take it any more and exploded, 'Try Willie.'

'Willie?' Mike stuttered.

Lindsey watched her friend warily.

'Yes,' Vivian persisted, 'as in McCovey, Kirkland and Mays, the greatest all-round player of them all. Willie.'

The next day, Ed was well enough to travel. Vivian, Lindsey and Willie came to the terminal to see them off.

'Your friend's potion was magic.' Mike patted Willie on the shoulder. 'But I think we should be pushing on. Fès doesn't seem to agree with Ed. How can I ever thank you?' Mike extended a white envelope. 'I, I'd like to give you something – to compensate for the balance of payments, you might say.'

Willie stood still and silent.

'Now, before you interrupt,' said Mike, 'I know you don't usually take money from travellers. I don't usually offer it. But I'd like to put this to, to your education. What do you want to do when you grow up, anyway?'

'I would like to be a doctor,' said Willie soberly. 'An eye doctor. Did you know that sixty per cent of my people have trouble with their sight?'

Mike pulled a hundred dirham note from his Marrakech leather purse. 'That's going to be expensive,' he considered. 'Let's say this is the first installment on tuition. There's so much we haven't talked about.'

Ed was whining and pulling on Mike's denim jacket.

'Maybe you'd let me help you with medical school,' said Mike, 'maybe we could write about some of the things we haven't had a chance to talk about?'

'Maybe,' said Willie.

The bus coughed to ignition, halting half-way out the garage door. The driver blasted his horn. Mike embraced Willie quickly, waved to the women and clambered up the steps after Ed. As the bus jerked forward, expelling dust, Willie took off his cap and waved goodbye. Then he folded the hat and stuck it in his back pocket.

'Given up on the Giants?' asked Vivian.

'You mean the hat?' he asked. 'It was getting too small. Anyway, my friend Ahmed wants to buy it. It's a good way to meet Americans.'

'And I reckon *you* don't want to meet any more Americans,' said Lindsey.

'No need,' said Willie. 'With the money from Mike, I will be able to save and go over by myself. To meet my father.'

Both women looked worried.

'I know what you think.' He sighed. 'I know what Mike thinks. But you are all wrong. I know my father's name.'

Vivian looked sceptical.

'My "medical tuition" isn't going to rob Mike,' smiled Willie. 'He'll feel better. I have not – as you say – pulled anything over Mike's eyes. He sees what he wants to see.'

'And even when you think you're seeing straight, there's not much you can do,' said Vivian.

'How do you plan to find your father,' asked Lindsey, 'once you've made it to San Fran-cis-co?'

'I don't know,' said Willie. 'Go around to his old address.' He brightened, 'Look him up in the telephone book!'

'There are lots of names in a city phone directory,' said Vivian.

Suddenly Lindsey asked, 'What *is* your father's name?'

'Hesse,' said Willie.

'What?' the two women asked in unison.

'Hesse,' repeated Willie. 'Hermann Hesse. Have you heard of him? It's funny, but my Milpitas friend and a man from Texas seemed to know him, too.'

'No, I don't think so,' said Vivian. 'Just one of those common names.'

'But the Giants,' said Lindsey. 'The Giants, have you given up on them?'

'I don't know,' said Willie. 'Mike kind of spoiled that for me. Besides, they haven't won a pennant since 1962.'

– Interval –

It wasn't the cigarette in the cut-glass ashtray that bothered me, even though you know I hate the smell of stale tobacco.

I could have forgotten it because I immediately get lost whenever I sit in your – womb – I want to say womb instead of room. The very first thing I noticed about the room was the African animal photographs. It was as though you had hung them in my honour. While I've never been to Africa, you know I've always been planning to go.

It wasn't the lipstick on the Spode cup that bothered me. I did notice that she drank coffee with sugar and cream, whoever *she* was. A certain contrast to my Spartan tea with lemon, don't you think? You always had the tea ready for me, and always before with a fresh linen napkin. Everything was thoroughly elegant – your basement Chelsea flat with the potted plants and the exotic prints, the ancient china and the Jackson's Darjeeling tea.

It was almost ready; I do understand. It would have been ready if the train hadn't been five minutes early. I saw the sliced lemon on the counter and I heard the kettle rumbling to a boil as I walked in today.

I'll tell you what really bothered me. It was that the footstool was in a strange position and the seat of the chair was still warm. Rive Gauche lingered. As you puttered in the kitchenette behind the charming Javanese screen, I wondered if you ever took time for notes after sessions.

At the price you charge, dearie, you might consider fifteen minute intervals.

– On The Way From China –

Monica learned about the Great Lakes as a Peking school girl in 1935. 'H-O-M-E-S: Huron-Ontario-Michigan-Eerie-Superior,' she practised for her visit one day. The American nuns made her nostalgic for those inland shores far from China.

Madame Chen sits on the edge of a borrowed wicker chair, savouring the accents of her two American guests and remembering the days she was called Monica. She grasps every moment of these two hours with the pale woman and the rosy one. How remarkable that they are writing about Chinese poetry, about her own work. Madame Chen is caught between listening and impressing them with her sophistication about American life. What do they all want from each other, she wonders.

*

Monica was a bright one, the nuns acknowledged. This scholarship girl who spoke English and French would go far. Certainly she would get to Chicago. But someone would have to explain she could not swim across the Great Lakes. Such an imagination, this Monica.

*

Madame Chen passes the nougat candies. 'Delicious,' says the pale woman. Now Madame offers English chocolates, wrapped in striped foil. 'My husband was the first to introduce Aaron Copeland to China,' she hears herself saying. 'Arthur Miller visited our house.' Watch the immodesty, she inhales, remember the taxi will fetch them soon. Three black cats peer into the parlour from a courtyard window.

*

Monica's long march led to Yenan, not university. Instead of packing for the windy city, she watched the nuns board ship. Father Foyle carried a chalice under his cape. 'This is my body. This is my blood.' Monica felt dizzy.

*

Madame Chen hears the familiar American accent. 'Do you still attend Catholic Church?' She recognizes this voice of innocent curiosity. She follows the rules with more subtlety these days. 'Thou shalt not bear false witness against thy neighbour.' Those she grew up calling 'neighbours' were now 'foreign friends'. 'No,' she answers, wondering if they hear her voice quaver.

*

Monica contributed to the countryside, nail by nail, her commitment fuelled with Actual Grace. Rising by the rooster, she recalled how Peter betrayed Him thrice before dawn. She remembered the martyrs. She promised Him and herself never to forget. Each night before sleep, she prayed, '*Agnus Dei, qui tollis peccata mundi, dona nobis pacem*. Huron-Ontario-Michigan-Eerie-Superior.'

*

Madame serves them bamboo shoots and marinated beef with her own chopsticks. She toasts them with Chinese rum. 'No, no trouble,' she insists. 'My daughter, Augusta, cooks while preparing for exams.' She watches the two Americans, pleased at their appetites. The rosy one is so like Sister Colomba, who was in charge of the rice.

*

Monica met her husband, Yu, in the countryside. 'Richard,' he whispered, explaining how he had been trained by the Jesuits before the Revolution. Together they said Hail Marys and obeyed two sets of commandments. They did not drown their daughter. They secretly baptized her Augusta.

*

Madame Chen checks the clock: in forty-five minutes the car will arrive for her guests. Still, she is unsure what she wants from this precious, private visit. Should she tell or listen or give or take? She wants a ticket on that old steamer; she wants to slip under Father Foyle's cape. 'No,' she answers the rosy woman quietly, 'I will not go to America. But my daughter Augusta has applied.' 'Augusta?' the visitor catches on. 'Why did you name her Augusta?'

*

Monica was lucky to find a flat with space for sleep and study. The two rooms, cramped with her husband and daughter, were not like the HOMES she had imagined. Still, Monica wrote to Sister Colomba through the sympathetic French officer, they were grateful. They did not forget.

Madame Chen hears her own voice again, high and urgent. 'Will you have another chocolate?' Fifteen minutes left. 'Susan Sontag came to our house.' The women nod uncomfortably, overfed perhaps. 'Many foreign friends have visited. Augusta will meet them in America. She has applied to Northwestern University. This is near Chicago. On the Great Lakes.'

*

Monica was not prepared for the Cultural Revolution. 'Bourgeois,' she was called because of the night school degree. So the family was separated into three provinces for two years. During this time Sister Colomba's letters failed to reach her. Monica's faith stretched only as far as her husband and daughter, as she willed them all back to that courtyard apartment in Beijing which was the only home she dreamt of any more.

Madame Chen's party is ending and still she does not know what she wants from these two American women. Books they give her, unsolicited. And addresses for her trip to the States, because they insist she must come some day. 'One more picture,' says the pale one. Polaroid creates an instant present. Here she slowly materializes in glossy colour, standing beside the one who resembles Sister Colomba. 'No, you keep it,' she declines. The rosy woman looks perplexed, but slips the photo into the pocket of her dark cape. A taxi honks. Madame Chen waves, sending Monica home.

– Smoking –

Mary had always wanted to go to Norway in June. Clean, green Scandinavia bathed in sun almost twenty-four hours a day. The people were supposed to be friendly, progressive and productive. When her boss offered to send her to the conference, all expenses paid, she could hardly refuse. Why would anyone hesitate? She was reluctant to leave New York where her father was recovering from pneumonia. But he did have two other children in the city. Truthfully she felt a little nervous, not of travelling, because her work took her all over the world, but nervous of going to paradise.

The SAS flight was not a good start. She began coughing almost immediately, for although she had requested a seat in the middle of the non-smoking section, she was placed in the seat directly behind the first-class smoking section. The flight attendant said she was sorry about Mary's bronchitis, but there were no more seats, what could she do? She handed her passenger an extra bag of peanuts. Mary shrugged sympathetically. Being a flight attendant was like being a producer – caught in the middle of impossible demands. She closed her eyes and felt grateful that the conference hospitality form enquired about smoking. She was looking forward to meeting her host, Sigrid Hannevig, an editor for Norwegian television.

Mary stared down at the ocean. Yes, Sigrid seemed very hospitable, even enquiring about what she liked to drink. She smiled to herself now at how alarmed she had been when Sigrid said in one of her letters, 'Your French friend, Lisette, asked to be placed in the same accommodation, so I am borrowing a bed from the neighbours.' Lisette, whom Mary had met briefly at a Swiss conference, was hardly her friend. Mary found the older woman charming, but overbearing. She knew Lisette perceived her as a 'contact', which startled her because Lisette was materially much more successful, with her Paris flat and the big house in Palm Beach that she won in a divorce settlement from her American husband. She did freelance projects, always penniless, always landing on her feet in the cash flow. Forget it, Mary was amused. Suddenly starving, she opened the bag of peanuts. Sigrid next wrote rather regretfully that Lisette was staying elsewhere in Oslo, with a friend of Madame Mitterand. So it would all work out – just she and Sigrid and her friendly drinks.

Mary dug into her briefcase for the proposal about a new documentary on European anti-nuclear groups. She hoped to meet distributors in Oslo. The station manager was getting tired of Mary's 'polemical programmes' on the environment, welfare mothers and Indian land rights. But Mary had won several awards and she knew deep down that he admired her work, that she might even be acting out his social conscience for him. Still, she had almost lost it with the documentary about Renée Lavirim, whose protests were a little too radical for American viewers. Come to think of it, Lavirim was how she met Lisette. She had wanted to translate the French interviews.

Mary noticed that there was only one smoker in the first-class section and that there were four empty rows ahead of him. Would he mind moving forward a row or two?

He looked through her, lighting another cigarette before finishing the one at hand.

Mary dipped into the peanuts, then picked up a conference catalogue. She was scheduled to screen her film the second day. Good. She would be recovered from jet lag and have a sense of the place by then. Resting her head back on the seat, she recited the litany silently: Oslo. Fjords, Midnight sun. Viking ships. Ibsen. Sandel. Munch. Grieg. Amundsen. Akavit. She could hardly believe it.

The flight was rocky. The man ahead smoked through the night, so she didn't get much sleep. She hurried off the plane, scanning the airport for tall, blond Sigrid. Her host was nowhere in sight.

Twenty minutes later, after all the other passengers had been met, a short, dark-haired woman came rushing forward. 'You must be Ms Conor. I'm terribly sorry to have kept you, but I couldn't locate a taxi. It's rush hour, you know.'

'Taxi?' Mary was confused. 'What an imposition I've been. When you offered to meet me, I made the very American assumption that you would be driving.'

'Ah, not to worry. Plenty of Norwegians drive cars too. But my beloved Nils always drove us, so I had no need to learn while he was alive.' She swallowed hard.

'I'm sorry,' Mary frowned. 'You've lost your husband recently?'

'Yes, just three years ago this month. He was still a young man, too, as you might imagine looking at me, although I've aged terribly since his passing.'

'I'm sorry.' Mary felt like a cactus in Siberia. Shifting the weight of her bags, she tried to get comfortable.

Sigrid coughed deeply. It was the kind of cough that frightened Mary, for she knew it was a smoker's cough. Sigrid caught her breath and hailed a taxi.

Once seated, Sigrid enquired kindly, 'Tell me, how was your flight?'

'OK,' Mary said, exhausted. 'What a beautiful city.'

'Oh, if you think this is pretty, you must see Bergen.' Sigrid reached into her purse. 'Do you mind?' She opened a pack of cigarettes.

Mary sighed. 'Actually, I have chronic bronchitis.'

'Oh.' A moment of panic crossed Sigrid's eyes. She tapped her collarbone. 'That is what you meant in your last letter, saying you were a "non-smoker". I was puzzled, you see, because the housing office did not enquire about smoking. I thought it was simply something Americans told each other. Is it a problem for you, that I smoke in my flat?'

Mary fought back the tears. How could she change accommodation now? Distributors had arranged to phone her at Sigrid's. Her station had sent tapes there. 'This is so awkward,' she stumbled. 'I did say very clearly on the form that smoke made me ill. It runs in my family; my father has . . .'

'Well, I shall just have to discipline myself.' Sigrid smiled almost convincingly. 'I can go to the veranda when I get desperate.' She looked tense, annoyed and apologetic.

'I hate to inconvenience you.' Mary wanted to respond in kind, offering to discipline herself. But she knew it was not a question of that. Besides, her life was already perilously long on discipline.

Sigrid gazed silently out of the taxi window.

'Tell me about your work,' Mary asked.

'Oh, I shall.' Sigrid recovered her hospitality. 'I've planned a tour of the studio. But first let me point out some of the sights for we are almost at my flat. There is the Royal Palace.'

Sigrid's elegant neighbourhood was like a fairytale – wide, tree-lined streets. Lilacs everywhere. Lilacs in mid-June. Mary reminded herself that spring came late to Scandinavia. Their taxi stopped outside a spacious block of flats.

Inside, Mary admired the lavish apartment – high ceilinged rooms, waxed hardwood floors, stunning eighteenth century botanical prints.

Sigrid was delighted by Mary's appreciation. 'It is too large for one person; but it was just right for two.'

'Is this Nils?' Mary nodded to a handsome oil portrait over the Victorian mantle.

'Yes, two years after we met. He was so handsome, blond and tall, so much more Scandinavian than I.' She paused to pick up a cigarette, but stopped herself. 'Discipline. I must remember.'

Mary's heart sank. She was exhausted, with no energy for remorse.

'A cup of coffee?' Sigrid offered. 'You must be very tired.'

'Thank you.' Mary shifted her bags. 'That would be perfect.'

'Let me show you your room.' Sigrid walked with a renewed spring in her step.

Mary was overwhelmed by the majestic boudoir. Windows open onto a quiet courtyard. She had her own fireplace, a luxurious couch and a large, flat, welcoming bed.

'But I've put you out,' she suddenly realized. 'This is your room, isn't it?'

'Oh, not to worry, since Nils died I haven't slept well here. I have my cubby-hole off the kitchen. I often sleep there when I'm all alone. The light is better. And I don't sleep many hours at a time.'

Mary disentangled herself from the coat and bags. She alighted on the bed a moment. Her attention was caught by a photograph of Nils wearing shorts and carrying a tennis racket. Sigrid noticed. 'Now let me get that coffee. The bathroom is just there, dear.'

Mary felt better having washed her face and hands. She changed clothes, brushed her hair, then unpacked the gifts – a corny Rye Beach dishtowel and the bottle of scotch.

'Oh, the *size* of this bottle,' Sigrid exclaimed gratefully. 'So thoughtful of you, for we have a terrible liquor tariff in this country.' She smiled in amusement at the dishtowel, setting it to one side.

Mary was overcome with well-being at she sat down at the pretty table, laid with cheese and cakes. The coffee smelled heavenly. Lifting the cheese knife, she remembered one like this in the home of her childhood friend Toril. Sigrid reminded her of Toril's mother. The same nose. Yes, she had that slightly distant friendliness, contained but kindly. Things would be fine here.

Sigrid warmed to Mary's careful appreciation. 'I hope to introduce you to my friend Kirsten Johansen. She is very interested in your work.'

Sigrid lay in bed thinking about the conference. Her friends warned her it was trouble to take in people. But as the oldest daughter in a large family, she had always been used to work. After marrying, she managed to entertain at Nils' foreign posts, to help him with the research and eventually developed considerable editing skills. But with Nils, nothing seemed like work. Every task was a brick in the great life they were constructing together. Then suddenly, he left her alone in an enormous, empty world. Her friends were tiring of the mourning, solicitously advising her to get on with things. Clearly they did not understand. Sometimes, she suspected they had never truly loved. Every day since his death, it had been an effort to rise from the bed. Every day, and she had watched this with a certain clinical detachment, she had been able to get up a minute or two earlier.

She stared at the light seaming the middle of the maroon drapes, considering how much she had looked forward to the conference. For the company. For the opportunity to be useful. To return the hospitality, because Americans often had been generous. The first person to ring after Nils' death had been an American. And the American Club had sent the largest wreath. She had spent weeks shopping for the perfect jams and cheeses and liquors. It *was* disappointing to receive this abstemious, young American.

Why, with all Mary had accomplished, one would have assumed her to be at least fifty. A senior producer, with several prize-winning documentaries, including the brilliant study of Renée Lavirim. She must be brave to handle such topics in America. Yet this woman was, well, she couldn't be more than thirty-five.

Mary was a funny one, so certain of her beliefs and uncertain of herself. Sigrid supposed that had something to do with class. Americans were interesting that way. Some of them had no background at all and moved into positions of high power by dint of intelligence and will. Much as she admired this, she wished the girl had a little more irony, a few more rococo edges.

There was really nothing *wrong* with Mary. But this smoking ban was dreadful. Frankly, Sigrid didn't remember anything on the hospitality form asking if she smoked. Perhaps she overlooked the question. And when the girl had written she was a 'non-smoker' she should have picked it up, knowing how pernickety Americans, even some Londoners, had become in recent years. But it was one of those things she preferred to ignore. Why was she letting this tiny problem undo her? So she had to open her window. It was midsummer, time to open windows. Time to change. She had been changing. Ever since Nils died she had been cutting down on the smoking.

She could have done worse in the guest lottery. And if she had wanted to host Lina Wertmuller, she should have specified. She would simply have to overcome her jealousy at Mary's accomplishments and her disappointment at Mary's age. The young woman was nice enough. It was time that she, herself, returned to the world. She had been very needy since Nils' death. If truth were told, her oldest friends were beginning to drift away.

Mary could not sleep. She knew she should close the curtains, however the late light was thrilling. If she did fall asleep, the dream might change. Images from this first Norwegian day screened across her mind. Cornflowers and rosy lupins. Sky blue and pink. The flowers were so much more tentative because of their late coming. People seemed relaxed, as if basking after the passionate climax of spring. How they soaked up the sun. Women walked bare-breasted through the parks. Everyone is so brown. They seemed to turn from white to tan overnight, from sugar to caramel without burning.

Still, they held ice under the warmth, reserving themselves. How much did this have to do with their geographic vulnerability – to the German occupation, to Chernobyl's recent 'friendship cloud'? Sigrid told her that Germans were frequent tourists these days. They would travel to the most remoted villages in Norway and say aloud on the street: 'That's where I lived during the war. That house. There.'

She picked up a postcard of Nansen's statue. Snow melted on the black marble head of the Arctic explorer. Water formed an icicle under his nose. Lines of water ran down the cheeks like sweat, drops gathering beneath the chin. Next to the statue, snow gathered on the tree, with no sign of melting, but this man's pulse was so strong that it would not allow snow to daunt his marble image.

Well past midnight now. She should sleep. Instead she wandered Sigrid's flat in her memory. Art on the walls from Greece, Italy, Spain, provided sun in the darker months. The windows shone as if they had been lovingly polished in anticipation of these long days. Mary was eating powdered-sugar cookies and smoked salmon. On the floor? She was alone on a mountain in winter. One hour of sunlight. One hour in which to write 'sos'. Did it mean the same thing in Norwegian? Or was it a German code word? Would she be bombed before she froze to death? A child's voice. Her friend Toril who moved from New York in the third grade. No, a real child. She started awake. A child from downstairs in the courtyard. She was really in Norway, Paradise at midsummer.

Mary yawned and got up to use the toilet. When she closed the bathroom door, she found herself staring at another picture of Nils – a line drawing by Sigrid, done perhaps ten years before. Shivering, she felt eager to return to bed, to be alone.

She wondered how her father was doing. She really should call him. He would get a kick out of how she could dial the phone at midnight without switching on the light. Well, why not? She gave it a try.

'What do you mean? You felt out the numbers on the dial? For a girl with four years of college, I'm supposed to be impressed?' His tone was more than usually brusque.

'No.' She tried to maintain a cheerful voice. 'I mean that it's so light here I can see to dial after midnight.'

'For this your station sends you all the way to Norway?'

'No, Dad, I just thought . . .'

'Ah, don't worry. I'm just a cantankerous old man. Cantankerous and sick. I would prefer to know you were calling from Riverside Drive, where you could also see to dial.'

Mary was walking alone through the Slottsparken after her first day at the conference. The Slottet was a small, graceful royal palace. King Olav V lived there, she reminded herself. Europeans always teasing her that Americans were romantic, but what did they think this reverence for monarchy was? She would ask Sigrid about the King. All day she had been saying to herself she would ask Sigrid this; she would ask Sigrid that.

The lilacs stung through the evening air and Mary felt something like bliss as she entered the block of flats. Climbing the well-worn steps, she imagined how many generations had lived here. She could hear voices from

Sigrid's flat. Good. She was up. Perhaps the other person was her friend Kirsten, the Swedish editor.

Mary hesitated at the door. Should she use her key or should she knock? After all, this was Sigrid's home. She had an amusing image of Sigrid caught in Kirsten's arms as she opened the door. Amusing because it would appall Sigrid. She turned the key and called, 'Hello there.'

'Welcome home!' Sigrid shouted.

'*Bienvenue*,' came another voice.

Mary's blood rushed to her face as she recognized the voice.

In the living-room, Sigrid smiled conspiratorially to Lisette. 'Well, we must put out these cigarettes, so she won't know we've been naughty girls.' Sigrid held the smile, enjoying the image of this French woman – dark, smelling of sweat, garlic and perfume. Pretty in a seasoned way. Wonderful crows' nests around her eyes. A neck that had been too tanned, ringed now with heavy jewellery.

Lisette smiled distractedly.

'Come into the front room, Mary. Join us for a drink.' Sigrid felt a long breath rag through her body. Delighted by her guest, Lisette was just what she expected from the conference: witty, worldly conversation. Thank God Lisette smoked – delicious Gauloises. Too bad they had to leave open the window because she adored the scent of Gauloises and dry red wine.

As Mary approached the living-room, her eyes watered from the smoke. Too bad, she thought, because she would have liked a nightcap. But it wouldn't be worth the trade-off of hacking her lungs inside out tomorrow morning. Lisette. She tried to calm herself with each step. There was no reason to be afraid. She simply did not understand the woman. She was probably envious of her aggressiveness. Deep down, she knew Lisette was politically committed and cared about her work. Her ability to understand (and manipulate?) people was evident in her intricate translations.

'Your friend has arrived,' Sigrid said expansively. 'Join us for a drink.'

'Hello, Mary.' Lisette drifted forward. 'I'm happy this worked out after all.'

'Hi.' Mary tried to sound neutrally cordial as she hugged Lisette. She was not going to pretend that she had been dying to room with the woman. Yet it *was* nice to see her, in a funny way. Her perfume was divine.

'Yes, you must hear Lisette's story about Madame Mitterand's friend.' Sigrid reclined on the couch, at home once more in her parlour.

'*Oui*, you would think a friend of the prime minister's wife would be more hospitable. But the French abroad, they are cold, entrepreneurial people. This Madame Bardot, she put me in a tiny, dusty attic room. I could not *bear* it. She did not offer a crust of bread. This, after I had brought a magnificent bottle of Pouilly Fuisse. So, I thought, Mary was always astute. I should follow my original instinct to stay with Mary and her friend.'

Sigrid smiled.

Mary wondered why her brain failed her. She was still trying to take it all in.

'Sigrid has been so kind.' Lisette beckoned Mary to the chair next to hers. 'As you can see – the olives, the pâté, the wine. Very civilized. Please, Mary, join in and tell us about the first day of the conference. I'm afraid I missed it with all the moving about.'

'I'd like to join you.' Mary tried not to breathe too deeply. Already she could feel the congestion in her lungs. 'But I'm a little jet lagged. I have an extra copy of the programme, though, which I brought for Sigrid. Perhaps you'd like to see it?'

Lisette grinned. 'Of course we both plan to see your film tomorrow. But I would love to see the rest of the programme, that is if Sigrid doesn't mind my borrowing it.'

'No, not at all.' Sigrid refilled Lisette's glass and her own.

'Good night.' Mary waved.

'*À demain*,' Lisette called.

Mary walked to the window in her room and tried to inhale the evening brightness. Why was her stomach in knots? She shivered although it was seventy degrees. What did

Lisette want? Well, she shrugged it off, just because they were sharing a room didn't mean they had to spend the conference together. Mary had a full schedule of appointments. They would just see each other at night and in the morning. The rest of the time Lisette would be sequestered with Sigrid in the parlour, sneaking a smoke. Ridiculous – Mary stopped herself – to be so petulant, to behave as if Lisette had kidnapped Sigrid. She was hardly destined to be best of friends with the Norwegian woman. Perhaps Lisette's presence was a gift. It would take the edge off Sigrid's loneliness and her disappointment at drawing an earnest American from the hospitality pool.

Sitting in Sigrid's comfortable bed, Mary reviewed the conference programme, grateful for the people she had already met. Several distributors expressed interest in her film tomorrow. She considered Lisette's skirt and blouse, draped over the desk chair, admiring the woman's flair. Lisette was like those girls at school who knew instinctively how to dress. Mary had improved her taste in the last twenty years. But she always looked a little studied. She switched off the light.

Maybe clothes would be the bridge with Lisette. She would ask fashion advice.

Closing her eyes, she remembered a lie Lisette told. A little white lie about a contract. And how could she tell Sigrid she had no money? She had managed to win grants from both the US and French governments for her work. She owned real estate in both countries. Agggh, Mary felt rigid and cranky. *This* is what she disliked about Lisette, the way she, herself, felt uptight around the other woman.

Sigrid was the first to rise the next morning, in her full flat. She had to refrain from whistling as she brewed the Italian roast coffee and set out the cheeses and fruits. Lisette would like this *chèvre*. Oh, Lisette was so refreshingly *urbane* compared to clean Mary. Lisette knew art and had travelled widely. Not that Mary hadn't travelled, but she harped on Third World places. Lisette had dared to win and lose a fortune and was trying again. She was, perhaps, a trifle arrogant in that French way, yet even that had a tart appeal. And such clothes. Sigrid, herself, could never put together pieces like that. Oh, she knew she was well-dressed enough, but in a conventional way.

Mary was wakened by Sigrid's movements in the kitchen. She wanted to go back to sleep, but the day was already bright. As she sat up, she sensed a slight nausea. Not a good sign. The first cough was heavy with phlegm. Maybe if she took a shower, breathed in the steam as Dr Kincaid had instructed . . . She went to the bathroom, smelling the delicious coffee on the way. But she could not stop coughing. Coughing and wretching from the phlegm. Silly condition, bronchitis. You drown in your own body's defences. She had always been overly defended. The coughs were deep; she would be robbed of energy for the rest of the day. The shower felt good. By the time she left the bathroom, she was simply tired.

The two women were laughing at the table. Laughing at eight in the morning, thought Mary. It was at moments like this she knew she must do something about her life.

Walking to the table, Mary tried to sound alert.

'You are all right?' Lisette stood as the younger woman entered. 'The coughing, it sounded very bad.'

Sigrid frowned. 'Yes.'

'Oh, I'm fine,' said Mary, hating the stalwart character who represented her at times like this.

'This is the bronchitis you mentioned?' Sigrid focussed sharply on her.

Mary nodded – partly defiant; partly ashamed.

'Here, drink some juice.' Lisette poured her a glass of golden liquid. She patted the chair next to her.

'Thanks.' Mary smiled at Lisette. 'Really, I'll be fine.'

Sigrid sat straighter and stared out the window, battling the feeling of intruding in her own kitchen. 'Well!' she picked up the conference schedule. 'Aside from Mary's session, what panels will you attend today?' She wished she had had the chance to study the programme last night.

'Panels!' exclaimed Lisette. 'I don't even know how to get to the conference centre. Is it far from here?'

'Just one transfer on the streetcar,' Sigrid jumped in.

'Here, I will give you streetcar tickets.' She reached for her purse and produced the first ticket, handing it to Mary.

'Oh, no, that's too kind,' Mary protested. 'I couldn't let you do that after you have provided all this hospitality. Besides, I have my own little booklet. I bought it yesterday.'

Sigrid shrugged and handed the ticket to Lisette.

'You are very *gentile*.' Lisette bowed.

Sigrid could not contain her smile.

They were sitting in the kitchen when Mary returned that night. She heard the women's laughter. Then a male voice. Making her way through the flat, she didn't even think to announce herself.

'*Mon petit chou*!' Lisette called from the table. 'The success of the conference. Everyone is talking about you. Brilliant! Courageous! Ground-breaking!'

Mary creased her forehead and blushed, surprised at how much she was affected by Lisette's praise.

'The mysterious Mary,' smiled the tall, balding man. 'Wonderful to meet you.' He had one of those international accents, the origin of which was impossible to determine. Mary imagined this as the speech of people born and raised in the United Nations building. Perhaps he was the child of a politically unfortunate liaison: Greek and Albanian; Panamanian and Cuban – left in a basket on the tenth floor women's room. A stateless son granted asylum in the concrete and glass structure.

Sigrid found another chair and poured Mary a Cherry Heering. 'Join us. Meet Teodor.'

'Hello, Teodor.' Mary hated herself for not being able to conceal the questions in her voice. She focussed on his ruddy face and wisps of sandy hair. He was an attractively animated, muscular man in his late forties.

'I found Teodor today,' Lisette explained. 'I got turned around on the way home and . . .'

'I knew I should have given you a map.' Sigrid shook her head.

'But it was, how do you say, "serendipity". Teodor was bicycling along and . . .'

'I knew she was lost. Something about this lady doesn't look Norwegian.'

Something about this man didn't seem Polish, thought Mary, wondering again at his speech in which she could now discern some Polish intonations.

'So he turned me around,' laughed Lisette. 'Actually I was only three blocks away and I invited him in for a drink. Now that was five hours ago. Sigrid was so hospitable. She insisted on broiling salmon and fixing those magnificent red potatoes with fresh parsley.' She put her fingers to her lips and kissed them. 'One word led to another and here we are.'

'Yes, here we are,' smiled Mary, unable to step onto the turntable at quite the right speed. She would need several Cherry Heerings to get in sync.

'Well, I know all about you, young Mary.' Teodor gave a wide grin. His teeth were straight, even and white.

'What do you know?' asked Mary, reaching again for the spirit of the evening.

'That you come from New York. That you are an inspired young producer. That your programme will be the most memorable event of the conference.'

The colour ran up Mary's neck. She was embarrassed by her embarrassment.

Lisette fidgeted with the top of the liquor bottle and poured herself another drink.

'Also that you do not smoke.' Teodor winked at Sigrid.

Sigrid looked down at her hands.

Mary asked, 'What should I know about Teodor?'

'He is a linguist,' Lisette said. 'First he hailed me in Norwegian. Then in Spanish. Greek. Russian. Polish. I don't know why it took him so long to get to French.'

'Teodor has lived all over the world,' Sigrid added. 'Even in your country without a work permit.'

'How did you do that?' Mary held out her glass to Sigrid. 'May I?'

'Of course.' Sigrid filled it to the brim.

'I was on a merchant ship and I swam ashore. I spent six months in Neeeew Yark. And a year in New Ahlins.'

'Stunning accent.' Mary was disappointed that despite

the Cherry Heering, she didn't like him. But she seemed to be getting along better with Sigrid tonight. Her mother, who often warned her never to impose on hospitality, simply did not have enough experience to know that people enjoy taking care of you.

Lisette and Sigrid argued about a panel they attended together. Teodor listened respectfully. Mary asked several questions. But she couldn't resist the fatigue. Glancing at her watch, she was amazed to read 'eleven-thirty'.

'The time!' she declared automatically. 'Can you believe that it's almost midnight. Look at that light!'

Sigrid beamed. 'Yes, isn't it wonderful. I have so much spirit at this time of year. I feel as if I could go on and on.'

'I envy that,' said Mary. 'But I'm exhausted. Please – don't let me disturb the party. I'll just sneak off to bed.'

Lisette looked disappointed but also concerned about her friend's health. *'Bon soir, ma chérie.'*

Before Mary was out of earshot, she heard a match striking.

'Ah, finally,' Sigrid whispered.

Two hours later, Lisette lay alone in bed reviewing the evening. *Très douce.* Teodor was amusing. No, she had not brought him home simply to test Mary's feminist instincts. *Fami*nist instincts they seemed to her at times, less to do with liberation than with repression. No, she brought him home for diversion. How often do you meet a bicyclist who speaks thirteen languages plus four American dialects? It crossed her mind that he might be an agent. But she had nothing to hide. And Sigrid had been charmed. She wanted to charm Sigrid.

Lisette held her neck back and let the tension drain from her pores. Was she getting too old – at fifty – for this international conference hopping? Speaking of age – here was Sigrid, sixty at most, ancient before her time, bowed with grief over her long dead husband. And weighed down by something Lisette couldn't quite discern.

From their initial correspondence, Lisette had sensed Sigrid's need to take care of someone. And she, herself, might as well benefit. Lisette knew she might never return to Norway and she was determined to savour this trip. The Scandinavians were a little cold and sharp for her taste, like their pickled herring. They could be officious like the Germans, but not so turgid. They were a pretty people, carried along on a pleasant sense of irony when the sun was shining.

Lisette reached for a cigarette and stopped herself, although Mary, who was sleeping soundly, would never know. Poor Mary – to miss the pleasure of smoking and worse, to turn other people's pleasure into her pain. No, Lisette didn't think it was psychosomatic. Mary looked like those consumptive Celts Lisette knew in London. But you would think that with all her American resources, she would take better care of herself.

She didn't understand her attraction to Mary. Part of it was her own ambition. Mary was very smart. A genius, according to one friend in Paris. She was rising fast and Lisette could use more American contacts. But there was also something irresistibly *good* about Mary. She was honest, reliable, steady, all the things Lisette wished she were. She once found these qualities in her husband, but he was also dull. Mary was far more intricate than Hugh.

Sometimes, however, Mary was tediously conscientious. Judgemental. And self-righteous about money. Lisette was tempted to lecture Mary about the difficulties of coming to adulthood in France right after the war, about how she had to scramble to gain skills, about getting pregnant and marrying long before she intended to. However, when she decided to have the baby, she made a vow never to use him as an excuse. Indeed, Roland had been more joy than burden. Strange to think he was only a couple of years younger than Mary. It was true that Mary had a less affluent childhood than she herself, but Mary was American and didn't understand that privilege. Besides, the girl was fifteen years younger. She had all that *time*.

On Midsummer's Night, Sigrid could barely contain her joy. Here they were in Nils' 'jalopy', with Teodor driving them to Boden for a swim and bonfire. She reflected on her day in the kitchen, preparing the picnic while Mary and

Lisette attended the conference. Why, she had actually been singing, thinking how lucky she was that Lisette met Teodor, how convenient that Teodor could drive Nils' car, how nice that he offered to take them to the fjord for Midsummer's Night. Ah, if she were only ten years younger. Sigrid caught herself. She hadn't had such a thought since Nils died. She glanced at his photograph on the refrigerator. Of course, this evening was what Nils had always wanted for her. He wanted her to on living. What a fine day, full of expectation.

Lisette and Teodor were in the front seat singing, *'Sur La Pont d'Avignon'*. Mary couldn't hear a trace of Polish in Teodor's French. Perhaps all linguists were chameleons. Lisette was always adjusting to her surroundings or adjusting the surroundings. Again, Mary thought about the lying. How could she tell Sigrid she had no money? Money! Mary returned to the day's obsession – the five hundred dollars her boss had wired from New York. She had cursed herself all afternoon for not taking it out in travellers' cheques. And now she thought she should have left the cash in Sigrid's flat, although when they were leaving town, it had seemed safer to keep it in her purse.

'Here we are,' announced Teodor. *'Si nous y allions?'*

Lisette was surprised by the crowds and the music. It was hardly the romantic Nordic night she had envisioned; it looked more like an American state fair. She glanced at Mary, pleased that the younger woman was also startled. She winked.

Mary raised her eyebrows in amusement.

'Ah, my favourite spot for midsummer,' Sigrid was saying, her arms open wide, basking in the seven p.m. heat. 'Come, let's swim first.'

Lisette's eyes widened.

'Oh, we don't need costumes,' Sigrid cajoled. 'I know a private place. It will be paradise.'

Sigrid found them a discreet rock, shaded by a small stand of trees. They unloaded their gear and lay silently on the granite, soaking up the sun. Mary sat up. 'This is remarkable. Do you know it's seven-thirty and I'm getting a sunburn!'

The others laughed good-humouredly.

Mary gradually focussed on distant clusters of people, lying about other flat boulders. She looked closer at the grey-blue water and noticed a number of people swimming. She loved swimming, but wasn't sure what it would do to her lungs. As this private debate proceeded, the others took off their clothes.

'Come swim, Mary,' said Lisette. *'Viens avec nous.'*

'Well,' she hesitated. 'I think someone should stay with the purses and watches. Why don't you all go in first.'

They needed no prompting. The three middle-aged children tiptoed over the rocks towards the fjord. Mary was touched by the aging firmness of Sigrid's body. The wrinkles laced a solid core. Here was a woman who ate moderately, walked to work and generally regarded her body as a tool. Lisette, on the other hand, reminded Mary of a fruit pastry, with many round and luscious parts. In the States, she would be considered flabby. Yet Lisette carried her body sensually, like an offering. Mary noticed Teodor last and saw him only from the back – broad shoulders, tight buttocks, the single imperfection being a varicose vein knotting along the left calf.

They chased each other in the water, whooping and gulping for air. Sigrid's stroke was strong and long. What Lisette lacked in coordination, she possessed in magnetism. Soon the other two were circling around her, pulling at her arms, splashing her face.

Mary ached to join them. She was so busy torturing herself that she didn't hear Teodor walk up beside her.

'I'll set watch a while, mate.' He was tying a towel around his waist. 'You go join the girls.'

The water was cold at first, but Mary soon realized, cold only in comparison to the air. She was distracted by splashing and laughter. Here she was in Eden, in Scandinavia where the sun sometimes shone twenty-four hours a day. The women were swimming in a small circle now, talking about other oceans.

Sigrid remembered the Indian Ocean off Mombassa; Rio's Atlantic; the Baja beaches between the Sea of Cortez and the Pacific. She told them about the haunting echoes of the expatriates' pool at the Jing Jiang Club in Shanghai.

Lisette reminisced about the Aegean near Crete and the cold, June Mediterranean off Marseilles and her favourite Senegalese beaches.

Mary heard herself describing the weekly workout at her Y in New York. No tedious city concerns here. No signs instructing, 'All women must wear bathing caps' and 'Slow swimmers keep to the right'. It was strange and exhilarating to be swimming in a world without lanes.

'I am a fish,' called Lisette, now on her back, her curly hair streaked straight by the water.

'I am an embryo,' laughed Sigrid, treading.

'I am a frog.' Mary puffed out her face.

Lisette was doing the breast stroke. Head below water, breathing out. Head up, breathing in. Legs in the scissor kick. Everything was slower now. As it should be. Water. Air. Movement. Everything was natural. She turned over to float.

Sigrid stroked slowly backwards through the water, each small effort squirting her further, her strong limbs the galley oars, ever reliable. The sun warmed her face, her belly, her thighs. She was six, eight, twelve feet above the rocks. Why did the water hold her? What had she done to deserve this respite? How safe was she? Enough. In a country which offered only a few months of sunlight, she had learned not to scrutinize warmth too closely.

The first to tire, Lisette started to shore, not wanting to disturb the reverie. Then she realized she did not want to be alone with Teodor.

'Ladies,' she shouted, masking her breathlessness, 'you will turn into mermaids after much longer. Come, let's dry off while the sun is still hot.'

Sigrid followed quickly.

Mary lingered a while before joining the other two.

Teodor laughed at them. 'Beautiful. *Très belles,*' he exclaimed.

They walked up the granite face, wincing at the sharp pebbles. Each woman collected a towel, retreating for a few moments to soak up the sun. Mary noticed new colours in the rocks as the light receded – patches of green and yellow, then dark seams of black and jade.

Sigrid broke the spell. She was, after all, the hostess, and what if the others were starving?

She dressed and began to unpack the picnic hamper. Thus alerted, Mary slipped into her clothes. She helped Sigrid set out the fish and cheese and salad and cakes.

'What a feast!' Lisette declared, sitting up on her towel. 'You have outdone yourself, Sigrid.'

Sigrid beamed.

Mary noticed, with pleasure, that she felt indulgent toward Lisette.

Lisette pointed to a bonfire on the far rocks. The sizzling yellow flared across the calm, grey water. From the top of the flames came a dark plume of smoke.

'Too early,' Sigrid protested. She fought her familiar annoyance with things imperfect.

'Almost,' said Teodor, who nodded to the west where the sun's reflection streaked a golden flame of its own in the opposite direction, burning through the water.

He uncorked another bottle of wine and the four of them toasted midsummer gods and goddesses.

Sigrid pulled herself from bed, still brimming with last night's pleasure. Midsummer was truly a magical time. But she must not neglect her guests. Someone was up. Mary, from the sound of it, for she had a lighter tread than Lisette.

Mary was trying not to panic. Perhaps she left her wallet in her sweater pocket. Perhaps it was in Sigrid's livingroom, where they all made a final toast at three a.m. She pretended not to have a headache. Everything would be all right. No high drama, she told herself. But she was in tears when she entered the kitchen.

'Oh, no!' Sigrid could not believe such a thing had happened in Norway. 'Have you checked your room? Perhaps in your briefcase?'

'I've looked everywhere.' Mary shook her head hopelessly.

'It's the tourists. You know, since the Americans are

avoiding Italy because of the bombings, the pickpockets have come to Oslo.'

Lisette woke with a raging hangover. She registered the anxious voices and could not return to sleep. Pulling on a wrap, she joined the others.

Sigrid was talking hectically. 'Perhaps you had it taken on your way home from the conference. On the streetcar? You must be careful on the streetcar.'

Mary resisted her annoyance. 'I did have it on the way to Boden last night. Remember I was showing you the picture of my family in the car?'

'The car,' Lisette spoke against all hope. 'Might you have dropped it in the car?'

'No, I brought it with me,' Mary moaned. 'I was afraid someone could break into the car. I had it in my purse on the beach.'

'And one of us was always with the belongings.' Sigrid understood the implication of this immediately and tried to conceal her horror.

Mary nodded.

'Well.' Lisette poured herself a cup of strong coffee. 'You must call and report your credit cards right away. That is the most important thing. I suppose that's what you had – credit cards and travellers' cheques.'

'Not exactly,' Mary lowered her head. 'I did have a credit card. And lots of cash. I thought it would be safer to keep the money with me.'

'Yes,' Lisette maintained a businesslike tone, 'You must report the credit card.'

'And Teodor is dropping in for a drink tonight.' Sigrid said. 'We will ask him if any suspicious characters . . .' She paused at the doubt on Lisette's face. 'Well,' her voice thinned, 'you never know.'

'You never know.' Lisette was furious with him. She walked to the window, opened it and lit a cigarette.

'We can ring him.' Sigrid spoke confidently as she dialled. The person on the other end had never heard of Teodor. 'Perhaps I have misdialled.' She tried again. Her face fell as the same clipped voice answered the phone.

Mary felt as if she would burst. She went to the living-room to be alone. She couldn't believe this had happened. She tried to be so responsible with the money. She had tried so hard, period. This trip had been exhausting. She never should have come. What a waste of time and now money.

Lisette hesitated, then followed Mary down the corridor. The girl took everything so *seriously*. In the long run of years, what was five hundred dollars? But it was more than that to Mary. Lisette stood silently in the doorframe.

Mary looked up, filled with rage at Lisette for spoiling her conference, for intruding on her shelter, for bringing Teodor into the picture to ruin things completely. She had never been able to conceal her emotions. Normally she was humiliated by such transparency, frightened of it, but now she didn't care at all. She had never felt so angry.

'It's your fault. *You* are the one who brought that jerk home. *You* are the one who invited him to Midsummer's Night. Why didn't you *think*?'

Lisette knew the best way to comfort Mary was to agree with her. Besides, she did feel a little guilty. Mainly angry at Teodor, but also remorseful about her own poor judgement. 'I am sorry. Will you forgive me, Mary?'

'Forgive you!' Mary let the force of her rage propel her to the far end of the room, as far away from Lisette as possible. 'Forgive you? How many times?'

Lisette inhaled sharply, then sat on the couch.

'For butting into Sigrid's flat, pretending you were a friend of mine? For taking up all this room with your stories and your smoking and your incapacity to negotiate the city? For introducing your larcenous friend to the scene? Just what are you apologizing for?' Mary stared out of the window, not believing that she could be this blunt. She felt the fury pulsing in her forehead.

Much as Sigrid hated friction, she was drawn to the living-room through a sense of duty. They were her guests. Whatever was happening, she should be there. She noticed she was carrying a dishtowel and paused, momentarily, to return it, then decided against the cowardly delay. Ah, Nils would have known what to do. She tried to summon his wisdom, a frequent help in moments of crisis. But her concentration was shattered by Mary's voice.

'You. You don't care about anyone except yourself. Your own convenience. Your contacts. Your pleasures. Did it ever occur to you . . .' Mary stopped, regretfully, for as much as she wanted to dump all her aggravation on Lisette, she knew she was stupid to bring her money to the beach. From the beginning, she hadn't trusted Teodor. 'You're a God-damned, selfish, manipulative *bitch*.'

Lisette was caught between satisfaction with Mary's passion – for this was the first time the younger woman had really engaged with her – and annoyance at the accusation. Ridiculous to be blamed for the theft. Still, she was washed with sympathy for Mary.

Sigrid coughed. What was there to say? 'Mary, I'm sorry for your loss. But you are being unfair. Lisette is not at fault . . .'

'No, no.' Lisette walked toward Sigrid and took her hand. 'Mary was right. I shouldn't have brought Teodor home. I must take responsibility . . .'

Sigrid was distracted by the word 'home'.

Lisette approached Mary and touched her shoulders, which rose on either side like the wings of a hawk. 'I'm sorry,' Lisette whispered.

Mary pulled away and moved to another window. She stared at the Slottsparken.

'I don't know what to say.' Lisette's eyes filled with tears.

Mary shook her head at Lisette's seductive talents. 'I'm surprised.'

Sigrid was twisting the dishtowel, unsure of the best move.

Lisette rushed from the room.

Mary watched the toy soldier guarding the Royal Palace.

Sigrid noticed a scratch on the oak table and a red wine stain on her couch. Perhaps she had been a fool to humour her loneliness this way.

Lisette reappeared. 'Here.' She handed Mary an envelope, 'Here is five hundred dollars.'

Sigrid's eyes widened.

Mary glanced distrustfully from Lisette to the envelope and back again.

'No, take it, I insist. I don't want you to be hurt because of me.'

Mary's wildest fantasy was confirmed. Teodor and Lisette were in cahoots. She took the envelope, opened it to count the money and found out this was not the kroner that had been in her wallet, but rather francs.

'No.' She was angrier than before because Lisette had somehow tricked her once again. 'Where did you get this?'

'It is my "pin money". I bring extra cash when I travel. For emergencies. And this is an emergency, no?'

Sigrid thought about the car tickets she had provided, the cigarettes, the restaurant lunches. She looked from one woman to another and wondered whether she knew either of them.

'No.' Mary flung the money down. The colourful bills scattered like leaves on the varnished floor.

'No!' she screamed, willing her pitch to shatter every window from here to the Royal Palace.

'No!' Yet even as she screamed, Mary knew she would take the money.

'Yes,' Lisette said kindly.

Two days passed. On the eve of their departure Mary and Lisette were cooking dinner in Sigrid's kitchen. They had invited several colleagues from the conference to a farewell party.

Mary washed the lettuce, thinking how the theft felt like a bad dream. She finally agreed to split the loss with Lisette, although she was not completely comfortable with the decision. The woman could be very persuasive. On a deeper level, Mary knew that she had needed someone to trust, someone to confirm she was not alone. Strange how this had brought them all together – yet with totally different reactions. Lisette was still steaming. She admitted that she was as mad at Teodor for not saying goodbye as for stealing the money. Sigrid took the loss the hardest, for it put a bad mark on Oslo, on midsummer, on her experience of the conference. Mary looked over at Lisette deep in concentration at the stove.

Sigrid sat in the living-room, smoking and doing needlepoint. While her friends were kind to fix dinner, she was unnerved to surrender the kitchen. She took a long drag on the cigarette, one of Lisette's blessed Gauloises. Perhaps not exactly *Lisette's* cigarettes but she would not have allowed herself this indulgence without Lisette's visit. Well, she considered the conference: it worked out fine. Lisette had been a treat. How nice that she wanted to come North to the cabin tomorrow. As she exhaled the smoke, her entire body relaxed. Even Mary had worked out fine. Once Sigrid had become accustomed to her ways, she had enjoyed talking with the provocative, original young woman. But how reckless to carry that much cash. Sigrid still had fond memories of Teodor, of the four of them singing at the top of their lungs in the car home that night.

Mary was washing the potatoes. She felt OK about being Lisette's scullery maid because she had a lot to learn about cooking. The other woman was in her element now, humming under her breath, conducting and choreographing at the same time. Although the basic ingredients were familiar: chicken, potatoes, squash, salad – this was going to be a very different dinner than she served at home. 'You know, Lisette, I hope you'll stay in touch if there's any work you can do for us.'

'Hmmmm,' Lisette smiled. 'Always thinking about work, Mary! Haven't we cured you of that yet? But yes, I should like that. I appreciate the invitation.'

Mary was surprised she didn't mind having made the invitation.

The doorbell rang. Lisette and Mary rushed to greet their friends and to introduce Eleanor and Donna to Sigrid. Sigrid's friend Kirsten arrived next. Lisette and Mary returned to the kitchen.

Sigrid was delighted to have her house full of intellectual talk and laughter. Yes, she was glad she signed up for the conference. You never knew how these things worked out.

Nils would have enjoyed these ladies. And they would have found him utterly charming.

The six women fit neatly around the antique mahogany dining-room table. Conference scenes passed before them. The dogmatic Swede, who railroaded her proposals through the final session. The Dutch librarian who ran off with the wife of the Spanish director on the first day of the conference. The incomprehensible American critic who talked so long he lost his audience. As they felt more at ease, they told stories about themselves.

Lisette talked about how her son had just fallen in love.

Mary felt badly she had asked Lisette so little about her family.

Kirsten recalled how she met Sigrid – on a holiday in Greece.

Sigrid grew melancholy, saying how much Nils would have loved this evening.

'If you don't mind my asking –' Eleanor sat forward '– Nils must have been a relatively young man – did he die in an accident?'

Mary was often stunned at the directness of other Americans. She, herself, had been curious about this for a week.

'Yes, he was only fifty-four.' Sigrid winced. She stood and began to collect the dishes.

Mary began to object to Sigrid working at her own party, then realized that her host was desperate to leave the room.

Lisette followed Sigrid to the kitchen.

Kirsten leaned forward and patted Eleanor's hand. 'It's all right. Not your fault. She's still sensitive, you see.'

Mary was covered with embarrassment, unsure of whether to go into the kitchen or stay here. Since Sigrid hated scenes it was probably best to remain at the table.

Kirsten whispered the explanation, 'Lung cancer. He went very quickly.'

Mary took a long draught of wine, remembering Sigrid's stricken face in the taxi that first morning, 'Is it a problem for you, that I smoke in my flat?'

'So sad,' said Eleanor, still unsure of her *faux pas*.

'Yes,' agreed Kirsten. 'So sad.'

Five minutes later Sigrid reappeared, completely composed and carrying a huge Wedgwood pot of coffee. Each woman tried for the intimacy and laughter of before.

The final morning Mary was surprised to find both Lisette and Sigrid in the kitchen drinking coffee. Sigrid had prepared a lavish going-away breakfast.

'Oh, you shouldn't have!' Mary declared. 'It's supernatural to get up this early, let alone to prepare a feast!'

'My pleasure.' Sigrid beamed, motioning her to the table. 'I have you and Lisette to thank for showing me there are *many* pleasures in life!'

Mary nodded to Lisette. 'And you! I know it's utterly unheard of for you to rise before six a.m.'

'Perhaps I am learning something of your work ethic,' she laughed, so tired she was unsure if her lips were moving in the right direction. 'However, I do think it is beyond the call of duty to rush back to New York for a meeting.'

'I agree,' said Mary. 'I'm not going to do it.'

'You mean we got up for no reason?' groaned Lisette.

'This way you can join us at the cabin,' Sigrid brightened. She realized she would miss Mary.

'No thanks,' said Mary. 'I've decided to take the train to Bergen this morning – for a little post conference holiday. I phoned New York last night after you went to bed and had my office change the reservations. A holiday – I haven't taken a non-working holiday in ten years. You two have had more influence on me than you know.'

'It rains all the time in Bergen,' Sigrid was frowning.

Lisette grinned, 'I'm sure Mary has an umbrella, *non?*'

'*Bien sûr.*'

After breakfast, Sigrid carried Mary's bags to the door. Lisette followed, more confident of her wakefulness with each step.

'*À bientôt.*' She hugged Mary. How small and compact she felt.

'Be well.' Sigrid kissed her on each cheek.

Mary could barely hold back the tears.

Lisette and Sigrid watched Mary until she turned out of sight on the landing.

They returned to the kitchen and poured more coffee. Lisette offered Sigrid a cigarette.

– *You Remember Sophia* –

'Despina, you remember Despina,' says the ancient woman as she sits on the stone steps frying sardines. 'Despina has four children. You remember Despina.'

'*Nai*,' nods Sophia in the Greek which comes easily to her head but slowly to her lips. Speaking the old language is like trying to communicate through Novocaine. Numbness. She feels such numbness. Her eyes are drawn down to the sea.

'And Eleni. She lives in that big stone house by the *kastro*. Her husband is a farmer and she has five boys.'

'*Nai*,' nods Sophia, searching for her mother in this bird wearing thin, black cotton. Her face is struck as coldly as those clay tourist medallions and her silver hair, knotted at the back, is like a miser's purse, deceptively small.

'Yes, Mama, I remember,' she wants to say. 'And Sophia has no children. But she has a life. Born of farmers on the Island of Lesbos, she is now a doctor in a big American city hospital. She lives with the woman she loves. But, Mama, you are too busy seeing what I am not.'

Sophia knew it would be like this. Despite the twenty years away, she knew in that part of herself which was deeper than memory. Which would sprout red poppies and pink daphne in dark dreams. She is dark enough to be taken for Chicana by the Americans. And Western enough to be taken for American by the shopkeepers here. Until they looked closely enough, to notice she is one of their own, a Greek woman returned to Lesbos.

'You are happy?' Mama considers this prodigal daughter in the crimson trousers and the boy-short hair. She looks into reflections of her own amber eyes and asks, 'You are happy, my little one?'

Sophia, the red giant, finds a tear on the edge of her smile. '*Nai*.' She feels the numbness wearing away.

After dinner, Sophia says she will visit the sea. Avoiding

her mother's hurt, confused glance, she walks quickly from the house. Mama cannot object. Their reunion is too fragile for demands. Questions cause enough strain.

Boys shout in the street. At first, Sophia is charmed by the chords of children's voices, a noise she never hears above the Los Angeles traffic. She is touched by the natural sound. And then she recalls her own childhood inside – practising quiet over the washing. Murmuring. Always murmuring, even the prayers. Now all around her, she can see boys. Replicas of her old friends, Christophe, Stevenos and Darius. Boys' voices. She cannot hear the silent, indoor girls. Perhaps, she laughs to herself, they have all gone to the sea.

Sophia can hear it still, the chorus of thirty years before. 'To go to school for a girl is luxury.' 'Your parents are peasants, not nobility.' 'The money belongs in your dowry.' 'Six grades is enough.' 'Why must you go to Petra, all the way to Petra for school?' 'It will turn your head.' 'It will . . .' Yes, they were right. Ever since Petra, Molivos was too small for her long legs and big feet. It was in Petra that she met Stellio who promised an automobile and a big house, like in the movies, if she would move with him to Los Angeles. After all, Los Angeles was where they made the movies. That she knew, even before Petra.

Walking down through the market now, all she can hear is the simmering of large black flies and fecund bees in the wisteria. The *tavernas* are quiet. Men are still at home eating meals which their wives have spent all day preparing. As she passes the shop called 'Agora', Sophia sees her hills have turned a California gold. Haze in the background (and beyond that, Turkey. Turkey is just eight miles away. Eight miles to the enemy. Eight miles of brilliant blue between Europe and Asia), reminding her of Los Angeles. Reminding her that it was never like the movies.

The rape scene was the only time Stellio resembled Clark Gable and he was disappointed she wasn't as grateful as Vivian Leigh. Their marriage lasted one year. But it wasn't a complete loss. It lasted long enough for her to learn about community colleges, to meet a few women friends.

Hard to write Mama about the divorce. Hard to read back

her shame, her bitter, 'I told you so.' How, then, could she write about going to college, about loving Myrna, about her dreams of becoming a doctor. Instead she wrote that she was well, working hard. She said she missed the bird music of Molivos. Mama asked the priest to read and write the letters. (She could have asked the teacher or one of the shopkeepers, Sophia knew, but she chose the priest.) Through Father's tense, spider scrawl, Mama wrote again and again, 'I pray for your safe return.'

Two American women at Stratos' *taverna* stare and smile. American. They have to be American with that size and bearing. Which she herself now shares. Almost. Their smiles blur into uncertainty as they regard each other, wondering if she is, after all, one of them. Sophia understands. She smiles hello. But she cannot reassure them. She does not know if she is American. Another time she might stop to talk ambiguities. Another time she might explain the banking hours and the best shops for jewellery and the statues of Greek women. But now she must reach the sea.

Gulls sail low, scouting the last catch. The sky is washed a dark grey which, Sophia remembers, precedes the false promise of sunset. Donkey shit on the cobblestones. How could she explain to Myrna that she missed this smell? Overripe plums are splattered on the roadside. Such richness. 'Star Trek' blares in Greek from an open doorway. The sea looks rougher than a moment ago, more determined, as if calling for the sun to set, summoning the moon to rise.

'A doctor now,' Mama wrote, the priest wrote, both comprehending nothing except new access to her. 'So now you can return home and do good.' How could she explain her choice to work with immigrant families in America – mostly Mexican or Asian – rather than with her own people? If you were a person, who were your own people? If you were a gull, you were not a dove. If you were Greek, could you be American? Was this the same water which washed through people in Tunisia and Israel and France?

These beach rocks hold her steadier than city pavement. Lapping waves soothe her deeper than Stratos' *metaxa*. Shadowed hills, now almost invisible, call her to join sleeping shapes in the distance. The hills. The sea. She had always been torn, even as a child.

Despina has four children.

Eleni lives in a stone house.

Mr Spock speaks Greek.

The priest admonishes.

American women nod in tentative complicity.

She knew it would be like this. Twenty years away and she knew she would be drugged by the flowers. She knew Mama would hold her at arms' length like a stranger, her eyes still full of longing for the daughter to return. Sophia knew she would return to the sea.

Here in the moonrise, she sees a face. Just beyond the cove, Sophia sees a moon face shining in the Aegean. Should she slip these fine lavender rocks into her red pants and wade out to this face?

Sophia does not have four children.

Sophia does not live in a stone house.

Closer yet, she finds a seductive smile, which does not question, which does not blur, a clear face beaming from the sea, a reflection not of the moon, but of Sophia.

Sophia has a face which shines in the sea. It has always been there. Waiting for her. Ever since she was 'odd Sophia with the books'. Now she has found it again.

She stands in darkness an hour, beckoned by this luminous face in the sea. Her own moon floating within reach.

Sophia, you remember Sophia. Finally, the face finds a voice. She watches for another hour and decides she does not need to go as far as the cove. She does not need to explain herself to the Americans at the *taverna* or to the priest. She will rest easily at Mama's tonight. She will return to Myrna in Los Angeles. She salutes her reflection and turns back to Molivos.

The face she carries with her, between the lands, behind the shadows, beneath the waters. Sophia, you remember Sophia.

Acknowledgments

I first knew Peggy Webb twenty years ago as a treasured teacher. Since then she has become a valued colleague and close friend. I am grateful for the splendid example of Peggy's own writing as well as for her unstinting support of my work. She has critiqued each of my books in manuscript, sometimes several times, has cheered me on during innumerable cloudy days and has generally given me courage to continue writing.

I would also like to thank other writers who generously read and commented on a number of these stories: Paula Gunn Allen, Sandy Boucher, Maureen Brady, Zoe Fairbairns, Judy Grahn, Helen E. Longino, Mary Mackey, Eve Pell, Susan Schweik and Madelon Sprengnether.

I am very grateful to Elsbeth Lindner for her editorial wisdom and to Leslie Gardner for her steadfast encouragement over many years.

Also available in Mandarin Paperbacks

By the same author
Movement

Movement captures ten years of changes in Susan Campbell's life. Draft dodger's wife, leftist activist, journalist, committed feminist – all these are part of her passage through the seventies. Travelling from the USA to Canada, Africa and Britain, we follow her search for self-knowledge in a decade of challenge and re-examination. Valerie Miner's skills as a storyteller and insights as a reflective feminist have never been stronger.

'I liked the form of *Movement* very much – it is indeed a novel of movement, political, personal movement from country to country and subculture to subculture ... vignettes and stories out of Susan's life, but never episodic, always carrying her development as a person and as a political personage a step further.'
Marge Piercy

'This is a compelling book, invigorated by Susan's idealism and enthused with her deep passion for life.' *Publishers Weekly*

Violet Trefusis
Echo

Sauge, an intriguing, evasive young Parisian woman, leaves her husband for a *séjour* in the remote Scottish castle of her aunt, Lady Balquidder, where she encounters her handsome young twin cousins, Malcolm and his devoted sister Jean. Both resent the intrusion of the newcomer. And then something happens. The charm, the feminine seduction of the young Parisian is irresistible . . .

One of Violet Trefusis' most teasingly allusive novels, *Echo* was published in France in 1931 and now sees its first publication in English. It reflects the author's deep, anachronistic attachment to Scotland, and in the personae of Malcolm and Jean evokes the androgynous sexuality of her own life. Sauge herself, perhaps a fascinating amalgam of the author and her erstwhile partner, is trapped in a sophisticated artificial society, which contrasts starkly with Violet's romantic vision of the Highlands. The tragic love affair which evolves in *Echo* ends with 'a sort of triumphant despair' and the haunting lines 'But me an' my true love/Will never meet again' – a refrain which itself pervaded the life of Violet Trefusis.

Alice Adams
Second Chances

In the tiny West Coast community of San Sebastian lives a group of friends whose lives have been inextricably linked for years. Celeste is the widow of Charles who years ago and on another continent was the lover of Polly. Polly, who lives alone with her cats and her bicycles, has recently embarked on an immensely satisfying clandestine affair. Dudley, wife to Sam, is probably Celeste's closest friend, and Edward, forever in the closet but happy with his companion Freddy, is a close confidant of them all.

Second Chances captures both the closeness and the secrets of this circle of friends, as it moves between their younger past and the present – a present still full of possibilities for sexual encounters and new relationships. Celeste, stylish and vivacious, finds herself involved with a man who might be working for the CIA; Dudley endures a terrible loss, but emerges to a new sense of what she wants from life; Edward is forced to confront his deepest fears, but discovers that he can do so and still survive.

Here is a novel which faces up to the imperfections of life and relationships, but is testimony to the individual's capacity to grow and change. Alice Adams, best-selling author of *Superior Women*, has people her new book with spirited, compelling characters whose encounters with life's rewards and tragedies make irresistible reading.

Zoë Fairbains
Here Today

She always knew men wanted her, as wife, secretary or lover. What if they didn't?

Antonia's life used to be perfect – she was temp of the year at the Here Today agency and had a happy marriage to come home to. Suddenly all that has changed. Her husband doesn't want her and nor, it seems, do the increasingly-automated offices of London. Her home and her health are under threat, and so is her knowledge of who she is.

Antonia's search for answers also becomes the search for Samantha, another office worker and a rumoured victim of sexual assault. Pursuing the truth about Samantha provides Antonia with answers to questions about herself she didn't even know she was asking . . .

'Her most successful novel so far – racy, crisp and yes, very thrilling.' **Tribune**

'Witty, provocative, ironic and, above all, lots of fun.' Sara Maitland, **New Statesman**

A Selected List of Fiction Available from Mandarin Books

While every effort is made to keep prices low, it is sometimes necessary to increase prices at short notice. Mandarin Paperbacks reserves the right to show new retail prices on covers which may differ from those previously advertised in the text or elsewhere.

The prices shown below were correct at the time of going to press.

☐ 7493 0003 5	**Mirage**	James Follett	£3.99
☐ 7493 0005 1	**China Saga**	C. Y. Lee	£3.50
☐ 7493 0009 4	**Larksghyll**	Constance Heaven	£2.99
☐ 7493 0012 4	**The Falcon of Siam**	Axel Aylwen	£3.99
☐ 7493 0018 3	**Daughter of the Swan**	Joan Juliet Buck	£3.50
☐ 7493 0020 5	**Pratt of the Argus**	David Nobbs	£3.50
☐ 7493 0025 6	**Here Today**	Zoë Fairbairns	£3.50

TV and Film Titles

☐ 7493 0002 7	**The Bill III**	John Burke	£2.99
☐ 7493 0055 8	**Neighbours I**	Marshall/Kolle	£2.99
☐ 423 02020 X	**Bellman and True**	Desmond Lowden	£2.50
☐ 416 13972 8	**Why the Whales Came**	Michael Morpurgo	£2.50
☐ 7493 0017 5	**Adventures of Baron Munchausen**	McKeown/Gilliam	£2.99

All these books are available at your bookshop or newsagent, or can be ordered direct from the publisher. Just tick the titles you want and fill in the form below.

Mandarin Paperbacks, Cash Sales Department, PO Box 11, Falmouth, Cornwall TR10 9EN.

Please send cheque or postal order, no currency, for purchase price quoted and allow the following for postage and packing:

UK	55p for the first book, 22p for the second book and 14p for each additional book ordered to a maximum charge of £1.75.
BFPO and Eire	55p for the first book, 22p for the second book and 14p for each of the next seven books, thereafter 8p per book.
Overseas Customers	£1.00 for the first book plus 25p per copy for each additional book.

NAME (Block Letters) ....

ADDRESS ....

....